WE'LL MEET AGAIN

RAY CHAPMAN

ANTRA PUBLICATION

To
George & Alice,
Judi,
Rachel & Anthony

Also in print by the same author:

Only As A Stranger

Order on the internet
www.antra.co.uk
or buy in bookshops

Antra Publishing

We'll Meet Again
First published 2003
This edition published 2004

ANTRA PUBLISHERS

33 Oakdene Park
Finchley

London N3 1EU

Copyright Ray Chapman 2003

A CIP catalogue record for this book is available
from the British Library.

IBSN: 0-9545899-0-4

Cover by Novel Graphic

Printed by Biddles Ltd,
King's Lynn, Norfolk,
England

ONE

Summer 2003

The man took another swig from the bottle of cheap sherry and settled back against the door in the recess of the boarded up shop. A long grey military coat covered his legs and another bottle neck protruded from a large, bulging plastic carrier bag. Many people slept rough in the docks area and this had been his home for the last few nights, watching and waiting.

It was a pleasant warm July night after the blistering heat of the day and sounds carried clearly in the still air.

Every now and again the doors of the small pub opposite opened and people came or went. Several crossing the road good naturedly tossed coins into the doorway and the unshaven man sullenly nodded his gratitude.

He huddled there, his eyes narrowed.

An hour later time was called and the final stragglers emerged from the saloon bar.

Ronald Woodcock stood out from the group of young men talking on the pavement. Seventy nine years of age his thin white hair was closely cropped short back and sides. There was talk of going to an Indian restaurant and the youths tried to persuade the pensioner to join them.

'No, I'm going 'ome,' he said. 'I've got some beer there and it's too late for me anyway.'

'Come on Gramps, it's a lovely night and we'll get a taxi back,' his grandson, Gary, said.

'It won't cost you anything, Woody,' chimed in another young man.

'No, I'm going 'ome.' The old man wasn't to be swayed.

'Okay, but don't put the front door bolt on. I don't want you locking me out again,' Gary said.

The man in the doorway opposite got to his feet and put on the long coat. He left behind the full bottle and carrier bag containing an old tattered blanket and clutching the other bottle left the doorway.

He staggered along the street away from the pub and started singing, every now and again taking sips of the sherry.

Woody took a brown flat cap from his jacket pocket, tugged it over his head and began walking. The group outside the pub had now departed in the other direction and he could faintly hear the drunk singing ahead of him.

The old man crossed the road leading to the alley he used every night on his way home from the pub. The alley meandered between the small back gardens of terraced houses and deserted commercial buildings. A high crumbling brick wall on one side and wood fences on the other, with just a couple of dim streetlights to show the way.

Nearly halfway along the alley the singing suddenly stopped and Woody vaguely saw the long coated man leaning against the wall. Then the man seemed to collapse and rolled over on his back.

'You all right, mate?' Woody called out as he came to within a few yards of the prostrate figure.

No answer.

'You okay?'

The old boy knelt down by the side of the man.

'I'm fine, Woody.' The man opened his eyes and grinned widely. 'And how are you?'

Puzzlement etched into the pensioner's eyes and stayed there in the last few moments of his life. A gloved hand holding an army bayonet appeared from under the grey coat and thrust with powerful force into Woody's right shoulder.

He groaned and was lifted upwards as the man on the ground got to his feet. The man gripped Woody's throat with his left hand and pushed him fiercely against the wooden fence.

'Traitre,' the man said clearly. 'Maintenant vous savez ce que c'est d'trê poignardé.'

Then he reverted back to English.

'Sorry I forgot, you don't speak French, do you? I said, now *you* know how it feels to be stabbed.'

The man pulled out the bayonet and thrust it into the chest of Woody's helpless body. A lung was punctured and blood mixed with spittle as it oozed from the slack mouth.

The eight inch blade was withdrawn once more and carefully placed under the pensioner's Adams apple. The man pushed fiercely and banged the heel of his hand several times hard against the hilt. He stooped, picked up a broken brick, and hammered it against the bayonet. The old man was already dead and didn't feel the metal go right through his neck and stick deep into the fence post.

He hung there like a lifeless puppet.

TWO

The dark green BMW slowed to a stop and the driver watched the man and woman leave the taxi. Challis had been shadowing the Member of Parliament and his mistress for over a month and during the last week they'd been getting careless. Staying in a London hotel rather than the country hideaway they usually used. Publicly holding hands in a restaurant. And now a visit to the shapely blonde's flat. At midnight the lights went out and the journalist patiently settled back. It was going to be a long night.

But thankfully it had cooled down after a scorcher of a day. The capital was in the grip of a heat wave. It had been that way for weeks now - and the temperature was still rising.

During the day it was a busy street, just five minutes from the shops in Queensway, and the large houses had long since been converted into flats with the extra population only adding to the chaos of parking. But at this time of night it wasn't a problem.

The spot was ideal for a stakeout and Challis used his mobile phone to contact his photographer.

The tree lined street slowly became silent as the hours elapsed with only the odd passer-by hurrying home in search of his bed to break the journalist's monotonous vigil. It seemed eerie that this incredibly noisy, bustling city could become so peaceful. Even if only for a short while.

The one problem Challis ever encountered on nights like this was if a nosy member of the public reported to the police that a biggish man with a broken nose had been sitting in a car for hours on end. His press card soon satisfied the men in blue, but he hated bringing attention to where he was parked.

Challis nestled lower in the driver's seat, but there wasn't much he could do about his profile, a souvenir from his days as an amateur fighter.

Only once during the night did the journalist get out of the car to stretch his legs, his khaki trousers and pale green shirt a mass of creases. He moved agilely, light on his feet for his six foot frame.

At six am Steve White had the taxi drop him off at the end of the road and he walked the last hundred yards to the journalist's car. Challis watched his friend approach. The tall, slim photographer easily recognisable with his dark designer stubble and matching short haircut. He was wearing his usual jeans and blue T-shirt, a large canvas bag slung over one shoulder, which he slipped off as soon as he reached the BMW. Steve grinned at Challis as he took out a bottle of water, chamois leather and proceeded to clean off the dust and grime from the windscreen.

Then the photographer got in the passenger side and checked his camera equipment. He'd remembered to bring a thermos and the two men sat slouched in their seats sipping coffee, their eyes never wavering from the front entrance to the flats as the street started to come to life once again.

Perspiration trickled down the side of Challis's face and he wiped away the irritating beads with the back of his hand. His jet black hair felt wet in the nape of his neck and over his ears. He must remember to get a haircut. He looked at his watch again. Seven forty five and already the heat was sticky, even with all the windows open. It hadn't rained for weeks. No doubt the water boards would soon be issuing drought notices.

Nearly eight o'clock and Challis flexed his legs in the driver's seat. He was feeling cramped. Then he tensed behind the wheel and pointed.

'That's them,' he said, as Tony Carter-West walked down the front mosaic tiled steps into the bright sunlight with the busty blonde. They were laughing and the man had his suit jacket slung over one shoulder.

The photographer quickly moved the camera he'd been cuddling in his lap to his eye in one fluid motion. One hand gently steadied the long telescopic lens while the other pressed the shutter release. Repeated clicks sounded in the car as the frames moved forward in spilt second sequences.

The MP was oblivious to the camera's scrutiny as he placed his briefcase on the pavement. He put an arm around the woman and as they kissed one stiletto foot bent upwards behind her.

'That's it, darling,' Steve said, as he snapped off more shots through the windscreen. 'Press up close to him.'

The couple broke apart and after a few words which ended in more laughter the man strode off in one direction and the blonde in the other. Challis knew she was heading towards the nearby tube station and another day's work as a receptionist for an exclusive estate agent near Bond Street.

Steve changed cameras and followed the well known public figure on the other side of the street, ducking behind parked cars, every now and again shooting more pictures. The MP hailed a taxi and Steve finished off the roll of film as he flashed past.

The photographer slipped back into the front passenger seat and smiled at Challis.

'Couldn't have been better,' he said. 'He never sussed a thing. When are you going to do a showdown with him?'

Challis turned the ignition key and slipped away from the kerb, his vacated space immediately taken by a big shiny Mercedes.

'I'm not sure if I will,' he replied. 'I've got enough evidence. Anyway, I'll leave that up to the paper.'

6

Challis was a freelance and had a reputation for landing the big exclusives. He made sure they were one hundred per cent accurate, with plenty of proof and photographs. Then it was up to the paper to top and tail it to their own fashion.

After all, they were paying. Paying plenty.

The journalist concentrated on the traffic and just off Praed Street turned into a mews yard where his friend shared a studio with two other photographers. Challis had nicknamed them the Paddington paparazzi.

Twenty minutes later Challis was driving down Park Lane, his fingers tapping in tune to the car radio, and was grateful for the fast flowing traffic. Then he hit a snarl of cars and his shirt was sticking to his back by the time he found a residents parking space near his mansion flat in Victoria. His eyes felt gritty through lack of sleep.

*

After a cooling shower to get his head together he phoned the news editor of the Sunday paper he'd come to a deal with and told him he'd got the snatch photographs of the MP with his mistress. He promised they would be delivered next morning with the finished copy.

They'd come to a price agreement weeks ago. Fifteen thousand pounds if Challis stood the story up. He had. Now his bank manager would be happy.

Journalism had been good to Challis in the last few years and gave him a comfortable lifestyle.

Now in his mid-thirties it had enabled him to buy the lease of this flat. His car was the latest model and there were plenty of clothes in his wardrobe.

But it was hard graft.

Being a freelance meant he didn't have the backup of a newspaper and he had to hustle all the time to find the stories himself.

He placed a large pot of freshly made coffee, along with a bottle of scotch on his desk, and spent the rest of the morning typing on his computer. Steve phoned and said the photographs had come out perfect and he'd deliver them in a couple of hours.

The two men went back a long way and their careers had followed similar paths. They'd met when they were teenagers working together on the same local newspaper and kept in close contact after they got jobs on different national newspapers.

Now they were both freelances - but not for the same reasons.

As the journalist pounded away on the keyboard he wondered if the MP would resign his seat. That would be another blow to the Labour party - or *New* Labour - as they wanted to be known. Even the name Carter-West sounded more Tory than Socialist. Definitely screw up his marriage.

For years it had been Conservative MP's forever in the headlines with stories of sleaze. But since Labour had swept to power, now in a second term, things had to change. Law of averages. Now *they* were under closer scrutiny than ever from the media, and the Prime Minister had already lost several key members of government, who'd been forced to quit their posts because of tarnished reputations.

It wasn't a good time for Mr Blair. The public weren't happy with the way he'd handled the Iraq war - and the weapons of mass destruction issue.

Challis was by nature fairly easy going but when it came to an exclusive story, that was different. That was food on the table. Money in the bank. And to survive as a top freelance in his business he had to be as hard as nails and just as devious.

The information about Carter-West's affair had come from an unexpected source and would sicken the MP if he ever found out. The informant had been passed on to Challis by one of his regular contacts and was too good to pass up. Challis didn't have many scruples but the way the affair had come to light still left a nasty taste in the journalist's mouth.

Challis eased his conscience knowing that if he hadn't done the story - another reporter would have.

It was always open season on politicians.

THREE

The man tightened the belt of his army greatcoat and pulled up the collar. He crossed the road and walked down a wide side street, keeping to the shadows of the tall hedges. He'd reconnoitred the street several times in the past month and knew exactly the residence he was looking for. He slipped into the driveway of the detached house and stopped, blending in with the foliage of a large conifer tree.

The house was old and the man could see lights through the leaded glass windows in one of the front downstairs rooms. He walked up the drive and rang the doorbell. A minute passed and then the solid mahogany wood door cautiously opened. The security chain still in place.

'Guten abend, Colonel Hardy,' the man on the doorstep said.

The frail old man peered through the narrow opening allowed by the chain. 'German? ' he queried. 'Who are you? What do you want?'

The man lifted up one leg and sent his heavy boot crashing against the door. The chain stretched taut but held, and the old man frantically tried to close the door. But he was too slow and too weak. The boot struck out three times in quick succession and the chain's mounting finally splintered from the door jamb. The sudden opening of the door sent the old man sprawling backwards to the floor. The man in the long coat quickly stepped inside and closed the door behind him.

'English, actually, old boy,' he said. 'Don't say you've forgotten me.'

The old man rose shakily to his feet and leaned against the wall. He gasped in air, breathing heavily, and stared at the intruder.

'I don't know you. I've never seen you before. Look, if it's money you want, I've got some in my study. Not much, but you can have it.'

'Your money or your life, eh?' the younger man smiled. Then his face hardened and he grabbed hold of the front of his victim's shirt with both hands, lifting him clean off the floor.

'Well, I don't want your money.'

FOUR

The headlines screamed out Tony Carter-West's misfortune from the news-stands.

MP'S SECRET MISTRESS was the Sunday tabloid's splash, continued on pages two and three. With exclusive pictures.

The story was lifted by all the other papers and repeated throughout the day on radio and television news. On Monday the dailies had a field day and the chase was on. The MP was reported to have fled to his villa in the South of France. The mistress hadn't left her flat since Saturday night and a score of reporters and photographers were camped on her doorstep.

Julia Carter-West tearfully denied any knowledge of her husband's affair and took their three children to her parents home in the Cotswolds. Her father appealed to the press to leave them alone.

A soft porn actress came forward and claimed she'd had a secret fling with the MP a year ago. He liked her to dress up as a tart and have kinky sex with her.

On the Wednesday Carter-West arrived back in England and said he hardly knew the actress. She was obviously trying to get some cheap publicity. He admitted the affair with the blonde but said his wife had forgiven him. His constituents were standing by him and he wouldn't be resigning.

He was sorry.

Challis read his comments and grinned. He was sorry all right, but only about one thing. That was getting caught.

*

Seton Travis phoned Challis Thursday evening.

'Very good story,' he said, in his softly spoken voice.

'Thanks, it didn't work out too bad at all.'

'Challis, I'd like to see you. As soon as possible.'

'I'm going on holiday the day after tomorrow, Seton. Can't it wait until I get back?'

'It's important.'

'Is it about a story?'

'I'd like you to meet someone.'

Challis paused, his mind quickly rearranging his plans for the following day. It was inconvenient but Seton was a good friend and if he said it was important then there wasn't much choice.

'Okay, but it will have to be tomorrow afternoon. About what time?'

'We'll fit in with you, but can you come to my place?'

'Three o'clock okay?'

'See you then.'

Challis replaced the receiver. They'd worked together on the same daily tabloid, before he'd gone freelance, and Seton had given him a lot of help and advice over the years. The old Fleet Street hack had retired last year to write his memoirs but they still kept in touch.

*

The next morning Challis remembered to get a haircut, but only a trim to keep his girlfriend happy. Keely liked his slightly curly hair *fashionable*, as she put it. Then she would, she was in the fashion business.

Challis preferred to wear it very short but Keely said it made him look too hard, with his broken nose and ridged scar under his chin. A legacy from a car accident.

Challis grinned to himself as he left the hairdresser's. Women. Still, Keely *was* special.

13

Just before lunchtime he went to his bank then caught a cab to a small pub just off Piccadilly. The journalist had many contacts, in fact, they were his lifeblood and without them he wouldn't be in business.

His contacts were a variety of people from all walks of life. But they all had one thing in common - money. They all wanted paying for their information.

And Challis could understand that. After all, he made plenty from their tips.

However, the person Challis was now going to meet was a different species. The lowest of the low. Hugh Carter-West was the MP's older brother - and he'd grassed up his own flesh and blood for a thousand pounds.

The brother was propped up at the bar as the journalist entered. He was drinking a large gin and tonic and it seemed to go in his mouth then immediately reappear as sweat on his fat face. He was a loathsome character.

'Ah, Challis, dear boy, what are you drinking?'

The journalist looked at the flabby figure in front of him dressed in a pin striped dark blue suit, white starched collar and pink tie, a deadpan expression on his face.

'Nothing,' Challis answered, and held out an envelope which Carter-West took and immediately opened.

'What's this then?' he asked, and quickly transferred the fifty pound notes to his inside pocket, then tipped the envelope upside down on the bar's surface. A small pile of ten pence coins formed.

'Thirty pieces of silver,' the journalist replied, and turned and left the pub.

*

Challis bought a couple of sports shirts in Selfridges department store, a new pair of sun glasses and then hailed a taxi to St John's Wood .

Seton was a widower and lived by himself in a flat close to Lords cricket ground. He opened the door on the second ring Seton was tall with a full head of grey hair, close trimmed beard and wore horn rimmed glasses. A pleasant man with an ever ready smile.

'Thanks for coming,' he said.

Challis followed Seton into the lounge, a spacious room with comfortable furniture. Glass doors, leading to a small balcony were open, vainly trying to capture a non-existent breeze. It was hot.

As they entered a man stood up from an armchair.

'Challis, this is Matthew Hardy, an old family friend.'

They shook hands.

Matthew Hardy was in his late forties, with a ruddy complexion, not from the weather, but from frequent boozy lunches. He was a director of a merchant bank in the City.

Seton gave Challis a cold beer, topped up the banker's scotch and poured himself a Pernod and water.

'Challis, Matthew's father, Colonel Roger Hardy, was killed last week. Perhaps you read about it. It happened in Totteridge.'

Challis gave Hardy a sympathetic look.

'Yes, I think I do remember something about it.'

Seton reached for some newspaper cuttings on the coffee table and passed them to Challis.

'It was in the Sun, Mirror and the Daily Mail,' he said. 'Not a lot, but the local paper covered it quite well. The trouble these days, violent death is all too common.'

Challis finished reading.

'The police seem to think it was a burglary which went horribly wrong,' he said. 'Your father was shot with his own gun, a Webley revolver he'd brought home as a souvenir from the war.'

The banker shook his head.

'I'm not sure the police have got it right,' he said. 'I think my Father's death was planned, not an accident.'

'What makes you think that?'

'Because nothing was taken. There was money in the house and the place is full of valuable antiques,' Hardy replied.

'Yes, but then, the burglar probably panicked after the murder,' Challis said. 'He wouldn't want to take anything that would connect him to your father's death. Burglary's one thing but murder is far more serious. His reaction is perfectly understandable.'

'My Father told me he thought he'd seen someone watching the house last month.'

'Well, burglars do watch houses,' Challis said.

'No, I'm sure there's more to it than just a burglary that went wrong,' Hardy said. 'The method of entry for one. Why would a burglar ring the doorbell and then kick open the door? Hardly a subtle approach for a thief.'

Challis shrugged his broad shoulders.

'Maybe it was a sudden spur of the moment robbery. A drunk who saw the lights on and acted without thinking it through.'

'Then who was watching the house?' Hardy asked.

'Do you know if your father had any enemies?'

'No, not offhand. But when you reach an old age like his, everybody's sure to have upset someone or other.'

'Tell me about your father.'

'Colonel Hardy had a distinguished record during the war,' Seton said, joining the conversation. 'He served the full six years, from nineteen thirty nine until forty five, and stayed on as a career officer. He retired about thirty years ago.'

'Any business interests?' Challis asked.

'The colonel was very wealthy,' his friend replied.

'My Father had a stockbroker he was in regular contact with.' Hardy said. 'And he also had overseas investments.'

16

'And your mother?' Challis asked.

'She's still alive, but my parents separated about ten years after my Father left the army,' Hardy replied. 'She complained he treated her like his batman. The split was amicable and they remained friends. They just couldn't live together. Twelve years ago my Father went to live in South Africa and he rented out his London house to an army general friend of his. Then a year ago the general died and my Father decided to return to England. He'd been back just nine months when he was killed.'

'Where is your mother now?'

'My Mother lives with me and my family,' he explained. 'I've got a large enough house near Hatfield in Hertfordshire and she gets on well with my wife. She dotes on her grandchildren, and I made sure my Mother and Father were always in contact at least once a week.'

By now Challis was beginning to wonder where this conversation was leading to. He'd asked questions out of habit but a niggling idea was beginning to form at the back of his mind.

It was as though Seton had been reading his thoughts.

'Matthew wants me to try and find out who killed his father,' he said. 'I told him I was retired but had a friend who was one of the best investigative journalists in the business. *You.*'

Challis was embarrassed by the exaggerated praise and realised his niggling idea had been correct.

'You're not suggesting, what I think you're suggesting, are you?' he asked in a slow and deliberate voice.

'Yes.'

'Come on Seton, you know I'm more involved in vice and scandal. Even showbiz. But I'm not into solving murders, that's police work.'

'I'll pay you,' Hardy said. 'I can afford it.'

'I assure you it's nothing to do with money,' Challis said, and took a swig of his beer.

'Newspapers love to expose bribery and corruption,' he continued. 'They lift the lid off sleaze and expose bent coppers. Reporters reveal the truth about prostitution rackets and perverts. And politicians are always news.'

Challis paused to emphasize his point.

'But journalists do not go around like Sherlock Holmes trying to solve murders. We work with the police insomuch as we report what they tell us. We also report court cases. Sometimes a murderer confesses to a reporter many years later about his crime. But that's about it. And the police get very shirty if you try to interfere in their work. Besides, there's too much else going on in the world that keeps us fully occupied. I really would leave it to the police if I were you.'

Seton rose from his chair and looked directly at Challis.

'I promised Matthew I would help him,' he said. 'And I said you would too.'

Challis returned his friend's gaze. He shouldn't have put him in this position. It was awkward, and Seton knew it, but then Seton had probably been put on the spot himself. He knew his friend wouldn't ask again. He had to make a quick decision. Challis was conscious of the two men waiting for his reply and bowed to the inevitable with a resigned grin.

'So okay, I'll play Sherlock Holmes for a couple of weeks. But it will have to be after I come back from holiday. And Seton, I'll expect some help from you.'

Seton poured more drinks and they worked out an agreement. Challis would spend two weeks looking into the murder after he returned to England, and if he didn't make any progress he would cease his investigation. He would only want his expenses reimbursed and wouldn't charge for his time. After all, there was the possibility he *might* get a story out of it. But only a slight one, was Challis's honest opinion.

And if he needed to use photographers or any other journalists then they would get paid the going rate, plus expenses.

Seton showed Challis to the front door and told him that the eighty four year old colonel was being buried the next day.

'How are you involved with the family?' Challis asked.

'My Father was a fellow officer in the same regiment as the colonel, the 2nd East Yorkshire's. He was quite a bit older but they became good friends. Also, I'm godfather to Matthew's son.'

'Well, you owe me one,' Challis said. 'You know this is an impossible job, and I will go through the motions, but *only* because it's you. Your friend would have been better off going to a private detective agency.'

'Perhaps, but he came to me.'

*

The funeral was a quiet one, just family and a few close friends.

As the mourners said their goodbyes and got in their cars nobody noticed the solitary figure in a long overcoat standing amongst the headstones. The man quickly walked from the graveyard into the street and opened the driver's door of an old blue Ford Granada. The car looked as though it could do with a paint job but the engine under the scratched bonnet was tuned to perfection. The man sat behind the wheel watching the exit.

There were no after funeral drinks at the colonel's house but if any of the mourners wanted to go back to Matthew Hardy's home in Hertfordshire, they were welcome.

The cars slowly left the car park in front of the small church and inched their way through the cemetery towards the wide open gates. Matthew Hardy steered his Bentley into the street and two of the vehicles tucked in behind him. The three cars kept within the speed limit as they drove through the suburban streets and cut through Arkley heading towards Stirling Corner.

By the time they reached the A1 heading for Hatfield the motorcade had become four.

FIVE

The crowds of people arriving at Heathrow Airport were in a buoyant mood. The weather in England was just as good as they had left in their holiday resorts and visions of tans not quickly fading away in dull, dismal weather brought a smile to their faces.

Challis was no exception. He was bronzed and his well built frame bursting with energy. His black hair gleamed in contrast to his blonde companion.

Keely Bowles and Challis had a special relationship. They'd both been through painful divorces and were quite willing to be partners in bed - but not on paper. They had contemplated living together, but decided against it. They were the best of friends, shared the same sense of humour and could depend entirely on each other. They didn't want to spoil things.

Long legged Keely was a magazine fashion editor with a better figure than most of the models she employed on fashion shoots. Her skimpy T-shirt and short mini-skirt brought looks of admiration as she pushed her luggage trolley by the side of Challis. She was used to it.

They shared a taxi to Challis's place because she wanted to spend another night with him. Work on Monday would come soon enough.

Challis opened the front door of his flat and stepped over a pile of mail. He helped Keely in with her bags and straight away began opening windows. He went into the spare bedroom he'd converted into an office and played back the messages on his answer machine.

Nothing urgent, but Seton had phoned a couple of hours ago with the time and a reminder to call him as soon as he returned.

Challis had intended to anyway and picked up the phone.

After politely enquiring about the holiday Seton asked if Challis had any idea how he was going to start the investigation into the colonel's death.

'I'd like to have a look around Colonel Hardy's house on Monday morning. Can you arrange that?'

'The colonel had a woman who came in every day to do the cleaning and cooking. More like a housekeeper really, but she didn't sleep over. She only lives about fifteen minutes away and I'll make sure she's there by nine o'clock to let you in.'

*

Monday morning and Challis was battling his way through the traffic. Fortunately he was going in the other direction to the commuters driving to work and the further he drove into the suburbs the easier it became.

It was nine twenty when he arrived at the house and parked in the U-shaped drive behind a mini metro. The large detached house, with ivy wandering over the red brick walls, was expensive, as were the others in the quiet road.

Mrs Goddard was a kind looking, alert lady in her fifties, who immediately insisted on showing Challis to the kitchen and pouring him a large mug of freshly made coffee. And to meet her son, Roy, a sturdy young man in his early twenties.

'I hope you don't mind, but I wanted someone with me when I came back here,' Mrs Goddard said with a slight shudder. 'I haven't been here since that morning I found poor Colonel Hardy.'

'If it's not too upsetting I would appreciate it if you told me what happened,' Challis said, and sat down at the large pine table.

Mrs Goddard lit a cigarette. She inhaled deeply, her other hand toying with a mug of coffee.

'I'd given up smoking for fifteen years,' she said. 'But now I'm back to where I started.'

She paused, and Challis let her take her time.

'I arrived here every morning at nine o'clock. My hours were from nine to five. Bit like office hours really.'

She smiled briefly.

'I cleaned, cooked and did the washing and ironing. I also did the shopping for the colonel. He had an account with a mini-cab firm so I didn't have to worry about carrying anything. And if the weather was bad the colonel insisted I got a cab home. He was good to me.'

Her eyes misted over.

'As soon as I got to the front door I saw there was something wrong. The door was ajar and the door chain was hanging down. I came inside and shouted the colonel's name. But there was no reply. I looked in the kitchen here and knocked on the downstairs toilet, in case he'd been taken ill. Then I went into the lounge...,' her voice faltered at the memory.

'I didn't see him first of all. But then I saw a wine table had been knocked over. The colonel was on the floor behind a large wing chair. He was laying on his back with blood all over the front of his shirt.'

She sniffled and busied herself lighting another cigarette. Challis had questions to ask but thought it better to wait.

He lifted himself from the pine chair.

'I'd like to look around the house,' he said.

'Oh yes.' She moved her seat back and stood. 'Mr Hardy said you were to have the entire run of the place and take as long as you like. And I wasn't to interfere.'

Challis gave a reassuring smile.

'You just relax and take it easy.'

Mrs Goddard forced a smile in return.

'Roy,' Challis said. 'Perhaps you could point me in the right direction. I take it you know your way around this house.'

The young man straightened up from where he'd been leaning against one of the work tops.

'I look after the garden and do all the odd jobs around the house,' he said proudly.

The two men left the kitchen and walked into the large square hall. The walls were wood panelled as were the walls going up the stairs.

Roy explained the various rooms downstairs and said there were five bedrooms and two bathrooms upstairs.

'You go and look after your mother,' Challis said, and the son returned to the kitchen.

The journalist walked up the thickly carpeted stairs and went along the wide corridor opening all the doors. Five bedrooms and two bathrooms, plus an extra toilet. All this space for just one old man.

It brought back memories of Challis's childhood and the tiny two bedroom flat where his mother had struggled to bring him up after his father died. There was always a shortage of money, but somehow they'd managed. People do.

His father had been taken into hospital to have his appendix removed, in what should have been a simple enough operation, but something went wrong and he died. It was something to do with the anaesthetic. The hospital denied negligence and there was talk of a cover-up. But, although a doctor resigned, nothing was ever proved.

Challis had only been eight years old when this happened and his father became just a distant memory, but his mother never got over the heartbreak, and never wanted to marry again. Instead, she devoted all her care and attention to her son.

It was she who encouraged Challis to go into journalism.

'Expose the bastards of the world,' she'd told him bitterly, and Challis had no doubts who she was thinking of.

Sadly, she died of cancer when he was twenty, just as he was starting to do well on the local paper in south London, and before he could start paying her back for the sacrifices she'd made over the years.

She'd been a good mother.

*

The journalist carefully examined the bedrooms, but it was obvious four of them hadn't been used for some time. The beds were made up but the wardrobes and drawers were devoid of any clothes or personal effects. They had the indifferent feeling of hotel rooms awaiting guests.

Challis looked out of one of the leaded glass windows. The back garden was enormous and it was hard to see where one garden stopped and another began. A perfect place for a burglar to remain unseen after dark.

The fifth bedroom, with bathroom en suite, was Colonel Hardy's. His wardrobe was adequate and the clothes were of the highest quality. Noticeable was his army dress uniform with rows of service ribbons and medals, all preserved under a protective clear plastic covering. The drawers contained shirts, socks and underwear neatly put away. The bathroom was the same. Normal.

Anyway, what was he searching for? Pity the colonel hadn't employed a butler. That would have solved everything.

He looked in the small television room and downstairs cloakroom. The dining room was very tasteful with a large yew table and chairs capable of seating ten people. He went into the lounge. It was expensively furnished with genuine antiques.

Maybe he should go around the room with a magnifying glass. He was beginning to feel ridiculous.

Challis had left the colonel's study to last which was situated at the rear of the house. More wood panelling with lots of bookshelves and prints of maps on the walls.

Challis crossed to the green leather topped desk in front of one of the windows and started to go through the drawers.

The large top drawer in the middle was full of the colonel's personalised stationary and his day by day diary. The journalist browsed through the pages. Not all that many appointments. There was nothing unusual for the day he died and the last entry was for a forthcoming Friday in October. His regimental reunion dinner.

Challis went through the four drawers on the left hand side of the desk. Nothing but business papers. The same with three of the right hand drawers. But the bottom one he pulled out and placed on top of the desk.

Inside were several boxes containing a variety of different calibre bullets. They looked old and were presumably war souvenirs.

The colonel had probably kept his service revolver there too.

Underneath the boxes were two brown folders which looked worn and tatty with age. Challis moved the boxes and carefully took them out. He opened one and saw about a dozen old newspaper cuttings, the paper turned brown and brittle with age. They dated from the outbreak of the Second World War in nineteen thirty nine to victory in Europe and the surrender of Japan in nineteen forty five. Challis read through the cuttings but there was nothing relating to the colonel personally, other than that his regiment was mentioned, along with others, in the D-Day landings in Normandy on 6th June 1944.

It seemed as though they were a reminder, more than anything else, that this is what happened to six years of the colonel's life.

Challis opened the other folder which contained a single shiny paper page torn from a magazine, dated August 1950. About a quarter of the page, outlined in blue biro, was devoted to a story about a wartime skirmish which happened in northern France. The article explained it was based on a story which had appeared in a French magazine the month before.

Paris July 1950

The graves of two wartime heroes have recently been discovered in the village of Roujan, ten kilometres south of Caen. The names of the two men are Henri Fabere and Giles Faraday, a British Army captain.

Captain Faraday had been working behind enemy lines with the French Resistance and he and Fabere were killed in crossfire between British and German soldiers seven weeks after D-Day.

The action took place in an orchard and was one of many as the Allies stormed across France. The 27-year-old captain had been listed as missing and it wasn't until new information came to light in the last few months that it was discovered where he was buried.

Captain Faraday had been with the Special Operations Executive, one of Britain's secret services created by the War Cabinet in July 1940. SOE trained nine thousand agents for missions in enemy-occupied territory during World War Two and was officially disbanded in June 1946. The captain had been with F section.

His parents died two years ago in a plane crash and his only remaining relative is a younger sister, Evelyn, living in Bath, Avon.

At the bottom of the story were two small photographs of Henri Fabere and Giles Faraday.

Challis finished reading and wondered if Captain Faraday had been a friend of the colonel during the war.

The journalist replaced the folders and drawer in the desk and went to a small filing cabinet. Nothing but more business papers. He swung back a hinged wall map to reveal a small safe. It was open and empty.

Challis looked at the framed print as he pushed it back against the wall. It was a detailed map of the designated areas for the D-Day landings. Utah and Omaha beaches for the Americans, and Gold, Juno and Sword for the British and Canadians. Feeling frustrated and disappointed Challis made his way back to the kitchen.

'Find what you were looking for?' Mrs Goddard asked.

The journalist shook his head. 'No, not really.'

'Are you doing a story about the murder?' her son asked inquisitively.

'Yes, something or other like that. I'm trying to get some background on the colonel.' Challis wondered if his reply sounded as hollow to them as it did to him.

The housekeeper had rinsed out Challis's coffee mug and she poured another from the bubbling percolator.

'Thanks,' Challis said, and took a sip. 'Mrs Goddard, during the few weeks before the colonel died, did either of you see anything suspicious? Did you notice anyone keeping an eye on this house? Any strangers hanging about?'

Mother and son looked at each other and shook their heads slowly.

'Nothing I can remember,' she replied.

'Do you know if the colonel had any enemies? Did you ever hear him arguing over the phone, or did he ever get any threatening letters?'

Mrs Goddard sat thinking.

'No, nothing like that. But then, don't forget, I wasn't here in the evenings. And that reminds me...'

She got up and went over to a tiled work top and picked up several letters laying next to the bread bin.

'These came this morning,' she said. 'I found them on the doormat when I arrived. I know Mr Hardy was here yesterday and he would have picked them up if they'd been delivered then.'

'Do you mind?'

Challis reached over and took the envelopes.

A couple of junk letters and two others. One brown envelope with the address typed and the other, a handwritten white envelope, which stood out because it had pencil markings and, *not known at this address,* scrawled on the front. There was a slight mistake in the post code and the sender had put *Street* instead of *Park* in the address. It had obviously been sent back to the post office before being re-delivered to the correct destination. The original postmark said it had been sent two days before the colonel's murder.

Challis left the kitchen and went back into the study, sat at the desk, and immediately dumped the junk mail into a wastepaper bin. It did briefly flash across his mind about phoning Matthew Hardy for permission to open his father's letters...but, what the hell. It wouldn't be the first time he'd opened someone else's mail to get information.

Laying on the leather top was a Second World War German officer's ten inch dagger, obviously used as a letter opener. It was a lethal looking weapon with an eagle and swastika on the metal crosspiece and Challis neatly slit open the two remaining envelopes.

The brown one was from an osteopath saying that they were now open longer hours and employed extra staff.

The journalist quickly discarded it and pulled out the contents from the white envelope, a lined foolscap page torn from a ringed exercise book, folded in four. He smoothed out the paper and looked at the address at the top of the page.

It was from Doncaster, South Yorkshire. The letter was short and read:

Dear Colonel Hardy,

You were one of my officers during the war and something has come to my attention that I think you should know about. I don't know if you remember Corporal Bernie Harris but he tells me that my life is in danger. Yours too. He don't go out much but he phones me now and again and he thinks someone is trying to kill us. Bernie says he's not much of a letter writer but he got your address from someone in the old regiment. It might not be anything but some of what Bernie says makes sense. If you are interested please write or telephone me at the above address.

Derek Watson (Private)

Challis read through the letter again. *The colonel's life was in danger.*

The journalist picked up the phone on the desk and dialled the given number in Doncaster. After about half a dozen rings the receiver was lifted and he heard a woman's voice.

'Hello.'

'I'm sorry to trouble you,' Challis said. 'Are you Mrs Watson?'

'Yes, what can I do for you?'

'Is Mr Watson there?'

'Yes, but he's in bed. He's not very well at the moment. Can I help you?'

'My name's Challis. I'm a journalist and I was hoping to have a word with your husband.'

'A journalist? Why do you want to speak to my husband?'

'It's about a letter he wrote to Colonel Hardy. Do you know anything about it?'

There was silence at the other end as the woman thought over the question.

'No, I don't know anything about a letter. My husband has mentioned the colonel to me though. They were in the war together.'

'Did he mention the colonel recently?'

'Maybe, I'm not sure. It's hard to remember.'

'And you're positive he didn't tell you he wrote to the colonel several weeks ago?'

'Would you like me to ask him if he wrote a letter?'

'Could you, if it's not too much trouble.'

Challis heard the sound of her receiver put down on a hard surface. Then silence for several minutes.

'Sorry, to keep you waiting,' she said on her return. 'Yes, my husband said he did write to the colonel recently. He said he gave it to our daughter to post.'

'Does your husband know that the colonel is dead?' Challis paused, before adding, 'He was killed by a burglar.'

'No, that's terrible, 'Mrs Watson said in a shocked voice. 'No, my husband doesn't know or I'm sure he would have said something.'

'It was in the papers, Mrs Watson.'

'My husband's been in bed for two weeks now and we don't have the papers delivered. He listens to the radio mostly.'

'What's the matter with your husband?'

'It's his heart. He's had two heart attacks and about ten years ago had a quadruple bypass. Then last year he had heart failure, and he's got worse ever since.'

'I'm sorry to hear that,' Challis said. 'Look, Mrs Watson, you might not think this a good idea, but I really would like to speak to your husband. Not on the phone, but in person. I'm phoning from London but could I come and visit him?'

'What's it about, Mr Challis? Are you doing some sort of story?'

'I'm a friend of the colonel's son and in that letter your husband said the colonel was in danger. I'd like to find out what he meant.'

'But you said the colonel was killed by a burglar.'

'That's what the police think at the moment, but I'm looking at another angle. Could I come tomorrow? I promise I won't stay too long, or upset your husband.'

There was silence again as Mrs Watson pondered the request.

'Could you be here by about eleven o'clock tomorrow morning? The doctor's coming to see my husband after lunch, so the morning would be the best time.'

'I'll be there tomorrow morning, Mrs Watson. And thanks.'

SIX

Challis checked his watch and figured he was an hour away from Doncaster. The traffic wasn't bad and the BMW quickly ate up the miles on the motorway. He'd been there a few times before but, like most towns he'd been to on stories, it was in and out as fast as possible. He remembered hotel rooms more than places. Doncaster was a busy industrial town and had a famous racecourse, but that was about as much as he knew.

He was still in plenty of time as he entered the town and stopped at a small cafe near the bus station for a late breakfast. After three hours driving his stomach needed more than the couple of cups of coffee he'd had before leaving his flat.

The address he was looking for was near the Royal Infirmary and after eggs and bacon asked directions from the young girl behind the counter.

It was five minutes to eleven as he drew up outside the old Victorian house divided into two flats. The Watsons lived on the ground floor and he rang the bell.

As soon as the elderly woman answered the door Challis sensed there was something wrong.

'Can I help you?' she asked.

'Mrs Watson?'

'No. Mrs Watson is inside. I'm a friend,' the woman stepped on to the front step and pulled the door nearly shut behind her. 'I'm afraid something has happened.'

Challis looked puzzled.

'Like what?'

'It's her husband,' she continued in a quiet voice. 'He passed away early this morning.'

'Oh, I am sorry,' Challis said. 'What happened?'

'Another heart attack. Derek had been poorly for the last couple of weeks and he was rushed into hospital just after midnight. He died about three o'clock. The doctors said his heart was just too tired to carry on anymore.'

'I had an appointment to see him at eleven,' Challis said lamely. 'I've just driven up from London.'

The woman touched his arm.

'Wait here a minute Mr...'

'Challis.'

The woman went inside and returned very quickly.

'Come inside Mr Challis. Edith said it's okay, and would you like a cup of tea? I've just made a fresh pot.'

Challis followed the woman through a small hallway into a neatly furnished lounge. Mrs Watson sat on the edge of a chintz covered armchair, a handkerchief in her hand.

'Take a seat, Mr Challis,' she said. 'Is tea all right, or would you like coffee?'

'Tea will be fine, thank you,' he said, and Mrs Watson's friend, Maisie, went into the kitchen. Challis sat in a matching chair opposite the old lady.

'I am sorry, Mrs Watson. I didn't realise how bad your husband was.'

'Don't worry, Mr Challis, my husband's death is no sudden shock. He's been ill for so long I was expecting it. If he hadn't died today, it would have been tomorrow, or the next day.'

Maisie reappeared carrying a large tray which she put on a coffee table between the chairs. She poured tea and passed the cups to Challis and Mrs Watson. But before she could take a drink herself there was a ringing in the hallway.

'The phone hasn't stopped all morning,' she said, and left the room to answer it.

'What exactly did you want to see Derek about?' Mrs Watson asked.

'Did you tell your husband that the colonel had been killed after I phoned?'

'No, I didn't. I thought it best you tell him because you would be able to answer any questions. Besides, I wasn't sure how much it would upset Derek.'

'I'm glad,' Challis said. 'I'd hate to think my news might have brought on his heart attack.'

Challis told her about Mathew Hardy and the police theory of a botched burglary.

'And then your husband's letter arrived. Your husband had posted it before the colonel's death but he'd made a mistake in the address and it wasn't delivered until yesterday.'

Challis took the letter from his leather briefcase and passed it to Mrs Watson. She took a pair of glasses from her handbag and began reading.

When she looked up, Challis asked, 'Do you know what he might have meant about his life and the colonel's being in danger?'

Maisie came back into the room and sat down on a worn leather settee. She sipped her tea and listened quietly.

'No idea, Mr Challis,' Mrs Watson said. 'But I see my husband mentioned Bernie Harris in the letter.'

'Yes, do you know him?'

'I know him all right. A strange man. Derek was in the army with him and after the war Bernie used to visit us quite a bit with one or other of his girlfriends. He never married and lives with his widowed sister in Sheffield.' Mrs Watson thought a moment. 'Sylvia Brown, that's the sister's name. She's nice but I hear Bernie's gone a bit funny in the head.'

'What do you mean?'

'Well, I haven't seen Bernie or his sister for, must be over twenty years, but he did phone Derek now and again. And

35

Derek told me, from what he gathered, that Bernie hadn't left his house for years and turned it into a fortress. Locks everywhere and all the windows barred. Always thought he was a bit odd.'

'Do you know the last time your husband spoke to him?'

'No, I can't really say. As I said, Bernie phoned here now and again, and I suppose Derek must have called him sometimes. But I know he's not phoned in the last two weeks, not since Derek was confined to his bed because I unplugged the phone in our bedroom so he wouldn't be disturbed. Anybody calling here would have had to spoken to me first.'

'Any idea how I can get hold of Bernie Harris? Have you got his address or phone number?'

She rose from her chair. 'Let's look where Derek kept his papers.'

Mrs Watson crossed the room and pulled down the flap of a writing bureau. She rummaged then found what she was looking for, a small black leather address book, and flicked through the pages.

'Here it is,' she said, and handed the open book to Challis.

Challis copied Derek Watson's neat handwriting of the phone number in Sheffield. No address.

Mrs Watson closed the bureau flap and pulled open one of the drawers. She took out a couple of photograph albums, sat down again, and started looking at the old photos.

'There's you and me when we went on that work's outing and I first met Derek,' she said to her friend, then continued turning over the pages. 'And there's you in that funny hat, never did like it.' She handed the album to Maisie.

'Looked a proper fright, didn't I,' her friend agreed, and quickly turned the page.

Mrs Watson began looking at the other photo album.

'Here's my husband with Bernie,' she said, her finger pointing.

Challis moved to her side and looked down at two young men in army uniform posing with broad grins for the camera. There were other pictures of men in uniform, the photos faded with age.

Mrs Watson pointed again at a large group photograph of about thirty men.

'That's Derek with some more of his friends,' she said.

Challis saw there were several officers standing on the edge of the photograph.

'Is Colonel Hardy there?' he asked.

'Yes, he's one of these,' she replied. 'Derek pointed him out to me one time, but I forget which one now. He was a captain then, I think.'

She continued turning the pages until she came to the end. There was a cardboard pocket on the hardback cover with a few odd photographs tucked in it. Mrs Watson pulled them out and a shiny piece of folded paper dropped into her lap.

She picked it up and said, 'I don't know why Derek kept this.'

Challis took the paper from her and placed it on the coffee table. He smoothed out the creases and stared at two familiar faces. It was the same 1950 magazine story with the small photographs of Henri Fabere and Captain Giles Faraday which he'd found in the colonel's study.

Strange. What was the connection?

'Did your husband ever tell you anything about this story?'

'No. But I did ask him about it because I saw him reading it several times.'

'What did he say?'

'Just said it reminded him of something that happened in the war. Nothing important really, and it was best forgotten.'

*

Challis sat in the driving seat of his car and phoned the number in Sheffield. He had thought of calling from Mrs Watson's flat and getting her to introduce him over the phone to Bernie Harris but felt that was asking too much. Her husband had died only a few hours ago and she had been kind enough to see him. To ask for more would have been pushing it.

'Hello,' said a female voice.

'Can I speak to Mr Harris, please?'

'Bernie don't speak to no-one anymore.' The voice was timid.

'Are you his sister?'

'Maybe I am, maybe I ain't. You'll have to write to him.'

'So, could you give me the address, please?'

'No. I ain't giving out our address, Bernie would kill me.'

'Then how can I write to him?' Challis asked, trying to keep the exasperation from his voice. He heard the click of an extension picked up.

'What's your game then? What do you want?' The man's voice was wheezy, and old.

'Are you Bernie Harris?'

'Maybe I am, maybe I ain't.'

Challis raised his eyes and wondered who coached who.

'Mr Harris I'm sitting in my car outside Derek Watson's flat in Doncaster. His wife gave me your number.'

'She had no right to give my number to a ruddy stranger. Wait till I speak to Derek.'

'I'm afraid that won't be possible,' Challis paused. 'I'm sorry to tell you Derek Watson died early this morning.'

'Died? What do you mean, died? Was he killed?'

'No, there wasn't any accident. He died of a heart attack.'

'I didn't mean an accident. Did someone murder him?'

'It was definitely a heart attack and he died in hospital. So what makes you think he was murdered?'

There was silence for a few moments.

'I warned him, I warned him.'

'About what?'

No answer.

'Colonel Hardy's dead too,' Challis said.

'I know.'

'Derek Watson wrote a letter to the colonel, but it didn't arrive until after he died.'

'*His* wasn't natural causes.'

'Agreed. In the letter Derek said you told him that his and the colonel's lives were in danger. What did you mean by that? Have you got any information?'

'Who are you?'

'I'm a journalist, Mr Harris, and a friend of Matthew Hardy, the colonel's son. He's asked me to see what I can find out about his father's death.'

'Well, I ain't seeing no-one.'

'Come on, Mr Harris, what about today? It won't take me long to drive to Sheffield.'

'You ain't got my address.'

'That's not a problem. I've got your phone number so I'll easily get your address.'

'If you come round here annoying me and my sister I'll call the police. You can't make me see you. I warn you, I really will call the police.'

'All right, I'll write to you instead. And if what you say is true then you might need help too. Maybe I'll be able to help you.'

'Do what you want, but I can look after myself. Don't bother me again. Goodbye.'

Challis took the mobile phone from his ear. Mrs Watson was right. Bernie Harris did seem a strange man. Or scared.

Challis dialled again to a contact who worked in British Telecommunications and gave him the Sheffield number. The contact said he would call him back in about half an hour with the address.

The journalist found a quiet pub and bought a chicken sandwich and a pint of lager. And that would be the only one until he got back to London. Five years ago he stupidly got drunk on a story, wrapped his car round a lamp-post, and was lucky to walk away in one piece. He was disqualified for two years and vowed he'd never drive over the limit again. He still got drunk, in fact, he loved a drink, but only when someone else was driving. No way did he want to lose his licence a second time. Those two years had been a bastard without a motor.

Challis tore a page from his notebook and wrote a brief message to Bernie Harris. When his BT contact phoned back with Harris's address he left the pub, bought envelopes and stamps from a newsagent and stopped at the first post box he saw.

SEVEN

The taxi drove into the rutted private road and stopped outside the small block of purpose built flats. There were three entrances, each leading to eight flats, making a total of twenty four. This once fashionable part of Islington in north London had gradually declined over the years and the flats had seen better days. Bare wood showed through cracked white painted window frames and the caretaker's flat had long been rented out to gain extra income for the landlord. A cleaner in a van appeared twice a week and spent five minutes on each stone tiled stairway with a mop and bucket, usually leaving more dirty streaks than when he started.

A well dressed man in his late thirties got out of the cab, paid the driver, and pushed through the swing doors of the left hand entrance. He walked up two flights of stairs and opened the heavy wood and glass panelled front door of the flat he'd rented for the last five years.

The run down condition of the block didn't bother him. The majority of the tenants were elderly and minded their own business and during all the time he'd stayed in the flat not once had he entered into conversation with any of them. He'd only seen the elderly man who lived in the flat opposite him a couple of times a year and the most they'd ever done was nod at each other. He preferred it that way.

Besides, it wasn't as though he *lived* here.

It was early evening and the sun was still shining but as soon as the man entered the lounge he drew the thick navy blue curtains and checked the windows were completely covered before turning on the lights. He went into the kitchen and pulled tight the dark curtains, once again making sure no light could escape through the window. He did the same with the half curtain covering the back door leading to a small balcony, also the bathroom curtain, then repeated the procedure in both bedrooms. The blackout was complete.

He returned to the lounge and looked through a selection of tapes. He chose one and inserted it into the side of the reproduction nineteen thirties radio, the cassette player being a modern addition. The sound of Geraldo and his orchestra followed the man as he went back into the larger bedroom and opened the mahogany wardrobe. He removed a British Army captain's uniform, laid it on the bed and went to a small chest of drawers, took out a newly laundered khaki shirt and regimental tie, followed by clean underwear and socks.

After a bath he quickly dried himself. He was in excellent condition, his muscles hard, the result of strenuous, regular workouts.

He carefully dressed in the uniform, went back into the lounge, opened a bottle of Johnny Walker whisky and poured a large drink into a crystal glass tumbler. He sat relaxed in an armchair and listened to a variety of his favourite music; Glen Miller, Joe Loss, Anne Shelton and of course, Vera Lynn singing, *We'll Meet Again.*

His eyes fastened contentedly on a group of framed photographs on the sideboard. His family.

An hour later he went to a small writing desk and opened the middle drawer. Inside were half a dozen cassettes that had been his conscience over the years. They were numbered with names, dates and times neatly written on the white labels. He selected one and stared at it. Usually he would listen to them all in sequence over a period of twelve months and only play this one once at the end. But he was impatient now and had found himself playing it more and more these last few months.

He inserted the tape into the player and poured another drink. Half an hour later the cheerfulness the music had instilled in him disappeared as his mind went back in time.

He listened intently to the voice coming out of the speaker. *His voice*, but oh so different. Tears coursed down his cheeks and his head slumped forward as he cried for his dead friend. Suddenly he stood.

'Bastards,' he shouted out, the word echoing eerily through the empty flat.

He took a handkerchief from his trousers pocket and blew his nose. He picked up his officer's cap from the small dining table, put it on his head and carefully adjusted it. He turned and stood crisply to attention before the mirror hanging over the tiled fireplace.

He saluted.

'Reporting for duty, sir.'

The reflection stared back at him.

'Your new mission begins tomorrow at 0600 hours.'

'Yes sir.'

EIGHT

The alarm clock burst into its piercing ringing noise. The machine said seven thirty and was on the other bedside table. It was supposed to wake Keely early so she would have time to go home before going to work, but she slumbered on oblivious of the noise.

Challis threw back the duvet and walked naked round the bed. The advantage of being a freelance was that he didn't need to be in an office at a certain time, and Challis would have liked to slept in this morning.

When he arrived back from Doncaster yesterday late afternoon Keely had phoned and said she'd got a last minute invitation to a film premiere. She wanted him to be her escort. Then there had been a party afterwards.

He silenced the clock and lifted up the duvet cover on her side, placed his foot against Keely's bare hip and pushed. She rolled over on her back, her long blonde hair spreading on the pillow. She yawned and stretched her arms and legs. She had a beautiful body.

'Keely, wake up. I've got a great idea.'

He prodded her once more and she sleepily opened her eyes.

'Let's take a shower together.'

She propped herself up on one elbow and looked at him.

'*You* need a *cold* shower,' and she turned back over and flopped face flat on the bed, one arm hanging over the edge.

Challis looked down at himself. She was right. He whipped the duvet completely off the bed.

'Keely, if you don't do as you're told, I'm going to ravish you.'

She spread her legs. 'Be my guest,' came her muffled reply from the pillow.

Challis looked at the provocative curve of her bottom. Then the phone rang. Challis couldn't believe it. He went back to his side of the bed and picked up the receiver.

'Yes operator, thank you,' he mumbled, and slowly put down the phone. 'You booked an early morning call. You couldn't have timed it better, you bitch.'

Keely got the giggles and a few moments later Challis joined in.

'I'll make us some coffee,' he said, and put on a white towelling bath robe.

A couple of coffees and glasses of fruit juice later they had their shower. Together.

Their relationship was so different compared to the journalist's brief fling at wedded bliss. It was only three months after Challis tied the knot that the complaining started about his unsociable working hours on the country's most popular daily tabloid.

Before they'd married his wife seemed to accept the fact that his was no ordinary nine to five job, but once the ring was on her finger she had other ideas. She wanted Challis to apply for the vacant job of deputy news editor and didn't like it when Challis told her he had no intention of being a desk jockey. He liked being on the road chasing up stories. Where the action was.

So they had arguments. Then he started drinking heavily and purposely staying out because he couldn't stand the nagging. More rows, so he quit the paper to give his marriage another chance, and became a freelance.

But the damage was too far gone and after just over a year they went their separate ways. Fortunately, they hadn't started a family.

*

When Keely left Challis sat down in his office and went over the last couple of days. He'd made notes but there wasn't a lot to show for it. Derek Watson was dead and Bernie Harris wasn't talking. He thought about phoning Harris but decided against it. Even if he had received the letter by now, there wasn't any guarantee he or his sister would speak to Challis. No, he'd wait until the end of the week, and if he hadn't heard by then, he would go to Sheffield anyway.

So what was he left with? The only intriguing thing he'd discovered so far was the 1950 magazine story about Giles Faraday. He'd seen it in the colonel's house and Derek Watson's. Just coincidence or was it important?

It mentioned a surviving younger sister, Evelyn. But that article had been written in 1950, could she still be alive?

It was worth trying to find her. He had nothing else to go on.

He picked up his briefcase, left the flat, and got in his car heading for The Family Records Centre situated near Exmouth Market and Angel. It was still baking hot and most water boards across the country had finally put a hosepipe ban on householders.

The Family Records Centre was an important part of any journalist's working life. The records of birth, deaths and marriages for England and Wales were kept there. Divorces and wills were kept in First Avenue House about twenty minutes away in Holborn and Challis had tracked down numerous people using these combined resources.

He placed his briefcase in one of the basement lockers and armed with a notebook and pen headed for the birth section. Births were in red books, marriages in green books and deaths were recorded in black books.

Giles Faraday was twenty seven when he died in July nineteen forty four and after a few minutes Challis found the birth entry for a Giles P. Faraday in the March quarter of nineteen seventeen. His mother's maiden name was Nolan and he'd been born in Bath.

Then he began searching forward looking for an Evelyn Faraday with the same mother's maiden name of Nolan. He found her registered in the September quarter of nineteen twenty three. She had a middle initial R and she too was born in the district of Bath.

So far, so good, but the search rooms were getting crowded with several coach parties of people doing their family tree. The Family Records Centre was a popular tourist visit for amateur genealogists. The air conditioning was adequate but lugging the large books to and from the shelves was still perspiring work.

Challis headed for the section where the marriages were kept. Evelyn R. Faraday would have been eighteen in nineteen forty one and he began looking in that year to see if she'd married. In those days a person was still a minor until they were twenty one and needed their parents permission to marry under that age. Even so, lots of girls married young, especially during the war.

However, as Challis worked his way through the forties he began to wonder if Evelyn had ever married at all. Then he found it in nineteen fifty two. She'd wed a man named George S. Nash and was still in the Bath area.

The next step was to see if there had been any children. He discovered she'd given birth to a boy in the December quarter of nineteen fifty three and a year later had a girl. The boy, Giles L. Nash, was obviously named after his uncle and the girl was called Rosemary, with W as a middle initial.

Challis looked at his watch. It was just after twelve. He was hungry but he wanted to get as much done as soon as possible.

Starting from the latest year available he began looking through the black books to see if Evelyn or George Nash had died. He worked his way back to nineteen seventy five without finding their names and presumed they were still alive.

He returned to the marriage section to see if their children had married. They both had. Rosemary in nineteen seventy seven and Giles in nineteen eighty one. Then Challis started searching for their children. The later the certificate, the more recent the address would be.

Between them the families sired five children and the last child he could find was a girl born to Giles Nash's wife in nineteen eighty nine.

It was now three thirty and Challis began filling in the marriage and birth application forms. Twelve in total.

The Family Records Centre operated a two tier system for ordering certificates. The normal way cost seven pounds each but took four working days before they were ready for collection, or there was a special twenty four hour *priority* service at twenty three pounds per certificate. Expensive, but a darn sight quicker and Challis was on expenses anyway, so he ordered them to be ready for the next day.

*

Challis spent the evening sprawled on his sofa drinking chilled canned lager and looking at videos. He was a keen boxing fan and had a collection of some of the greatest bouts to have ever taken place.

Over the years he'd spent a small fortune getting the best ringside tickets for live matches in this country and the States. He'd travel anywhere to see a good fight.

Challis had been a pretty good amateur in his teens and had taken up boxing initially at school because he didn't have a father around to fight his battles. Then the gang of teenagers he hung about with began getting into trouble with the police, so he started to study in his spare time. Challis wanted to be able to use his head as well as his fists and was determined to get out of the slum area he lived in.

The boxing club Challis belonged to had produced some good boxers and for a time he was one of the most promising. He became an ABA junior middleweight champion and then fought in the senior rankings as a light-heavyweight. He was good, and at one stage there was talk he might turn pro, but deep inside Challis knew he never had that something extra to make him a champion. And when his mother got really sick and then died Challis lost his enthusiasm for training, so he quit.

Besides, he'd discovered the opposite sex by then and didn't want any more damage done to his face. He'd already had his nose broken a couple of times. But girls told him that added to his attraction, and being a reporter on the local rag didn't do his pulling power any harm, either.

Looking at the flickering images on the screen Challis felt guilty because when he worked on a story, it was usually a non stop work schedule until he'd finished, with no time for knocking back beer and watching videos.

But Challis was bored and hoped the two weeks passed quickly so he could get his life back the way he wanted.

*

The next morning Challis stood in the shower and slowly turned the spray to cold, letting the water play over his muscular body. He wasn't in bad shape, considering he didn't get as much exercise these days as he should.

He spent a lazy couple of hours reading through the newspapers then met Lucy Barnes in a little bistro near Whitehall. A lunch he'd been promising her for ages. Lucy was a journalist now in semi-retirement due to the fact she'd married and was expecting her first child. Her husband, Mark, had left the police force after ten years service, a very disillusioned copper, and now ran his own successful private detective agency. Challis often used him.

The two journalists were great pals and had worked together on several stories over the years. Lucy was a good looking, ballsy woman who had taken more risks than a lot of male reporters Challis knew.

And the two hacks spent the next couple of hours enjoying a leisurely meal, reliving past stories, and discussing mutual friends in their business. An old journalist habit.

'What are you working on at the moment?' Lucy asked.

'Not much,' Challis replied, and went on to explain about the commitment he'd given to Seton Travis. A job he wasn't sure if he'd be able to stand up.

Then it was time to say goodbye.

'Don't forget to let me know as soon as your kid's born,' Challis said, as Lucy got in the first taxi.

'Of course,' she replied, and kissed Challis on the cheek through the open window before the black cab sped away.

A minute later Challis was in another taxi on his way to The Family Records Centre.

*

The girl behind the collection desk took his ticket, pulled a sheaf of papers from a drawer and shuffled through them, separating the pinned application forms from the certificates, making sure they were all present and correct. Three marriages and nine births.

Challis took the green and pink documents, sat down on a nearby bench seat and put them in the right order. It was fascinating that he could trace the family from the dead parents of Giles Faraday right up to the grandchildren of Evelyn, his sister.

Challis left the search rooms, retuned to his flat, and once inside selected the birth certificate of the youngest grandchild, Sara Jennifer Nash. She was born on September 8th 1989 and her parents address was in Trowbridge, which wasn't too far from Bath.

The journalist dialled directory enquiries and asked if the father, Giles L. Nash, was listed under the address.

He was and Challis scribbled down the number as it came through the earpiece.

He switched on the tape recorder attached to the telephone and dialled the number.

'Hello,' a woman's breathless voice said. 'Hang on a minute.'

Challis heard the voice shouting at someone to be quiet.

'Sorry, about that,' she said. 'My kids and some of their friends are eating. It's like a war zone here.'

Challis remembered it was the school holidays and she had another two children as well.

'What can I do for you?'

'Well, actually, I'm trying to locate your mother-in-law.'

'Evelyn, what do you want with her?' caution creeping into the woman's voice.

'Don't worry Mrs Nash, I'm a freelance journalist and I'm doing research for a book about the Second World War. It's to do with your mother-in-law's dead brother, Giles Faraday, and I'd like a word with her.'

'How did you get my number?'

'It's a long story, but I assure you I'm genuine. If you like I'll give you my number, I'm phoning from home, and you can call me back.'

'No, that's all right,' she said slowly. 'But I'm still not sure if I should give you Evelyn's number.'

'Well then, let me give you my number anyway and get her to phone me. I think she lives in the Bath area and I could track her down myself. But it would take much longer.'

'Okay, that sounds fair enough. But you haven't told me your name yet.'

Challis gave his name and number and Mrs Nash promised that either she or her mother-in-law would call him within the next fifteen minutes.

His phone rang within ten.

'Hello, is that Mr Challis?'

It was a different voice.

'That's right. And I assume you're Mrs Evelyn Nash.'

'Correct,' she replied. 'I believe you're writing a book or something like that, and you're interested in my brother. At least, that's what my daughter-in-law told me.'

'Yes, I am doing something like that.'

'So, how can I help? My brother's been dead for well over fifty years. He wasn't famous or anything.'

'Have you ever heard of a Colonel Roger Hardy?'

'No, can't say I have. Why?'

'He wasn't a friend of your brother? Or maybe your family knew him during the war.'

'The name doesn't mean a thing to me, but don't forget, we are talking about a very long time ago. If I ever did meet him, I certainly can't remember.'

The journalist was disappointed but the answer wasn't unexpected.

'Would it be okay if I came and saw you?'

'Well, yes, I suppose so. You're in London, Mr Challis, when were you thinking of coming?'

'Where exactly do you live, Mrs Nash?'

'Bradford-on-Avon.'

'What about later today? I could be there by five o'clock.'

'Today?' She sounded surprised. 'I was thinking more of next week, something like that.'

'Mrs Nash, I promise I won't take up much of your time, but it's really important I see you.'

'No, I'm sorry Mr Challis, but I can't possibly see you this evening. I've got friends coming for dinner.'

'What about tomorrow?'

'I'm busy during the day but, all right then, let's say five o'clock tomorrow afternoon.'

She gave him the address and told him it was off Thorsey Road.

Challis swore as he put down the phone. Keely was out of town for a couple of days so it meant another night drinking beer and watching videos.

NINE

The three bedroom terrace house was in Millbank, in the Northam district of Southampton, near the docks and wharfs which had been in use since Victorian times. It was in one of the oldest parts of the city and the house had been neglected over the years. The small backyard had long ago given up trying to support any plant life and was littered with old car and motorcycle parts. A rusting water tank was wedged against a tiny shed, no doubt holding it up.

At the end of the yard was a dilapidated brick wall topped with broken glass. Pointless really, because the large wooden gate leading to the back alley was hanging off its hinges.

The man in the long grey military coat and heavy boots peered through the opening and quietly eased himself through. He took a pair of black running shoes from the coat's large pockets and, after exchanging footwear, placed the boots and coat behind the shed.

The figure crouched looking at the back of the house. There were lights on in every room, but the upstairs were curtained and didn't throw much illumination into the backyard. The main light was coming from the kitchen and the man silently made his way to the window. His head was now completely covered in a one piece woollen mask, with holes for his mouth and eyes, his long sleeved two piece track suit jet black. The man cautiously raised his head above the window sill and looked in.

*

Gary Woodcock sat at the rickety table holding his head in his hands, his elbows resting on the scratched blue Formica surface. He'd cried at his grandfather's funeral today and still found it hard to believe the way the old man had died, skewered through the neck and left hanging on a wooden post. The police said the murder weapon was a World War Two issue bayonet and Gary knew his grandfather had been in that war, which made it all the more eerie.

The Woodcock family were well known to the police. Woody, as his grandfather was called, had lived in Southampton for over fifty years but had been born in Bethnal Green, in London's East End. He'd moved north with his parents to Barnsley in the late thirties when he'd first got into trouble with the law, then the war came along and he joined the army. When he'd been demobbed he moved to Southampton and married a local girl.

Woody had been a small-time thief, fence and burglar. He'd done a couple of six month sentences inside and been lucky not to have done longer. He was a public pest more than a hardened criminal, but he certainly didn't deserve to die like he had. Nobody did. Not even Gary's father, Billy, who was in the next room. And he *was* a hardened criminal who'd done a lot of bird.

Billy had only been set free from prison eight days ago, three weeks after his father's murder.

The coroner had delayed the release of the body until Billy finished a seven year sentence for armed robbery and was able to make arrangements for the funeral which had been held at eleven o'clock that morning.

Gary had drunk too much beer and felt rough, and looking around the small kitchen didn't help matters. Plates with smears of mustard, pickles, and bits of salad and pork pie were jammed in a pile against the wall by the sink. The water in the bowel had a thick layer of grease with pieces of soggy food floating on top. Bottles of sherry, whisky and gin, their contents long gone, were stacked by the back door, next to empty beer crates.

Somebody had attempted a clean-up but there were just as many plates and beer cans in the living room where his father lay spark out on the sofa.

After the burial of Gary's grandfather in Hollybrook Cemetery a lot more people than expected came back to the house to eat, drink and talk over old times.

It was now ten thirty and the last of them had only just staggered out. Then Gary remembered, there was still one left, Rosie, who'd gone upstairs a couple of hours ago for a lay down. He hadn't been up to the bedroom to check on her, but she'd probably end up staying the night.

Rosie was in her late thirties and married but had been separated from her husband for so long hardly anybody could remember him. She loved drinking and men, and it didn't matter in which order. She was free and easy with her favours and had taken most of the young men's virginity in the area, Gary's included.

*

At that moment Rosie was just waking from a heavy sleep and it took a few moments to collect her thoughts. During the day she'd drunk so many glasses of gin and tonics she'd lost count.

The light was on and as she moved off the bed she caught her reflection in the dressing table mirror. Her black dress was badly creased and wrinkled so she undid the buttons and slipped it over her head. Underneath she was wearing a black lace suspender belt, brief matching panties and sheer black stockings. Stiletto heels added inches to her height and the black half cup bra highlighted the whiteness of her ample bosom.

Rosie knew she was getting on a bit but nature had been kind to her face and body, and she knew how to excite the opposite sex.

She looked at herself again in the mirror and decided to go downstairs just as she was. Nearly all of the women had already left when she'd gone for a rest and she didn't expect any to be there now. But if there were any men still about, well, she'd give them a treat. She'd often been gangbanged by three or four at the same time. And enjoyed it. She took a brush from her handbag and pulled it through her long black hair. She felt randy.

*

Gary stood up from the table and yawned, he must have dozed off for a few minutes. He walked into the living room and surveyed the mess. He shook his head, and decided he couldn't face doing any clearing up, it would have to wait until tomorrow. His father was snoring like a steam train with his legs dangling over the end of the too short sofa and Gary stooped and adjusted the cushion under his head. He shouldn't have bent down so quickly because he suddenly felt dizzy and nauseous. He reeled back into the kitchen, opened the back door and stepped out into the fresh air. He tried taking deep breaths but still couldn't stop himself from being sick. He finished retching and straightened up.

He'd just placed one foot on the doorstep to go back inside when he felt a hand clamped tightly over his mouth and nose from behind. Gary's eyes opened wide in shock, but before he could defend himself, his head was jerked sideways and a double edged knife plunged into his neck. The man in the black tracksuit pulled the commando knife free and thrust the tapered blade hard into Gary's back. Then he pushed Gary forward with his left hand so his body slipped off the steel and crashed face first onto the lino covered stone floor. The man stepped inside the kitchen and his foot kicked against the whisky and gin bottles sending them flying.

'Merde,' he cursed, and quickly went into the living room, just as Billy struggled to rise from the sofa, his feet nearly touching the floor.

'Wassup,' he slurred. 'Wass going on?'

The man stood behind Billy, grabbed his chin, forcing his head backwards over the sofa's arm and savagely drew the seven inch blade across Woody's son's throat. Twice.

As the man let Billy's head flop forward the door opened from the hallway and Rosie entered. At first the scene was too horrific to comprehend, then realisation set in and she drew the back of her hand to her mouth. But before she could scream the man pushed past her and kicked the door shut. He grabbed Rosie, twisted her around so her back was pressed tight against him, and shoved a hand over her mouth.

Where had this stupid woman come from? He was sure all the guests had left half an hour ago.

'Silence,' he commanded, and pushed Rosie into the middle of the room. He hooked a wooden dining chair with his foot, pulled it towards him and sat the trembling woman down.

Billy had fallen off the sofa into a sitting position and was making gurgling noises. He limply lifted one hand to his severed neck and felt his fingers go inside his throat. His arm flopped down and stopped moving as the dark red blood continued gushing over his chest, down his stomach, forming a pool between his crotch.

Rosie averted her eyes but spotted Gary face down through the open doorway in the kitchen. A pool of blood spread in a circle like a red halo around his head.

Now Rosie knew what fear was. Real fear.

The man stepped in front of her and she looked through the round openings of his black mask and stared into his cold brown eyes.

58

'Shush,' he said and pressed his right forefinger hard against her lips, his gloved hand still gripping the knife. She gaped at the bloodstained weapon with its slightly S-shaped crossguard and wet herself. She didn't look down but could feel her warm urine spread through her knickers, against her bare thighs and over the wooden chair until it reached her stocking tops.

'Shush, silence.'

She noted the man spoke the second word with the French pronunciation.

Her gaze was riveted to the blade as it moved down the front of her and the point settled on her bra. Then with a quick flick the material was cut in two and her large breasts sprang free.

The man moved behind her and dragged the bra backwards over her arms, forcing her hands behind the chair where he firmly tied them.

Rosie decided to break her silence.

'Please don't kill me,' she said. 'Please don't kill me. I'll do anything you want. You can fuck me if you want, I don't mind. As many times as you want. Any way. I won't tell anybody. I'll do anything, anything.'

Rosie's words became desperate as she pleaded for her life.

'I do a great blow...'

The man's hand shut off her flow.

'Silence,' and his voice sounded more menacing this time. He bent down and placed the knife on the threadbare carpet. He released Rosie's right stocking from her suspenders, pulled it down her leg, removed her high heeled shoe and dragged the stocking free. Then he wedged her foot behind the chair leg and securely tied it with the black nylon hose.

He repeated the procedure with her other limb, forcing her legs wide apart, and noticed the puddle in front of her lace knickers.

'Cochon,' he said.

He put two gloved fingers in the urine and then dragged them across her cheek. 'Cochon,' he spat out the word as he called her a pig, and put his fingers once again into the yellow liquid.

He pushed his hand against her lips forcing them apart, and she opened her mouth wide fearful of accidentally biting him and tasted herself.

The man grabbed several crumpled paper napkins from the small dining table and shoved them in her mouth. He pushed in more until she could only breathe through her nose.

He picked up the knife from the floor, grabbed a handful of her long hair and cut it free from her scalp.

'Collaborateur,' he grunted out, and continued hacking off handfuls of hair.

Rosie made squealing noises from the back of her throat each time her hair was savagely pulled.

Finally the man stopped and left the room. He ran up the stairs, found what he was looking for in the bathroom and returned to his victim.

He looked around, picked up a half full bottle of white wine and poured some over Rosie's head. Then he sprayed shaving foam over her shorn scalp and started scraping her head with a safety razor. He nicked her several times and, as the blade lost its edge, pieces of flesh were torn out. Thin rivulets of blood ran down the back of her neck.

He finished with the razor and poured the remainder of the wine over her head washing away streaks of foam.

He stood in front of Rosie and lifted her chin upwards with the tip of the knife. Her mascara had run in streaks down her cheeks which were puffed out with paper and her bald scalp looked red raw. Her eyes gazed fearfully into his wondering what was coming next.

It was deathly quiet. Billy had stopped gurgling an eternity ago.

'Collaborateur,' he said, and dropped the point from her chin and stooped down.

He pulled up his right leg track suit bottom and slid the Fairbairn Sykes fighting knife neatly into its leather sheath strapped to his calf.

Then he turned his back on Rosie and casually walked into the kitchen, stepped over Gary's body and left the house.

TEN

There wasn't much in the morning newspapers about the murders in Southampton, just a few paragraphs in some of the later editions. The murders had been discovered too late for much coverage in the dailies but breakfast television was highlighting them as one of their main news items.

If he was up early Challis always switched on to catch up with overnight events. And as he munched his way through tinned tomatoes on toast and watched the programme he remembered reading about Ronald Woodcock's grisly death just before he went on holiday. Now someone had brutally butchered his son and grandson on the day of his funeral. And a woman had been found tied up with her head shaved at the scene of the murders. Most macabre.

The story was a news editor's dream and the tabloids were certain to give it plenty of space the next day. The local news agencies in the Southampton area would make a small fortune if they acted quickly, especially if they got their hands on family photographs.

Challis spent the rest of the morning on the phone trying to discreetly find out information about a TV chat show host who was cheating on his wife. He'd been given the tip-off just before he went on holiday and was itching to get stuck into the investigation. He phoned his contact and said he hoped to be able to give the showbiz story his full attention in just over a week's time.

The contact was an ex-con now working in a club in the West End and had fed Challis a lot of good leads in the past.

Challis was welcome in quite a few late night drinking clubs used by villains and showbiz people, even though he wrote for the papers, simply because he was discreet in his use of information. Some things he heard he conveniently forgot.

The journalist didn't want to end up on the bottom of the River Thames. No story was worth that.

*

After a burger in the local McDonalds he went back to his flat and packed an overnight bag. The weekend was starting next day and Challis had decided to drive to Sheffield and see Bernie Harris after his meeting with Evelyn Nash.

At two thirty Challis drove to Chiswick and joined the traffic on the M4 motorway. It was just over a hundred miles to his destination and shouldn't take him more than a couple of hours.

The journey was uneventful and at junction 17 he turned off the motorway, drove past Corsham in the direction of Trowbridge, and then cut across country to Bradford-on-Avon.

It was a beautiful town with Bath-stone houses and a medieval bridge which crossed the river Avon. Challis got lost so he phoned Evelyn Nash on his mobile and she guided him in. She lived in a quaint thatched cottage that looked as though it should be on the front of a picture postcard, with climbing roses growing over the front door porch, and two black Labrador dogs dozing in the shade.

Evelyn Nash was a charming lady with silvery curly hair framing a tanned freckled face. Gold rimmed half moon glasses perched on the middle of her nose gave her an inquisitive look. Challis had her birth certificate and knew she was seventy nine, but if he hadn't had that document and been asked to guess her age, he would have said at least ten years younger. She looked exceptionally fit and well.

She led Challis through the cottage out through the lounge French windows into a pretty country garden and showed him to four white wrought iron garden chairs grouped round a matching table.

'Just a minute, Mr Challis,' she said, and went back inside.

She returned very quickly with a jug of ice cold home made lemonade and two tall glasses. She put the tray down and opened the table umbrella to give welcoming shade. Challis took a large sip and swirled the ice cubes around.

'Very tasty,' he said, and meant it.

Before Challis could begin his questioning an elderly man in tan slacks and cream coloured jacket appeared through the French windows.

'Mr Challis, meet my husband, George.'

Challis stood and shook hands with her husband. George was three years older than his wife, it said so on their wedding certificate, but he too looked remarkably fit and young.

'I'm just off darling,' he said, and gave his wife a gentle kiss on her cheek.

'Sorry I can't stay, Mr Challis, but I've got a bowls match on this evening.'

'A healthy looking man, your husband,' Challis said, as George walked to his car in the drive. 'I hope I look as good as that when I'm his age. You look very well too.'

Mrs Nash smiled graciously at the compliment. 'Thank you. I get a lot of fresh air gardening. I think that keeps me fit.'

'Your brother would have been three years older than your husband, I believe,' Challis said.

'Yes, that's correct. But how do you know?'

'I did some digging and I found your brother's birth certificate.'

Evelyn Nash didn't say a word and her silence forced Challis to carry on. 'As a matter of fact I did a bit of a family tree, that's how I traced you.'

'Very industrious, Mr Challis.'

The journalist explained about Colonel Hardy's death and his visit to Doncaster to see Derek Watson. He said he was intrigued that at both addresses he'd found the same magazine story about her brother.

'Now you've come to the third place that's got the same story. So what do you think of that?'

'Well, I'm not surprised you've got a copy. After all, you are mentioned in it.'

'It all sounds very intriguing, but I don't see how my dead brother fits into what you've told me. I really do fail to see the connection between a present day murder in London and Giles. Are you really writing a book?'

'Truthfully, I'm not too sure what I'll be writing about. But I would like to learn more about your brother. His background, and things like that. Do you mind?'

The old lady smiled.

'No, I don't mind. Anyway, it's so long ago.'

'Is it okay if I tape record you as well as taking notes?'

'That's fine.'

Challis opened his briefcase and took out a small Olympus tape recorder.

'Tell me about your brother. From the beginning, in your own words,' he said.

Evelyn explained her father was a doctor and her mother taught French at an exclusive girls school in Bath where she and her brother, Giles, were born. There were no other brothers or sisters.

'Of course, my Mother gave up teaching as soon as she married,' Mrs Nash said.

'I had a very happy childhood and we lived in a large house which always seemed to be a meeting place at weekends for medical friends of my Father. Giles and I were both fairly clever and my brother took after my Mother for learning languages. Giles was at Oxford University when the war broke out and he volunteered for the army just a few weeks later.'

'What was your brother studying at Oxford?'

'Modern languages and English history,' she replied. 'I was hoping to go to university myself but the war changed all that. I wanted to be an archaeologist but I decided to go into nursing instead.'

'What happened after your brother joined the army?'

'He joined the Royal Fusiliers as a second lieutenant and I didn't see him for a couple of months. Then he went to France and returned to England after Dunkirk. I remember he came home several times during the next two years but I didn't know what he'd been doing. In those years it was impressed upon us all that careless talk cost lives. The last time I saw my brother was Christmas nineteen forty three. He'd been promoted to captain by then and he brought one of his friends to stay with us. He had two weeks leave and left a couple of days after New Year.'

'Were you close?' Challis asked.

'I adored him, but I think a lot of girls feel that way about an older brother.'

'Did he marry?'

'No.'

'Any girlfriends?'

'No one special. He was a good looking man and I'm sure he would have had several girlfriends, but not any that I can remember.'

'It said in the article your brother was with the Special Operations Executive. That was one of our wartime secret services. A spy, actually. Did he ever mention anything to you?'

'No, nothing at all. As far as I knew he was in the army, and that was it. I must say it came as a surprise to me. It seems my brother was quite a hero. Pity our parents didn't live long enough to find out.'

'They died in a plane crash, didn't they?'

'Yes, they were holidaying abroad. They went to Italy and Greece, then flew to Turkey, but they never got there. Their plane crashed in the Aegean Sea. It was tragic.'

'How did you find out about your brother?'

'Through the War Office. Originally, we'd been informed that Giles was missing in action. Then in nineteen forty six we were told that no trace had been found of him and he must be presumed dead. But then in nineteen fifty I was contacted by the Ministry of Defence and told that they had been informed by the French authorities my brother had been killed in July, nineteen forty four, and his grave was in a small village called Roujan, in northern France. They also told me Giles had been on a special mission behind enemy lines when he died. But they didn't say what.'

'Have you ever been to the grave?'

'Yes, when I got married we had a honeymoon touring in France and went to Roujan. The villagers were very nice to us once they discovered I was Giles sister. Henri Fabere was from the village and was a member of the French Resistance. He and Giles were killed together and that's why my brother was buried there.'

'Why did it take so long for the British authorities to find out what had happened to your brother?'

'The people in that village and surrounding area are a tight knit community and keep very much to themselves. It only came to light because some French author was writing a book about the Resistance, otherwise I don't think I would have ever known. On my brother's headstone it doesn't say *Captain* Giles Faraday or that he was in the British Army. It only gives his name and the date he died.'

'Did your husband know Giles?'

'Yes, but not very well. They met a few times before the war. They were in the same tennis club, but when the war started they joined different regiments.'

Evelyn Nash stood up.

'I won't be a minute,' she said, and disappeared inside the cottage.

Challis paused the tape recorder, topped up his glass of lemonade and had just taken a swig when the old lady returned with a large chocolate box.

She took the lid off the box and Challis saw it was full of photographs.

'I've got boxes of these,' she laughed. 'I keep promising myself one day I'll put them in albums. This box covers my childhood, then right through the war years up until I got married.'

She quickly searched through the pictures, every now and again placing one on the table. She found an envelope and handed it to the journalist.

'There's your story,' she said.

Challis opened the envelope and saw the same 1950 magazine story about her brother.

'And here's Giles.'

Challis spent the next ten minutes looking at snaps of the Faraday family and the different stages of Evelyn and her brother's life through adolescence to maturity. There were some very good ones of Giles, especially one that was taken on his last visit home at Christmas in nineteen forty three.

From the pile Challis selected several photographs of the parents, and Evelyn and her brother.

'Would it be all right if I borrowed these and had them copied? I'll get them returned to you as soon as possible.'

'Why yes, of course,' she replied.

Challis pulled his wallet from his trousers back pocket and took out his business card.

'Just so you know where I am in case you want to get hold of me.'

'That's what the other journalist said.'

Challis looked at her in surprise.

'Other journalist? You mean another journalist has been here to see you?'

'Yes, but it was a long time ago, about five or six years, maybe longer. He wanted to know all about my brother too. He also borrowed some of my photographs and I got them back through the post a couple of weeks later. He sent me twenty five pounds as well.'

Challis smiled at the gentle hint and asked, 'Do you remember his name?'

Evelyn looked thoughtful but after a few moments shook her head.

'No, I'm sorry but I can't remember.'

'Did he say which paper he worked for?'

'No, I think he said he was a freelance, like yourself.' She stood again. 'I might still have his card somewhere.'

She went back into the cottage and returned with a smaller cardboard box in her hand.

'My husband says I'm a hoarder, but I keep most of the business cards I get, even cards that come through the front door. You never know when they might come in useful.'

She pulled a small white card from the pile. 'Yes, here it is. Now I remember.'

Challis took the card and read the name. John Mason, and the address and telephone number was in Bristol. He copied the details into a small notebook.

'Do you know if a story about your brother ever appeared anywhere?' he asked.

'I honestly don't know. The journalist said it was for a magazine and he would let me know when it was coming out, but I never heard from him again.'

Challis turned off his tape recorder and put it in his briefcase, along with the small notebook and borrowed photographs. He finished his glass of lemonade, stood up, and gave Evelyn Nash a warm smile.

If the journalist had a weakness, it was nice little old ladies. It was a pity his mother hadn't lived to be a little old lady. Life could be cruel.

'Thanks,' he said. 'You've been most helpful.'

ELEVEN

The Sheffield trip to see Bernie Harris was put off until the next day and Challis used his road atlas to work out a route to Bristol. Depending on the traffic he should be there in under an hour.

Before he left Bradford-on-Avon he called Seton.

'Have you ever heard of a freelance journalist called John Mason, from Bristol?'

'Not offhand, no. There are a couple of big news agencies in that area, maybe he works for one of them.'

'No, I don't think so. I've seen his business card and I'd say he operates by himself. I'm on my way to Bristol now, so see what you can find out about him.'

'Bristol? What are you doing there? I hope you're still working on the colonel's story.'

'Yes Seton, I'm still on that.'

'Ah, so you're making progress then.'

'Not very much, but I am enjoying the countryside.'

'I've got great faith in you, Challis. Keep plugging away and I'm sure you'll come up with something.'

'Thanks, that's most reassuring.'

Challis gave his friend the freelance's address and phone number and said, 'I'm going to spend the night in Bristol so as soon as I get somewhere to stay I'll phone you.'

'Speak to you soon,' Seton said

Challis had stayed in Bristol several times and knew that at this time of the year all the decent hotels in the centre would be full, so he pulled into the first motel he came to on the outskirts. There were vacancies and as soon as he was in his room phoned Seton back.

'John Mason is well known in the Bristol area, Challis. He's in his fifties and worked for twenty years on the local paper, then edited several trade magazines before they folded. He started a small local giveaway paper and was quite successful. Then one of his rivals bought him out about five years ago so he went freelance. He does odds and sods for the nationals, mostly their consumer pages, and he does research for one of the local radio stations.'

'You found out a lot in a short time, Seton.'

'Yeah, I was lucky. One of the first people I spoke to has known him for years. He's a nice bloke from what I hear, and loves a drink. What's your interest in him? Is he involved in this?'

'I'll tell you after I've spoken to him.'

Challis called the local number he'd written in his notebook and a man's voice answered.

'Hello.'

'John Mason?'

'That's right. Who are you?'

'My name's Challis. I'm a journalist, like yourself, and I think you might be able to help me with something I'm working on.'

'Peter Challis? The reporter who recently did the story on the Labour MP?'

'Yes, that's the one.'

'I'm pleased to talk to you. I see your by-line all the time and that was a great story you did on Carter-West. I always thought he was a smug little bastard.' Mason paused. 'You said I might be able to help you.'

'Yes. I'm in Bristol at the moment and I'd like to have a meet with you.'

'What about?'

'About a story you were involved in quite a few years ago, about five or six, I think. I've been to see an old lady today called Evelyn Nash in Bradford-on-Avon and she told me you interviewed her about that time. It was to do with her brother, Giles Faraday. Do you remember?'

'Yes, that's right,' Mason replied slowly. 'Yes, most strange that was, and I remember it well. Where do you want to meet me? Where are you staying?'

Challis gave him the name of the motel and, after they exchanged descriptions, arranged to meet in the bar later in the evening.

'Oh, and no need to drive,' Challis said. Get a cab both ways and I'll put it on my expenses.'

Challis had a shower, changed into a fresh pair of lightweight khaki trousers and blue denim shirt, then went to the motel restaurant. After a thick fillet steak, washed down with lager, he headed for the bar.

The room wasn't very busy and ten minutes past the arranged hour John Mason entered and looked around.

Challis got off his stool.

'John Mason?'

'That's me,' he answered with a broad grin. 'And you must be Peter Challis.'

'Just call me Challis, everybody else does. I only ever use my first name on by-lines.'

Mason had a friendly round shaped face and was bald on top with grey curly hair sprouting over his ears. He was about two stone overweight and looked as though he'd enjoyed putting it on.

'Okay then, Challis, what would you like to drink?'

'No, tonight's on me. I'm working and on expenses.'

Challis brushed aside Mason's protests, gave the barman his room number, and told him to put all the drinks on his bill.

'I'm drinking large ones,' Mason said.

'So am I,' Challis echoed. 'Scotch?'

'Of course.'

They took their drinks to a table within easy eye distance of the barman and sat down.

'Evelyn Nash is a nice old lady and somehow I always had the feeling I hadn't heard the last of her. Working on anything big?'

'I'm not sure,' Challis replied. 'It's a bit complicated to explain at the moment, and I'm not sure how she fits into the picture. But it appears you were asking the same questions then, as I was today.'

'About her brother, Giles?'

'Yes. Do you mind telling me what your interest was?'

Mason took off his sports jacket and folded it on a spare chair. The buttons strained on his check shirt and a few more added pounds would mean going up a larger size. He took a gulp of his whisky which nearly drained the glass and Challis immediately caught the barman's eye and motioned for two more drinks.

'I used to run one of these freebie local papers and I was doing pretty well. So well, in fact, somebody bought me out. And that's why I remember Mrs Nash. I sold the paper in June six years ago and decided to go freelance. I went on holiday for a couple of weeks and when I got back, July it was, I got a phone call from a man who said his name was Paul Phillips and asked if I would do some research for him. He said he was doing a book on the Second World War and he would like me to interview Evelyn Nash about her brother, Giles.'

'Did he know where she lived?' Challis asked.

'Yes, he gave me her telephone number and address in Bradford-on-Avon and her husband's name.'

'What did he want to know about Giles Faraday?'

'Well, it wasn't just about the war, because as it happens, the sister didn't know much about his war years. She knew her brother was in the army and after the war she discovered he was some kind of special agent. But she was a bit vague about it all.'

'Did she show you a magazine article about her brother and some Frenchman? It was written in nineteen fifty.'

'Yes, she did.'

'Had this Paul Phillips mentioned the article to you?'

'No. He gave me Giles Faraday's date of birth and when he died, but he didn't say anything about that article. As a matter of fact I photostatted it and sent it to him.'

'Did he make any mention about a Colonel Roger Hardy, or maybe that name, but with a different rank?'

Mason thought for a moment then shook his head.

'No, not a thing.'

'You said he gave you a date for Faraday's death. The exact date?'

'Yes.' Mason picked up his coat and extracted a reporters notebook from a side pocket. 'Twenty eighth of July nineteen forty four. He died in France. And if you're wondering why I'm so efficient and could put my hands on my notes so quickly, the answer is because it was my first freelance job after selling the paper, and this notebook was still in my first file. You're lucky.'

'Did his sister verify the date?'

'Yes, she told me she'd visited his grave and that date is on the headstone.'

'I wonder where your Mr Phillips got it from,' Challis said half to himself. 'What else did you talk about?'

'Well, that's where it got a bit strange. Phillips had sent me a list of details about Giles and Evelyn's early days and growing up together. Giles was six years older and he taught her to ride a bike, roller skate and swim. Things like that. Things that jogged her memory and led her to speak about other things.'

'Anything specific?'

'No, not really. It was all small talk domestic stuff, But what I found strangest of all was, all the events I brought up were bang on the nail each time. Even Mrs Nash commented I seemed to know as much about her brother as she did.'

'Did you tell her about Phillips?' Challis asked.

'No. I told her I was doing a piece for a magazine about forgotten heroes and they had done research on her brother. But the more I talked with her the more I got the feeling Phillips knew near enough everything about the Faraday family anyway, and was just using me to confirm what he already knew.'

The barman brought over another pair of double whiskies and placed them on the table.

'Cheers,' Mason said as he lifted his glass. 'I'm just starting to get the taste.'

Challis grinned back at him and took a drink.

'Then what happened?' he asked.

'I asked Mrs Nash if I could borrow some photographs to be copied and also the magazine piece. She said yes and I left.'

'How did Phillips get hold of you in the first place, had you ever met him?'

'No, never. Not even to this day. He phoned me out of the blue and said someone had recommended me. He said he'd pay me two hundred and fifty pounds plus expenses to do the interview with Evelyn Nash and to try and get copies of family photos. He said he'd send me the questions he wanted asking in the post and would rely on my journalistic prowess to expand the interview. Journalistic prowess,' Mason chuckled, and took another sip. 'Drinking prowess is all I've got left these days. I always wondered who recommended me.'

'How did you contact Phillips? Did he give you a phone number or address?' Challis asked.

'After I agreed to see Mrs Nash, he said he'd write to me, and a couple of days later sent me the questions, along with one hundred pounds in cash as advance payment on my fee. He told me to send the results of the interview to the enclosed address and said I needn't write it as finished copy. He wanted it in memo form, more like questions and answers.'

'Where was the address?' Challis signalled the barman again.

Mason looked at his notebook and flicked a few pages.

'Nottingham.'

He ripped an unused page from the back, copied the address and phone number, and gave it to Challis.

'When I phoned Phillips to tell him I'd got what he wanted a woman answered and said she would pass on my message to him. And the next day he called me.'

Mason took another drink and a handful of peanuts from a small china bowel.

'I told Phillips I would have the photographs copied for him, there were eight, and I would post them to him, along with the interview and my expenses as soon as possible. I said I was also enclosing a photostat of an old magazine article that might interest him and thought it would be a good idea to send the old lady something for being so helpful. I suggested twenty five pounds and he agreed.'

'And that was it?' Challis asked.

'Well, he must have been pleased because when he sent the rest of my money he gave me fifty pounds bonus. All in cash as well.'

'Did he write you a letter?'

'Yes, he thanked me for doing a good job and said if he needed anything else he'd contact me. All typed, even his name on the bottom.'

'He didn't sign it?'

'No, just typed.'

'What about the questions he sent you, were they also typed?'

'Yes, and those, unfortunately, I can't find.'

'When you spoke to him on the phone, what did he sound like? Young, or old?'

'Difficult to say, really. He didn't sound like an old man, but he didn't sound like a teenager either. Twenties or thirties, maybe even forties, but I couldn't swear to it because it's such a long time ago.'

'Any accent?'

'A well spoken accent as I seem to recall, but not posh or lah de dah.'

'Can you remember anything else about him?'

'Yes, I can. About eighteen months later I was staying with some friends in Mansfield, which isn't far from Nottingham, and we went there shopping. I know the area fairly well and remembered the address, so I thought I'd take a look. It turned out to be offices above a dry cleaners, obviously an accommodation address and looked a bit shabby. I was going to have a look inside but it was Saturday and they were closed. Anyway, when I got back to Bristol I gave them a call and they told me they didn't know a Paul Phillips. I suppose he wasn't using them anymore.'

'That was years ago,' Challis said. 'I wonder if they're still in business?'

Mason smiled. 'Yes they are, and that's why I was a bit late arriving. I checked through directory enquiries, gave them the address and they came back with the same telephone number.'

Challis picked up his glass and rubbed the rim thoughtfully against his lips before taking a drink.

'A lot of people who use accommodation addresses, do so, because they don't want anyone to find out who they really are, and where they really live,' he said. 'I wonder what Paul Phillips, or whoever he is, has got to hide?'

78

TWELVE

The newspapers and coffee were delivered to Challis's motel room at seven thirty, just as he was carefully shaving over the ridged scar under his chin. He'd nicked it with his razor more times than he liked to remember.

The journalist stared at his reflection, the hangover not helping. He looked a mean son of a bitch at times. Handy occasionally, when doing a showdown, but the journalist preferred to talk his way out of trouble if possible. Much more civilised.

Challis spread the newspapers over his bed and, as he expected, they were dominated by the savage Southampton murders. There were pages and pages of copy and pictures, and they had rehashed the grandfather's murder again. The woman, whose head was shaved, wasn't sexually assaulted, and said the killer was masked. Although she didn't see his face he spoke in a French accent and from her description the murder weapon was thought to be an army commando knife. There was a lot of speculation about the three deaths but the police said they were baffled. It was Saturday and Challis knew the Sunday papers would be hard at it trying to get an exclusive.

There weren't any other big stories in the papers but he did note that MP's wife, Julia Carter-West, had announced she was separating from her husband. And the mistress had decided to tell all. For a lot of cash, of course.

Challis ate a fried breakfast in the motel restaurant and by nine o'clock was on the road, heading for Sheffield. He drove on the M5 motorway then skirted around Birmingham and picked up the M1.

The evening before had ended up a boozy one and it wasn't until midnight when Challis ordered his new friend a taxi and insisted he accept fifty pounds for his time and cab fares. John Mason certainly had a thirst once he got started and then they discovered they had a few mutual contacts and shared similar views on matrimony. When Challis told Mason his marriage had ended in divorce, Mason said, 'I'm lucky because I've got a wonderful wife, I haven't seen her for twenty years. She pissed off with my best friend, poor sod,' and then dissolved into laughter.

Mason added that when he first got married his wife was always on at him to give up drinking, so he went teetotal for a whole year because he couldn't stand the nagging. Challis agreed that boozing was the cause of many journalists divorces, and asked Mason what he thought was the hardest thing about giving up drinking.

'Shagging the wife sober,' Mason had replied with a straight face.

Challis was still chuckling at the memory when his mobile phone rang.

'Challis here.'

'This is Bernie Harris.' The voice was wheezy and easily recognisable.

'Yes, Mr Harris, what can I do for you?'

'Have you read the papers today?'

'Yes.'

'About the murders in Southampton?'

'Yes. What about them?'

'I got your letter, Mr Challis.'

The journalist waited.

'I got your letter and I'd like you to come and see me. As soon as possible.'

Challis decided to be tactful because he wasn't sure what the old man's reaction would be if he said he was already on his way, determined to see him anyway.

'This really is a coincidence Mr Harris because at the moment I'm on my way to see some friends in Birmingham. In fact, I'm not very far from there now and if you like I'll phone them to say there has been a change in plans.'

'I'd appreciate it, and you won't be sorry.'

'See you soon,' Challis said.

He wondered what had made the old boy change his mind. And why had he mentioned the Southampton murders?

Challis stepped on the accelerator, turned up the radio and watched the miles fly by. When he reached Sheffield's outskirts he stopped at a petrol station to fill up and get directions. He was told the address he wanted was near a cemetery and disused quarry in the Meadow Head district.

Thirty minutes later, and after stopping again for directions, Challis pulled into the small drive of an Edwardian detached two storey house. There were about a dozen similar houses on either side of the wide tree lined avenue. The one striking difference was the iron bars covering all the windows, securely cemented into the brickwork, and the heavy wood front door with two deadlocks as well as a Yale lock. Two spy holes had been drilled through the door at different heights. Challis rang the bell and waited.

'If that's Mr Challis please speak into the intercom,' a woman's voice said.

Challis put his face close to the small grill and confirmed it was him.

After about a minute he heard a key turning in the locks but the door remained closed. Then after about another minute the woman's voice said, 'You can come in now.'

There was a slight electric whirr and the door clicked opened. He stepped inside into a small porch, only to be confronted by another wooden door several feet in front of him, but this door was already half open with an old woman's face peering at him.

She looked like Norman Bates dressed as his mother in the film, *Psycho*.

'Come in here, Mr Challis,' she said in her timid voice, and crooked her forefinger, motioning him toward her.

Challis smiled and asked, 'Are you Mr Harris's sister?'

'Yes, that's right.'

'Your brother is expecting me. Could I see him please?'

'Oh, yes, of course. But I'll have to lock up first.'

Mrs Brown walked to the heavy front door, securely locked it and did the same with the inner door. Then she crossed the small tiled hall and walked up the stairs, holding her drab grey dress with both hands.

She stopped outside one of the bedroom doors which also had two deadlocks.

'This is my brother's room,' she said, and nervously adjusted her metal frame glasses.

She rapped hard on the door and a man's voice from inside asked, 'Who is it?'

Challis couldn't help a small grin. Who the hell did Bernie Harris think it was? Even Houdini would have had trouble getting this far.

'It's me, Bernie, and I've got Mr Challis here as well.'

The door opened and her brother smiled at them. He was a lot bigger than Challis expected. Even with a stoop he matched the journalist's height.

'Come in, Mr Challis,' and the two men shook hands. 'It was good of you to come at such short notice.'

'That's okay Mr Harris, as you know, I wanted to see you anyway.'

Challis looked around the large room. It was furnished like a bed-sitter with a curtained off area for a small cooker and sink, and behind a plasterboard partition a bath and toilet. All very compact and self-contained.

Although both the large, barred windows were open wide there was still a slight haze and strong smell of cigarette smoke in the room, and the overflowing ashtrays explained Harris's wheezy voice. He was a chain smoker.

Harris relocked the door and motioned the journalist to one of a pair of large armchairs on either side of a low round table, in front of one of the windows.

'You're very security conscious, Mr Harris,' Challis said.

'And I have every good reason to be,' he replied.

The journalist opened his briefcase, took out a notepad, pen and his tape recorder. Harris didn't say a word and lit up a cigarette.

'Do you smoke?' he asked.

'No, I've never felt the need to. It'll kill you in the end.' Like it did his mother, Challis remembered.

'Oh, I don't know. I think it's a toss-up really to see who gets me first. Maybe the cigarettes, or maybe him.'

'Who's *him*?' and Challis clicked on his recorder.

Harris smiled but ignored the question.

'You were interested in the letter Derek Watson sent to Colonel Hardy,' the old man said.

'That's right, but he died before I could speak to him.'

'Derek was lucky. At least he died of natural causes.'

Challis looked puzzled,

'We're all being killed off one by one,' Harris said, and bent forward and put his hand under the front of his chair. He straightened up and Challis saw he was holding a German Luger pistol.

'Never thought I'd need a gun to protect myself in this country.' He placed it on the table. It looked clean and well oiled.

'Took it off a German officer in the war.'

'Why do you need to protect yourself?'

'Derek thought I could have been right about some of the things I told him.'

'About what?' Challis patiently asked.

'It started five years ago. Eleven dead now. Nine of them murdered, but the police still haven't put two and two together.'

Harris leaned forward and flipped open the cover of a large cardboard file lying on the table. Inside were newspaper cuttings and lined foolscap pages covered with handwritten notes. The old man pulled out a page torn from a magazine and offered it to Challis. It was the 1950 cutting.

'Read this,' he said.

'I already have, I saw Giles Faraday's sister yesterday. As a matter of fact, yours is the fourth copy I've seen of this same article. Colonel Hardy and your friend Derek also had a copy.'

'So did they all.'

'Who are *they*?'

'It all goes back a long way. Right back to just after the D-Day landings on the 6th of June, nineteen forty four.'

Bernie Harris lit another cigarette and told Challis that he was in one of the two leading companies of the 2nd East Yorks who landed on Sword beach which ran from Lion-sur-Mer to Ouistreham at the mouth of the Oran Canal.

The fighting was fierce and, even though the Allies had superior air power, the German resistance was stronger than anticipated. The British put 29, 000 men ashore at Sword beach but failed to reach one of their over-ambitious D-Day objectives, Caen. In fact, it wasn't liberated by the Canadians and British until 20th July.

Caen was important because it opened the direct route to Paris. The Germans knew this and put up fanatical opposition, and the final few days saw some of the most savage house-to-house fighting of the Normandy campaign.

'It was hell, something I'll never forget. Bomber Command had dropped over two thousand tonnes of bombs on the city and three quarters of it had been razed to the ground, but still the Jerries kept fighting. We lost a lot of good blokes.'

The old soldier put another cigarette in his mouth and lit it from the stub of the other one now nearly burning his nicotine stained fingers.

He explained that after the capture of Caen their next target was south to Falaise. He was in a platoon which had gone ahead to scout out the land and was between a small village called Roujan and St Martin de-Fontenay.

'It was the twenty eighth of July,' Harris said. 'I remember the date because the day before had been my birthday. Twenty two I was, and felt more like forty. The countryside was hedge-lined fields with booby-traps everywhere. For the last couple of days we'd been in fire-fights with small pockets of enemy stragglers, still fighting like crazy.'

Bernie Harris said that his platoon was on the edge of a field trying to decide if a ruined farmhouse two hundred yards away was sheltering Jerry soldiers. It was close to a small orchard of fruit trees which offered good cover for snipers and they had been laying motionless in a shallow ditch for nearly an hour, watching for any sign of movement.

He was just starting to stand when his arm was grabbed and he was pulled roughly back to the ground.

THIRTEEN

'What's the matter you prat? You nearly pulled my bloody arm off,' Bernie said to his friend, their dusty faces only inches apart.

'Saved your bloody life more like it. Look...,' and Derek Watson pointed towards the far edge of the trees.

Bernie looked across the field, the earth crisscrossed with tyre tracks, and saw a small group of civilians just emerging from the orchard. They were being herded along by a German officer and two soldiers.

Bernie nudged the man on his other side, Shorty Swales, and whispered, 'Pass it on. Ask the captain to come up here.'

The three men were in the front of the platoon and their commanding officer, Captain Roger Hardy, was twenty five yards away behind a large tree with the wireless operator. They were trying to contact headquarters to see if they could call up any artillery to shell the orchard.

The officer joined his men and asked, 'Have you seen any more Germans besides those?'

Bernie shook his head and replied, 'No. So why don't we take them out? There's only three.'

'Supposing we hit the civilians. It's a bit risky.'

'If they've any sense they'll dive on the ground as soon as we start shooting,' Derek said.

'I contacted HQ and we should get some back-up pretty soon,' Captain Hardy said.

'Well then, the bloody shells will get them even if the Jerries don't.'

'Okay Corporal Harris, pass the word along, after you fire, the rest of the men begin shooting. And make sure you get one with your first shot.'

Bernie Harris was one of the best marksmen in his regiment and he carefully looked through the sights of his .303 Lee-Enfield rifle. He swung the barrel across the civilians, three men and one woman, trying to focus on the field-grey uniform of the German officer. Bernie was just about to squeeze the trigger when the woman blundered into his vision.

He cursed and moved his rifle a couple of inches and quickly sighted upon one of the steel helmeted soldiers. He snapped off a shot and saw him fall as the rest of the platoon opened fire. But, instead of the men and woman hitting the ground as thought, they began running in the direction of the British soldiers.

'Viva la France,' one of the men shouted, then was flung forward and fell heavily, his white shirt turning blood red.

'Stop firing, stop firing,' Captain Hardy shouted, immediately echoed by Corporal Harris.

The British guns stopped but shots still rang out from the direction of the Germans. Another man was hurled violently forward in mid-stride as bullets tore into his back.

Bernie Harris strained his eyes to get a look at the enemy on the other side of the rutted field as the remaining man and woman sprinted towards him. Just fifty yards away he could see the terror in their faces as they tried to zig-zag. Thirty yards, then twenty and Bernie thought they were going to make it and started firing at the spot where he'd seen the German soldier fall.

Then the woman seemed to somersault forward as a heavy calibre rifle bullet punched through her back. She rolled to within a couple of yards of Bernie, her lifeless eyes staring blankly at the sky. She was only in her early twenties…and pretty.

The lone survivor leapt into the ditch as the British soldiers poured fire towards the other side of the field.

'Viva les Tommies,' the Frenchman gasped out, his eyes wide with fear.

Suddenly the firing stopped and a deathly silence hung in the air, the sinking evening sun casting long shadows over the field. Slowly Bernie and Derek Watson slipped out of the ditch and inched their way forward. They felt confident because if there had been any other Germans in the ruined farmhouse or orchard they surely would have shown themselves before now.

The two khaki clad soldiers had covered about fifty yards crawling on their bellies when they heard a shout. They looked up and saw the German Oberleutnant stand up about one hundred yards away with his hands in the air. Bernie raised his rifle and took careful aim at the officer's chest. 'You bastard,' he breathed.

'Corporal Harris, stop,' Captain Hardy yelled, 'we need him as a prisoner. Don't shoot. That's an order.'

Bernie swore and got to his feet, swiftly followed by Derek. The two men walked towards the German, the rest of the British soldiers catching up. As they neared their captive Bernie's eyes were riveted to the Knight's Cross around his neck. The officer smiled and looked as though he was about to say something but froze as the corporal rammed the rifle barrel under his chin.

'Shut it,' the Englishman hissed.

The soldier Bernie had shot lay on his back in a little hollow. He was dead. The other soldier was propped up against the shallow bank, the front of his grey tunic stained a dark crimson. He had been shot in the chest and the colour was slowly draining from his face. His rifle and steel helmet lay uselessly on the ground beside him. He knew he was dying.

He was only in his late teens but his eyes showed no fear. He smiled weakly at the British soldiers staring at him but then his face hardened and patches of red showed in his cheeks as he strained his right arm upwards and pointed.

'Traitre,' he said clearly in French.

The surviving Frenchman, in his forties, who'd managed to dodge being shot in his dash across the field shouted harshly back at the soldier. The rapidity of the words meaningless to the Englishmen.

The stocky Frenchman suddenly dropped to his knees in front of the youth and, before anyone realised what he was doing, pulled a knife from his trouser pocket and flicked open the blade. He grabbed hold of the teenager's hair, pulled his head back and drew the knife across his throat.

Then a single shot rang out and the Frenchman was knocked sideways as the bullet smashed into his skull. The group of soldiers looked in amazement at the German officer holding a 9mm Luger pistol in his hand. Two lives extinguished in a matter of seconds. It had happened so fast the soldiers were stunned by the thought that they hadn't prevented it.

Then one of the men drew his bayonet from its sheath hanging at his side and thrust the shiny steel through the officer's right shoulder, making him drop the pistol.

'No more, Private Woodcock,' Captain Hardy said, as the soldier looked as though he might repeat his action.

'You shouldn't have done that,' the German said in a perfect English accent, his face grimacing with pain.

'Hey, listen to him. A kraut that speaks better English than you do, Woody,' Corporal Harris said.

'Well, that's not fuckin' 'ard, is it?' the cockney grinned.

The corporal picked up the Luger and stuck it in his belt. 'You won't be needing this anymore, old son,' he said. 'Your war's over.'

Private Chris Thomas got on his knees and examined the young German soldier and Frenchman. Then he looked up grim faced.

'Both dead, sir.'

Captain Hardy nodded and turned to the officer, 'Where did you learn to speak English like that?'

Before he could reply there was a whooshing sound as a shell slammed through the air and exploded about a hundred yards away in the trees. Quickly followed by another, and another.

'Blimey, we're being shelled.'

'Make for the farmhouse,' Captain Hardy shouted, 'and bring the prisoner. *Alive.*'

The ruins were about seventy five yards away and the British soldiers ran towards them in a crouching position, the German pushed and prodded to keep up with them, losing his cap in the rush.

The bombardment continued as they reached the crumbling walls and took what shelter they could. The bullet scarred stones showed they were not the first to seek refuge and they hugged the ground praying their gunners would concentrate only on the orchard.

Then, as suddenly as it started, the shelling ceased and the soldiers grinned at each other with relief. They were still in one piece. Most of them lit cigarettes and inhaled deeply.

'Wonder if there's a wine cellar here,' Shorty Swales said. 'Some nice plonk would go down a treat right now.'

Minutes later they discovered there *was* a cellar, but not surprisingly, no wine. The trapdoor had long disappeared but the stairs leading to the large underground room were still intact. Holes gaped in the ceiling and craters in the floor showed the results of previous shelling.

Captain Hardy camped his men in the room and stationed three sentries up top as lookout. The German officer had been put at the far end of the cellar as one of the soldiers put a field dressing on his shoulder wound.

'He'll live, sir, more's the pity,' Private Bob Barratt reported to his captain. 'Woody's bayonet went in and out clean enough and I put some stitches in. A bit crude but they'll do until he sees a doctor.' The private grinned,' I don't think he liked it.'

'I know, I heard him cursing.'

'Strange that sir, it was all in English. Knows nearly as many swear words as Woody.'

'Bring him here.'

The private returned with the German who took up a position leaning against the wall, his jacket hanging loosely over his shoulders, one arm in a crude sling.

'I am an Englishman,' the prisoner said.

Captain Hardy looked at him in surprise and several soldiers standing nearby moved closer.

'An Englishman?' the captain queried. 'Englishmen don't shoot people in the back. And definitely not women.'

'No, you're a Jerry all right,' Derek Watson said. 'You're a murdering bastard who's lucky to be alive.'

'Not for long,' another voice growled.

'My name is Captain Giles Faraday and I'm with the Special Operations Executive. For the last couple of months I've been working with the French Resistance, the Maquis, and since D-Day we've been blowing up bridges and trains. My job has been to cause as much trouble and distraction as possible.'

'And I suppose the other Jerry soldiers were Englishmen too,' Captain Hardy said.

'No, they were Frenchman, in the Resistance,' was the reply. 'The men and woman we killed were collaborators. They had been helping the Germans for a long time and were responsible for the deaths of many of their countrymen. We were taking them to a village not far from here where they would have been executed anyway. They were traitors and the

91

French like to take care of their own problems. It was none of your damn business.'

'Don't listen to him, sir,' Private Jimmy Kemp said. 'The bugger's lying, just to save his skin. We should shoot him now, just like he shot that woman.'

'You can see how my men feel. They want you dead, and from what I saw, I can't say I blame them. Anyway, supposing your story was true, how could you possibly prove it?' the British captain asked.

'Take me to Roujan, it's not far and there are plenty of people who will vouch for me.'

'No, we're not going to any village or any other place you might say. We've got other plans, orders to carry out.'

'Then send me back to your headquarters as a prisoner. I'm sure it won't take me long to convince your superiors.'

Captain Hardy knew he couldn't take the German, or whoever he was, with them as a prisoner, but he couldn't spare any men to take him back to HQ either. He was already short a sergeant who'd been killed yesterday. It would be easier probably to leave him in the cellar as just another casualty of the war. God knows, any one of his men would kill him without the slightest hesitation.

But Hardy couldn't allow that to happen. He was a British Army officer and murder was murder, even under these circumstances. No, there was another way.

'Private Kemp,' he said to his wireless operator. 'I want you to try and contact headquarters, give our position and say we're leaving a prisoner in the cellar. Tell them he'll be tied up securely so there's no need to come in shooting. Have you got that?'

'Yes sir.'

'Oh, and add, he's dressed as a German officer but says he's really an Englishman. Claims to be a special agent.'

'Yes sir.'

92

That'll cause a few raised eyebrows, Captain Hardy thought.

He turned his head as he heard movement overhead and a civilian clumped down the wooden stairs closely followed by Private Chris Thomas, rifle at the ready. The civilian was in his twenties, dressed in dark blue cord trousers and blue work shirt.

'He's French sir, and doesn't appear to speak any English,' the soldier said. 'He suddenly came from nowhere. Lucky I didn't shoot the blighter.'

The Frenchman smiled at Captain Hardy and spoke quickly in his native tongue, none of which the captain could understand. Roger Hardy, although he'd had a good education, had a mental block where it came to foreign languages. He could tell the difference between German and French, but when it came to understanding the meaning of words, he was completely lost. As far as he was concerned, one didn't need to learn a foreign language to play rugger or cricket.

'Sorry, old man, don't understand a word you're saying,' the captain said. 'Don't parlez vous the lingo.'

'Hello Henri.'

The sun had set and the basement room was getting darker by the minute. The Frenchman turned his head and strained his eyes in the direction of the voice.

'Giles? Giles, is that you?'

'Yes,' replied the prisoner, and the civilian moved the few yards to his side, both of them talking in French.

'You're injured.'

'Yes, but it's not too bad. It's stopped hurting anyway.'

'Where are the others?' the Frenchman asked, referring to the two men dressed as German soldiers.

The wounded man hesitated, knowing one of the men was Henri Fabere's younger brother.

'They're both dead,' he replied. 'I'm sorry.'

'Did these soldiers kill them?'

'Yes, but you can't blame them, they thought we were the enemy. They weren't to know the difference.'

Henri stared at the floor and sighed.

'And they wounded you?' The Frenchman moved his friend's jacket gently and looked at the bandaged shoulder.

'Yes.'

Giles Faraday quickly explained the events leading to his capture and the difficulty he was having trying to make them understand who he really was.

'I wonder what they're rabbitin' on about?' Woody said. 'They're probably both a couple of bleedin' Jerries.'

'Well, they're speaking French, not German,' Derek Watson said. 'That much I do know.'

Captain Hardy had a nagging feeling in the back of his mind as he heard the Frenchman and the man who said he was English talking in such a familiar way. Supposing the man really was a British officer. He had to admit he spoke perfect English. But then, he'd met several Germans before the war who'd been brought up in England, and they spoke English as well as their mother tongue. But before he could ponder further the Frenchman turned and directed a tirade towards the soldiers.

'What's he saying?' Captain Hardy asked.

'He's saying, why have you wounded another Englishman. I'm on your side,' Giles Faraday replied. 'In fact, we both are. My friend is a good man.'

Suddenly there was an explosion nearby and dust showered down from the ceiling. Then the ruins took a direct hit up on top and the captain heard his sentries yelling.

'Have you got through to HQ yet?' he shouted at his wireless operator.

'Yes sir,'

'Then tell them to stop shelling us.'

Moments passed then Private Kemp shouted back, 'It's not them. They say it must be the Jerries. There's been reports of Panzer tanks in the area, trying some sort of breakthrough, sir.'

'Everybody up on top, quick,' Captain Hardy said. 'You two as well.'

The Frenchman got behind his friend and steadied him as they climbed the stairs. There were more explosions close to the ruins and the sound of small arms fire as they reached the open air. The night was black with shafts of moonlight flickering through the clouds.

'Keep your heads down,' somebody shouted as bullets ricocheted off the stone walls.

'Johnson's dead, sir.'

Eric Johnson, from Rotherham, was just nineteen and the youngest son in his family. His two other brothers had already been killed in action.

'Blast,' Captain Hardy said. When this war was finally over he hoped the loss of young life was justified.

'Where are the Germans?'

'In the trees, sir.'

The captain looked in the direction of the orchard and saw flashes of yellowy orange from automatic weapons. His men were firing back but they might just as well have been aiming at shadows. Another shell exploded close to the ruins and mud and stones showered the crouching soldiers. They were like sitting ducks.

'Doesn't sound like tanks, sir, more like mortars.'

The captain shouted Corporal Harris's name.

'We'll have to retreat,' he told him. 'You pick one man to stay with you and give us covering fire. We'll go back to the nearest hedge and wait, then cover for you. We'll go back field by field until we meet up with our own men. Okay corporal?'

95

'Yes sir.' Harris pointed in the direction of their prisoner and the Frenchman. 'What about them?'

'They come with us when we go.'

The captain explained the situation to the man in the German officer's uniform and told him to translate for the French civilian.

'We would be much better off if we went to Henri Fabere's village. It is less than two kilometres from here and the villagers will help us. Take my word, it will be much safer for us. I really am an English officer, you know.'

Captain Hardy stared hard at his prisoner, wishing he could believe this man. But he had to put the safety of his men first, beyond any reasonable doubt.

'No,' he said. 'We go back towards our own troops.'

Corporal Harris chose Derek Watson to stay with him and three British soldiers, led by the captain, clambered over the shattered walls, heading for the hedgerow in the opposite direction of the orchard. Giles Faraday and Henri Fabere were prodded after them and the rest of the soldiers silently followed, all moving in a crouching run.

They had only gone fifty yards when a flare exploded above the ruined farmhouse illuminating the soldiers, who immediately dived to the ground. Mortar shells hit the ruins and Captain Hardy shouted back to Harris and Watson.

'Change of plan. Run for it.'

The two soldiers vaulted over a ruined wall and joined the men on the ground who were starting to move on their stomachs towards the hedge. It was just beginning to darken when another flare lit the sky. The mortars changed their aim and clumps of earth were thrown through the air as shells exploded in the field. The brightness showed a hedge just under a hundred yards away.

'We'll have to run for it before the mortars get our range,' Captain Hardy said. 'Group on the other side of the hedge.'

96

The captain looked at his men. 'Best of luck.' He rose to a crouch. 'Now let's go.'

As they started their run two mortar shells exploded directly in front of them, temporarily halting them. It was in that panicking moment Giles Faraday and Henri Fabere made their break and sprinted away from the direction of the hedge. Another shell exploded and the heavy crackle of machine gun fire joined in. Then the two men were spotted.

'The Jerry bastards are escaping,' one of the soldiers shouted, his mind immediately made up on whose side the fleeing men were on.

'Shoot the buggers.'

The British soldiers, hatred for the enemy over-riding their fear, turned their anger on the two men as fingers tightened on the triggers.

A flurry of shots rang out and the two figures stumbled and fell. Then one got up and tried dragging his friend but it was impossible with only one good arm.

There was a brief few seconds silence and the upright man cupped his hand to his mouth.

'Bastards!' The one word echoed across the field, then another burst of firing rang out and the man was hurled back onto the ground.

The mortar fire increased in its intensity and the British soldiers continued their desperate scramble to save themselves, instantly forgetting the two crumpled figures left lying in the field.

FOURTEEN

The old man took another draw of his cigarette and looked at Challis.

'It was a brutal and bloody war,' he said.

Challis had sat engrossed as he listened to the old soldier's first hand account of what happened to Giles Faraday nearly sixty years ago. Bernie Harris had made it sound so vividly clear the reporter almost felt he was there in person.

There were a lot of gutsy old age pensioners out there, their bravery and sacrifice long forgotten.

'Who else knows about this? Were the authorities ever told?' Challis asked.

'No,' Bernie replied. 'You see, after that night there was nearly another year of war, and that incident was nothing compared to some of the fighting I saw. I'd forgotten all about it until six years later when I read that magazine article, and it was only then I realised we must have killed a British officer.'

'But nobody would have blamed any of you in the circumstances you've described.'

'Maybe, but we decided to let sleeping dogs lie. There was no point raking up the past. The war was over and it was best to forget it.'

'You said *we*. Who were the others?'

'I saw the story first and contacted the others who'd been lucky enough to come home alive, which was easy enough because the regiment had a yearly reunion and we'd kept in touch. There were eight of us, including me and the captain, who'd been promoted to major by then.'

'You mean Colonel Hardy.'

'Yes.'

'There is a possibility Giles Faraday and the Frenchman were killed by German bullets.'

'No, I don't think so. We all fired at them, and we were nearer to them than the Germans, so it had to be one of us.'

'Well, if you did kill them, at least none of you will ever know for sure who it was,' and Challis shrugged his shoulders. 'It could have been any one of you.'

'That's not much consolation.'

'I should imagine quite a few soldiers were accidentally killed by their own side during the war. Nowadays they call it *friendly fire*. It said in the article they were killed by British and German crossfire, so it would appear the person who wrote it wasn't sure. And that story originated in France.'

'Well, somebody's sure all right. That's why we're all being killed off.'

'And you're saying that's because of what happened to Giles Faraday?'

'Yes,' replied the old man, and spread the contents of the brown folder over the coffee table.

'And Colonel Hardy was killed for this reason too?'

'That's correct.'

'Who's doing the killing then? '

'Maybe Faraday had a son.'

'No, he wasn't married.' Challis said.

'Perhaps some other close relatives. Or maybe some army friends of Faraday's from the SOE. They were a pretty tasty lot.'

'No, I don't buy that, they'd be too old now. And why would anyone wait so long? Why didn't the murders start nearer nineteen fifty when that article appeared?' Challis paused. 'Anyway it said in the papers the murderer in Southampton spoke with a French accent.'

'A lot of people speak French, Giles Faraday spoke it fluently. Or it could be someone's just trying to confuse the police.'

The two men fell silent with their thoughts for a moment.

'Maybe Henri Fabere had a son,' Bernie said.

'Yes, that's a possibility,' Challis agreed. 'But another thing, supposing your theory is correct, how would the person know which British soldiers were involved that night, and which ones returned safely to England after the war?'

'That's easy,' Bernie said, and picked up a lined page of foolscap paper. He handed it to Challis who saw it was a hand written list of names.

'The first name on that list is Jimmy Kemp, he was the first one murdered. But before he died he was tortured, and I believe he gave all our names, addresses and whatever information he had to the person who killed him. The police never caught the murderer. They said it looked like the work of a sadist, maybe something to do with Black Magic.'

'But how would the killer have found out about Kemp in the first place?'

'The year before he was murdered, Jimmy was featured in a lot of the national newspapers as a hero. He foiled an armed bank robbery and the papers were full of praise for the old age pensioner. He was even interviewed on television. Of course, they went into his army background and the fact that he was in the D-Day landings and fought in the battle for Caen. Made him out to be quite a war hero. You'll find some of the stories in that folder.'

Challis looked down the list of names, numbered from one to eight. Some of them had other names listed in brackets after them.

'These were there that night in France,' he said.

Bernie nodded in agreement.

'And the names in brackets?'

'Sons and grandsons. I haven't included daughters or granddaughters because it seems the murderer is only interested in the male offspring. Maybe some code of honour, or something like that. Anyway, the whole list adds up to fourteen names, eleven of them now dead. Two from natural causes and nine murdered.'

'Then why haven't you been to the police?'

'Because I didn't think they'd believe me. The killer has been very clever and the first five murders happened at the rate of just one a year. They happened in different areas and the police never discovered the common denominator. It's only now I think they might believe I'm right.'

'Colonel Hardy, Ronald Woodcock, his son and grandson all died in the last few weeks.'

'Exactly,' Bernie said. 'The recent murders have nearly doubled the total. It looks like the murderer's changed his pattern. It seems he's in a hurry now.'

Challis studied the list.

1. Jimmy Kemp, murdered 20th July 1998, age 75. He was tortured, throat cut and body found in local canal. No children.

2. Brian 'Shorty' Swales, murdered 1st August 1999, age 75. Stabbed while walking his dog in woodland. Murder weapon never found but described as a double edged knife. (Not married.)

3. Chris Thomas died from natural causes, cancer of the bowel 18th March 2000, age 76. (His son, Michael, was murdered 26th July 2000, age 45. Stabbed in neck and back when taking short cut through alley).

4. Bob Barratt murdered 3rd August 2002, age 80. Killed by repeated blows to head. Body found on allotment and he was killed by his own garden spade. (His son, Paul, 51, had been murdered the year before, 29th July 2001. He'd died of

multiple stab wounds and been found in a deserted street in the early hours of the morning.)

5. Ronald 'Woody' Woodcock, murdered 25th July 2003, age 79. Killed by army bayonet. (His son, Billy, 45, and grandson, Gary, 22, were murdered 15th August 2003. Both were killed by knife wounds.)

6. Colonel Roger Hardy, murdered 30th July 2003, age 84. Shot in the chest by Webley service revolver. (One son, Matthew, still alive. One grandson, Ralph, still alive.)

7. Derek Watson died from natural causes, heart attack 13th August 2003, age 81.

8. Bernie Harris, still alive. (Not married.)

It seemed amazing but the old boy's theory certainly was plausible, interesting to say the least. Challis wondered what the police reaction would be.

'There is another common factor here,' he said.

'I know,' Bernie said. 'All the murders have happened during the summer, the months of July and August.'

'And Giles Faraday was killed in July.'

'So you believe me? You think I'm right?'

Challis didn't reply straight away but sat looking at the old man, the Luger pistol still visible on the table.

'I know I've certainly got enough to write a piece,' he said. 'The nineteen fifty article, the murders over the last five years and your story would make a sensational read. I take it I can quote you.'

'Of course.'

'It all ties in with the Southampton and Colonel Hardy's murders which are current news. It's a different angle and the timing couldn't be better. But...'

Challis had another week to go on the promise he'd made to Matthew Hardy and he wasn't sure exactly what was expected of him. Would his progress so far satisfy the colonel's son?

No, he didn't think so. There were still a lot of unanswered questions and besides, he was no nearer to finding the identity of the killer than when he started.

'I'd like to dig a bit deeper before I write a story,' he said. 'However, there is one thought that bothers me.'

'What's that?' Bernie asked.

'Your safety. Supposing you are right about what you've told me, then your life is in danger. I'll try and have a word with the police down south and see if I can get you some protection up here.'

'They'll probably think I'm some decrepit old nutcase who should be locked up.'

'Well I don't,' Challis said.

'You don't have to worry about me.' Bernie patted the pistol. 'I've got an advantage because I'm expecting something to happen and I'm ready for trouble.'

'What about your sister?'

'As I said before, none of the female relatives have been harmed, just the men. The woman in Southampton who had her head shaved was unlucky, I think she was in the wrong place at the wrong time. Mind you, her treatment does seem to fit into the pattern of things. After Europe was liberated, women who'd collaborated with the German occupation forces had their heads shaved, as traitors.'

'Yes, I remember reading that somewhere,' Challis said.

'But don't forget Colonel Hardy's son and grandson on that list, their lives are in danger too.'

Challis was well aware of that fact.

'Besides Derek Watson, did you discuss this with any of your other old army pals?' he asked.

'No. And I didn't tell Derek until about five or six weeks ago.'

'Have you got the addresses of all the people named on this list?'

Bernie picked up another sheet of paper. 'Some of them might be out of date but they'll put you in the right direction.'

Challis started to replace the scattered papers on the coffee table into the brown folder.

'Can I take these with me?' he asked.

'Of course, my sister copied those for you,' Bernie replied, and lit another cigarette.

Challis borrowed some wartime photographs of Bernie taken with his pals and used his small Canon Sure Shot camera to take a couple of up to date pics.

The journalist left Bernie with the guarantee he would phone in a couple of days at the latest. Challis was full of admiration for the old soldier who reminded him of his mother's father, the only grandfather he'd known. He too, had done his bit during the war and had captivated the young Challis with tales of bravery and courage against the enemy.

His other grandfather had been in the merchant navy but died of malaria five years after the war ended. It seemed his family didn't have much luck on his father's side.

*

As soon as he was outside in his car Challis called Seton.

'Don't ask any questions, just listen,' Challis said when his friend answered. 'Get hold of Matthew Hardy immediately and tell him to go home. No ifs or buts, tell him he has to do as he's told.'

'But he might be in an important meeting,' Seton protested.

'Matthew's son, where is he?'

'Ralph, he should be at home, but I'm not sure. He could be on holiday. I know he's starting university pretty soon, but that won't be until the new term starts.'

'Find out from his father. If he's out of the country then don't bother, but if he's anywhere in Britain, he must go home straight away.'

'What's up Challis?'

'Then I want you to get hold of Gerry Cassidy and arrange immediate round the clock protection for Matthew and his family. Tell Gerry it could be dangerous and someone is possibly going to try and kill Matthew and his son.'

'Challis is this true? What's going on?'

'Seton, I'll explain everything when I see you, and I think it would be best if we met at Matthew's place in Hertfordshire. I'm just leaving Sheffield now and I'll drive straight there.'

'Challis will you please tell me what this is all about.'

'Seton, just make sure you do what I've asked, and I'll see you in a few hours.'

Challis clicked off his phone and started the car. He hoped he wasn't being too dramatic and Bernie's theory was nothing more than an old man's imagination running wild. What he'd just asked Seton to do was expensive and would cost Matthew Hardy a pretty penny but Challis consoled himself with the thought that the banker had wanted some action over his father's death. Now he was getting it.

*

As Challis put his car in gear and drove off the man lying on the long grey army coat watched his departure through a small pair of powerful binoculars. His blue Ford Granada was parked several streets away and he lay completely hidden in the long grass on the spare plot of land at the end of the road, close to the overgrown pathway leading to the disused quarry.

He had already written down the journalist's car number while Challis was inside talking to Bernie Harris.

FIFTEEN

Matthew Hardy's house was five miles from the town of Hatfield, set in several acres of cultivated land. There were stables near the house for three horses and on the other side, about two hundred yards away, were two large greenhouses.

One hundred and fifty yards from the rear of the house was half an acre of woodland. The perimeter of the estate was a mixture of hedges, stone walls and wood fencing, the entrance set between two large brick pillars with seven foot high iron railings extending for about a hundred yards on either side before disappearing into prickly hedges. It was an open entrance, with no gates, leading to a long driveway.

But as Challis drew up he saw a Range Rover and a large black saloon car blocking the entrance. He stopped the car and waited. A full minute went by but the journalist knew the cars weren't abandoned and sensed he was being observed. Finally, a powerfully built man in his thirties appeared from behind one of the brick pillars carrying a walkie talkie. He moved lightly on soft leather boots and was wearing black jeans and tee shirt under a lightweight black short jacket.

'Mr Challis?' he asked.

The journalist nodded.

'It's all right sir, I relayed your car number to the house and Mr Travis said it was you.' The man spoke into the walkie talkie. 'Confirmed. I'm letting Mr Challis through.'

Challis's mobile phone rang. It was Seton.

'Security all right for you?' he asked, and Challis could hear the amusement in his voice.

106

The Range Rover reversed leaving Challis just enough room to squeeze past. As he went by he saw another man dressed in black crouched behind a tree watching him.

Gerry Cassidy was an ex-soldier turned mercenary wheeler dealer who could fix up anything to do with security. He supplied bodyguards for visiting film stars, royalty, politicians and some of the richest men in the world. Rumour had it they carried guns on special jobs. Totally illegal of course, but Challis hoped Seton had emphasised this was a special job. The journalist had an uneasy feeling.

The journey from Sheffield had taken Challis a lot longer than it should have because of several road works on the motorway slowing traffic to a crawl. The stifling heat didn't improve matters.

He parked his car in the large space in front of the Georgian style mansion. There were six other cars parked on the gravel surface.

Another guard opened the white painted front door, Seton standing behind him.

'What's this about, Challis?' he asked, as they walked over deep pile carpet towards the double doors leading to the drawing room.

'Seton, I don't want to go over it twice, so let's wait until we're all together.'

They entered the large elegantly furnished room and Matthew Hardy came straight across.

'Is your son here?' Challis asked.

'No, he's in California, staying with friends. He won't be home for three weeks.'

'Good, then that's one less to worry about.'

As well as the banker and Seton, there was another man in the room, John Conway, who was Gerry Cassidy's right hand man.

'Where's the rest of your family?' Challis asked.

'My wife, my two daughters and my mother are in the TV lounge,' Hardy replied.

'Any servants?'

'Husband and wife, Mr and Mrs Peters. She cooks and is general housekeeper and her husband does all the odd jobs and doubles as our chauffeur. They live in a self-contained flat above the garage. I have a full time gardener, who doesn't live in, and two women who come every day. One who does the cleaning and the other helps with the horses.'

Challis shook hands with John Conway. They'd met before, and the journalist remembered, it was like shaking hands with steel. Conway looked a quiet sort of man, even inoffensive, but Challis knew different. The security specialist was a former sergeant in the SAS and had gone behind enemy lines during the first Gulf War. One day Challis hoped to do a story on him.

'How many men have you got on the job?' the reporter asked.

'Two on the gate, two patrolling the grounds and one in the house,' Conway replied. 'There will be five men on duty at all times, changing shifts every eight hours. There will probably be at least ten men on call at any one time. At least half of them are ex-paras, and there's me of course, I'll be co-ordinating everything.'

'Where will they sleep?'

'That's no problem,' Hardy said. 'There are eight bedrooms and three bathrooms, plus there's a swimming pool with extra showers and sun loungers which can be used for sleeping on.'

Matthew Hardy's housekeeper arrived with cold drinks and sandwiches. After wolfing down a couple of ham sandwiches and a glass of chilled Perrier water the journalist began speaking. Challis started with Derek Watson's letter to the colonel and his meeting with Watson's wife, then went on to describe his visit with Giles Faraday's sister. When he got to

John Mason he explained his intention was to try and find out more about the mysterious Paul Phillips.

Challis concluded with his arrival on Bernie Harris's doorstep and related in great detail the old soldier's story. After he'd finished he looked at the three men who'd listened intently to his narration.

There was a long silence as they digested his words.

'You're talking about a serial killer,' John Conway finally said. 'You're saying that someone's going around the country murdering people like the Yorkshire Ripper did, only he's killing men instead of women.' The security man shook his head. 'I find it difficult to believe.'

'Challis, the sort of person you've described, fitting in with the information you've given us, would be an old man now,' Seton said. 'You're not suggesting there's a geriatric killer on the loose, are you? Mind you, it would make a good story.' He gave a short laugh.

'I know it sounds far fetched, but I've been giving it a lot of thought as I drove here,' Challis said. 'The amazing thing is everything fits. So far the murders have been treated as one-offs, but when you couple them with the link to what happened in the war, then it all slots in. Surely you can see that, Seton?'

'Yes, the theory for the motive sounds fine from what you've told us, but if we took every murder separately I'm sure we could probably come up with different conclusions,' he replied. 'Anyway, how does it help catch a killer? Who are we looking for? The murders in Southampton were supposedly committed by a man with a French accent. But the woman might have been completely mistaken and the accent was really Italian or some other language. It could be anybody.'

'Or, as Bernie Harris pointed out, it could be an Englishman trying to confuse the police,' Challis said.

'Precisely.'

'My first concern was for the safety of those involved, that's why I insisted your family had protection, Matthew. I could be wrong but, on the other hand, I could be very right. The fact is, do you want to take that chance?'

'No, you did the right thing, Challis.' The banker rose from his chair and crossed to a drinks trolley. He poured himself another scotch. 'If this Bernie Harris has got his facts correct then I'm grateful you acted so promptly.'

'But how long will you keep the guards here? A week? A month? Six months?' Seton asked.

Matthew Hardy smiled. 'As long as it takes for the murderer to be caught.'

'My security men are clearly noticeable at the front entrance so maybe the killer might think he's been rumbled, and be put off,' Conway said.

'Somehow, I don't think so,' Challis said. 'If this theory is right then he won't stop until everyone on that list is dead. So we've got to find him.'

'What about the police? Shouldn't we tell them?' the banker asked.

'I've been thinking about that,' Challis replied. 'But I think it would probably sound better coming from you, Matthew. I should imagine you know some of the police around here.'

'Yes, I do. As a matter of fact, I know the Chief Constable quite well, and I've met a few senior officers at various functions...the only trouble is, how do I explain it to them? It's going to be a bit hard convincing them that something which happened in the war all those years ago is the motive for these murders occurring right now...but I will have a word.'

'One thing though, Matthew. I'd prefer you not to mention my meeting with John Mason because I want to find out about Paul Phillips myself. I'd still like to get a story out of this and I don't want the police stepping on my toes.'

'But I will have to tell them about you, Challis. Won't I?'

110

'Yes, that's fine. Give them my phone numbers and say they can call me anytime. And obviously, the police will want to have a word with Bernie Harris, so tell them I promised I'd try and get him some protection. Make sure you impress that point on them.'

'There is another factor as well,' Seton said. 'It comes down to finances. Supposing your theory is correct, Challis, then it means a lot of different police authorities would have to be involved.'

He spread his hands.

'But who's going to pay for it? Only one force can be in charge of the investigation and set up a headquarters to co-ordinate all the inquiries. And who would it be? The Metropolitan Police because one of the murders happened in London, or Southampton because three of the murders took place there? And what about the other murder areas? Everything is run on a tight budget these days and the cost could be enormous. So I don't think there will be many volunteers.'

'What about the safety of the public? I'd have thought that was the most important issue,' Challis said.

'Of course it is, but I bet it would take a lot of convincing to get the police to spend money like this.'

Challis stared hard at his friend.

'What would they want? Another murder?'

SIXTEEN

The sound of thunder woke Challis at three in the morning and he lay there watching the flashes of lightning brighten the bedroom. He closed his eyes tight and buried his head in the pillow but the heavy downpour lashing against the window panes stopped him nodding off again.

The first rain in weeks and he should have been grateful but he cursed as he tossed and turned. He hadn't gone to bed until after midnight and it had taken some time before he'd fallen into a deep sleep. Now he was having the same trouble as his mind went over and over the events of the last week trying to put the pieces together.

One thing Seton had certainly been right about was that, even if the wartime theory was correct, it still didn't reveal the identity of the killer.

Maybe Giles Faraday wasn't dead after all and had been planning this for years. Or maybe it was his ghost. Weird thoughts went through his mind as he tried to get back to sleep. Maybe his sister had found out and was employing someone to do the murders. Or maybe it was somebody from Faraday's army days. Maybe it was somebody who had been connected with the Special Operations Executive.

Maybe, maybe, maybe...

Challis suddenly opened his eyes wide as a thought struck him. He had a friend, Nigel Thompson, who'd married a French girl and now operated as a freelance from Paris. He'd contact Thompson and get him to dig out what he could on Faraday and Henri Fabere.

Dawn was breaking before Challis managed to drift off again and he slept through until mid-morning. He awoke with a start and as soon as he saw it was ten-thirty headed straight for the bathroom. Keely was coming over at mid-day and they were going to a barbecue.

The next thing Challis did was call his friend in Paris but got his answer machine. He left a message and wished he had Nigel's new mobile number, so sent an E-mail instead.

He dressed in jeans, short sleeved shirt and sat at the kitchen table drinking coffee, reading the Sunday papers. The Southampton murders had been relegated to the inside pages and, other than more speculation, the coverage wasn't much different from the previous day.

Half an hour later he phoned Paris again. Still the answer machine. Then Keely arrived wearing a plain white blouse and cotton skirt, her long blonde hair tied back in a ponytail. She looked girlishly gorgeous.

'How's the story going?'

Challis gave a crooked smile.

'I think it's starting to take off.'

'So, you're not bored anymore?'

'No, I'll tell you about it in the cab, but I must make a phone call before we leave.'

Challis called France once more and left his third message.

*

The barbecue was just off Fulham Road. Stuart Jones was a top features writer and more a friend of Seton's, but when Jonesy held a party it was open house for half of Fleet Street. Anyone was welcome as long as they arrived with a bottle, or two...or three.

Challis once again related Bernie Harris's story in the taxi.

'But it's too ridiculous to think it could be an old man,' Keely said. 'It's got to be someone younger.'

113

'I agree.'

Jonesy lived in a basement flat with a high red brick walled garden and when Challis and Keely arrived there were already about twenty people there. The barbecue was professionally built and the large grill was covered with sizzling sausages and steaks, the aroma mouth watering.

The sun was shining intensely hot from a cloudless blue sky and the storm during the night was forgotten. It had helped clear the stuffiness and the air felt fresh, but the ground was already bone dry. No doubt the gardeners were praying for more rain.

Seton was already at the party and as soon as he saw them came over.

A few minutes later the men were drinking cold cans of lager with Keely sipping gin and tonic from a plastic cup.

'Have you spoken to Matthew today?' Challis asked.

'Yes, and he told me to tell you once again that you did the right thing,' Seton replied.

'And he doesn't mind the expense?'

'Challis, I don't think you realise just how rich he is. I know for a fact Matthew is worth about twenty million and his father will have left him another couple of million. Money is the least of his worries. Your trouble is, you never read the financial pages. If you did, then you'd know he's one of the City's top business brains.'

'In that case I won't worry about my expenses,' Challis grinned.

'Have you told Keely everything?'

'Yes.'

'About Paul Phillips too?'

'Yes.'

'Have you thought of the possibility that, although Giles Faraday wasn't married,' Keely said, 'he could have had an illegitimate child by someone. Maybe even in France.'

114

'I don't know about that,' Seton said. 'In those days it was regarded as a real stain on a woman's character if she had a baby outside of marriage. Parents would throw their daughters out into the street if they got pregnant because of the shame it brought on their family. It was very strict in those days, nothing like as free as it is today. So women were much more careful.'

'Even during wartime?'

'Umm yes, maybe that might have made a difference,' the older man conceded.

'But there is a problem with that,' Challis said. 'Faraday wasn't married and if he had given a woman a baby then she would have to register it under *her* name. And what would that be? Smith? Jones? Brown? The kid could be under any name.'

'Why not Faraday?' Keely asked.

'Well, it could have been,' Challis replied. 'If they weren't married then the baby should have been registered under *both* surnames, but it would need the father's consent to do this. Anyway, I'm sure if Faraday had got a woman into a situation like that he would have married her. He was an officer and came from a good family. No, I think we can rule out an illegitimate son bent on revenge. However, I'm contacting someone in France to do a bit of digging for me and I will mention that possibility to him.'

By three o'clock there were about forty people in the garden chewing on chicken legs, other barbecued meats, and knocking back a variety of drinks.

Steve White arrived at four. The photographer was en route to do a job in the Hilton hotel, a picture spread on the latest pop group sensation for one of the Sunday magazines, and he'd arranged to meet Challis at the party. They spent half an hour in conversation and Challis told Steve to keep as much time free as he could for the next week as he would most probably need him. Challis said he would get paid for being on standby and briefly explained what he was involved in.

Challis and Keely left at seven even though people were still arriving. The barbecue had now turned into a full blown party and would go on until the booze ran out, which would take some hours yet, or when the neighbours complained about the loud music.

As soon as they arrived back at Challis's flat he tried the number in Paris. Once again the answer machine.

*

It was half eleven when the call came through. Challis sat upright in bed and it took a few seconds for him to clear the sleep from his head and answer the phone. It was Nigel Thompson.

'I hope it's not too late Challis but your messages did say it was important and to phone as soon as I got in,' he said.

'No, no, that's fine,' Challis replied.

Keely stirred and rolled on her side.

'I've been in Nice for a few days,' Thompson continued. 'Michael Caine is making a new film down there and I was commissioned to interview him. I haven't been home more than fifteen minutes.'

'Thanks Nigel, I appreciate you getting back to me. I'm working on a story and part of it concerns an incident that happened in France during World War Two. I'd like you to check up on a few facts for me if you've got the time.'

'What do you want me to do?'

'I want you to go to a village near St Martin de-Fontenay. It's called Roujan, do you know it?'

'Not specifically, but I do know the area, and it won't take me long to drive there. Then what?'

'Have you got a fax machine where you're talking from ?'

'Sure.'

Challis wrote down the number.

'I'll fax you over a copy of a story which first appeared in a French magazine in nineteen fifty. In it you'll read about a Giles Faraday and Henri Fabere. They got killed and are supposed to be buried in Roujan, and that's what I want you to check up on. Make sure they are dead and try and find out anything you can about them. Talk to any friends or relatives that might still be alive. Try and find out if Faraday had a girlfriend or got married over there and had a baby. The same with Fabere, find out if he was ever married and had kids, and if he's got any brothers or sisters. Faraday is buried in the local cemetery according to his sister. I spoke to her only a couple of days ago. Henri Fabere should be there too.'

'Okay Challis, but some of the country people in that part of northern France are pretty tight lipped and resent strangers poking their nose about. Especially foreigners.'

'Come on Nigel, we're all supposed to be Europeans now, the Common Market and all that crap. Turn on the old English charm. Anyway, when do you think you'll be able to do it?'

'Tomorrow I'm busy, so that's out, but possibly Tuesday. If not, definitely Wednesday. Okay?'

'If you can do it Tuesday it would be better. Tell you what, do it Tuesday and shove an extra couple of hundred quid on the bill. I really am in a hurry for the information.'

'Challis, I can be bribed.'

'Thought you could. I'll fax over that magazine story right now.'

SEVENTEEN

The call of nature got Challis out of bed five minutes before the alarm was due to go off. As soon as he was dressed he went into his office. The small clock on his desk said seven forty five and he picked up the phone and called Steve's number.

'I'm leaving home now and I'm going to drop in an envelope at your studio. Inside you'll find the photo's I want copied and also a cheque for fifty quid made out to Evelyn Nash. Send the originals back to her with the money.'

'What about her address?' the photographer yawned into the mouthpiece.

'It's on a piece of paper in the envelope. And do two copies of each pic.'

'Yes boss.'

'Am I disturbing your beauty sleep?'

'Bloody right. I'm going to have a long lay-in this morning seeing you're paying for it.'

Challis put down the receiver and went into the kitchen. He poured a glass of fresh orange juice, walked into the bedroom and woke Keely. She gratefully accepted the drink and immediately took a large sip.

'It's getting on for eight o'clock,' he said, as he pulled the drawstrings and opened the full length curtains.

Sunlight flooded in and Keely shaded her eyes.

'You leaving now?'

'Yes,' he replied. 'I'll call you during the day if I get a chance.'

'I think I'll stay over again tonight.' She threw back the duvet and stood. 'That okay with you?'

Challis gave her a peck on her lips.

'I'll look forward to it.'

*

After dropping off the envelope in Paddington Challis drove through north London and got on the M1 motorway heading towards the midlands.

A couple of hours later he arrived in Nottingham, famous for its lace making, and put his car in a public car park near Mount Street, not far from the address John Mason had given him. It was in a small parade of shops and the dry cleaners Mason had mentioned was now closed with *to let* signs plastered on the windows. A door to the side of the shop leading to the upstairs offices was wide open and Challis walked up the fraying stair carpet until he came to a frosted glass panelled door.

From previous experience Challis knew accommodation address offices usually fell into two categories. Straight or dodgy, the latter being the type that handled pornography mail order and con trick companies where you sent money but never received the goods you ordered. These villains normally used an accommodation address for just a couple of months then moved on to another one. And the owner of the office address could rightly say it had nothing to do with him, whether it was true or not.

Hardcastle Business Services was printed in large black capitals on the glass and Challis turned the round plastic knob and entered. A bleached blonde wearing heavy make-up stopped reading a magazine and looked up. Only the top half of her was visible behind the desk and she was wearing a green low cut sweater, her large bust threatening to pop out of its uplift bra. She looked no more than twenty.

'Hello, can I help you?' the young woman said with a beaming smile, aping Marilyn Monroe's breathless voice. He looked a lot more interesting than most who came here, she thought, as she gave the journalist a quick once-over. Quite a hunk, in fact, and loved the way his hair fell over his forehead. Lovely tan too.

Nothing like most of the dirty old men who used the facilities on these premises.

'Hey, you're nice,' Challis said. 'Didn't expect to see such a good looking girl like you in a place like this.'

He looked around the cluttered office. One wall had rows of pigeon holes with name tags written in blue biro, underneath were two wooden tables covered with letters and small parcels, yet to be sorted. Grey metal filing cabinets were stacked against two other walls. Everything looked seedy and the office was desperately in need of decoration.

'I'm a model really. I've only been here a couple of months,' she said, pleased with the compliment. 'I'm just helping out Mr Hardcastle for a while. He says he can make me famous.'

'Does he. Well, you've certainly got what it takes to be a page three girl.'

'Thank you. Mr Hardcastle's got a photographic studio above this office and he runs a private camera club.'

'Is that so.' And Challis immediately knew what category this business fell into. 'Is it busy?'

'Sometimes I pose for as many as six or seven men at a time.'

'I take it you're not a shy girl.'

'No,' she giggled.

'Ever pose for any naughty ones?'

'Sometimes,' she giggled louder. 'Mr Hardcastle says lots of stars had to do it before they got to the top.'

'What's your name?'

'Natasha, but everyone calls me Tasha. What's yours?'

'Challis.'

'Nothing else?'

'Nope. That's what everybody calls me.'

'Well, what can I do for you?'

'Is Mr Hardcastle about?'

'No, he's just popped out to see someone, but he shouldn't be long.'

'People use this place as an accommodation address, don't they?'

'That's right.'

'Well, an old friend of mine was using this place six years ago because he didn't want certain letters sent to his house in case his wife found out.'

'Oh, lots of our clients have the same sort of problem. But that's a long time ago, I was still at school then.'

'I know it's a long time but I've been working out of the country and I've lost his telephone number and can't remember his address. So, I was wondering if you could help me.' He gave a toothy smile.

'What was his name?'

'Paul Phillips.'

'Wait a minute.'

She moved from the desk and opened a door to another room. She disappeared for a good five minutes then teetered back on her high heels carrying a large ledger. She put it on the desk and began flicking through the pages.

'Sorry to keep you waiting but I had trouble finding the right book. Paul Phillips you said.'

'That's right.'

'And it was definitely six years ago?'

'Yep, about July time.'

She stopped at a page and was just about to speak when the door opened and a man entered.

'Jennifer, what are you doing?' he asked.

'It's Tasha, Mr Hardcastle. I'm Tasha now.'

'Yes, yes, of course.' He bent forward and closed the ledger. 'That's confidential, Tasha.'

Challis nearly swore out loud. Just another minute and he'd have had the information.

'And who are you?' Hardcastle asked.

Hardcastle was about forty with slicked back hair at the sides and the top a carefully arranged set of railway lines trying to hide his baldness. He was clean shaven but a pencil thin moustache would have suited him. He was skinny and his eyes shifty. A right *face*, the journalist thought.

'Mr Challis is looking for one of his friends, Mr Hardcastle,' Tasha said.

'That's right,' Challis said.

'Who's that then?'

'His name's Paul Phillips and I know he was using your services six years ago. The thing is, I've misplaced his real address, and I was wondering if you could help me.'

'Out of the question, that kind of information is confidential,' Hardcastle abruptly replied.

Challis looked dismayed.

'Is it possible to have a word with you in your private office, please,' he said in an affable voice. 'I won't keep you long, and you might find it to your advantage.'

'Really?' and Hardcastle looked at his wristwatch. 'Oh, all right then, but it will have to be quick, I'm expecting an important phone call soon.' He picked up the ledger and walked into the other room. Challis followed and closed the door behind him as Hardcastle sat behind his desk.

Challis pulled up a metal tubular chair with a torn plastic covering and sat down. There were another couple of metal filing cabinets against one wall and a fan, obviously broken, perched on a scratched wooden chair under the window. Half a dozen cardboard boxes were stacked in one corner of the room. The top one was open and Challis saw a video cassette sticking out which immediately gave him an idea.

'So you're interested in one of my clients,' Hardcastle said.

'That's right.'

'Now, you know I can't reveal any information to you. It's not ethical.'

'Do you have any information about Paul Phillips?'

'Probably.'

'Do you mind looking in that book of yours?'

'Look, I told you...' Hardcastle stopped in mid-sentence when he saw Challis take a small tape recorder from a side pocket of his linen sports coat, switch it on and place it on his desk.

'What the hell's going on?' and he stopped again as Challis produced a small notebook and pen.

'What's your first name Mr Hardcastle?' Challis asked in a steely tone.

'Who are you? What's this all about?'

'Oh, I'm sorry. You don't know do you?'

Challis dug into his back pocket, took out his wallet and leaned over the desk. He flipped it open to reveal his NUJ press card, then pulled his hand back to the side of his face and smiled.

'See, it's me in the photograph. I'm a journalist.'

'A journalist? Who do you work for? '

'I'm a freelance, Mr Hardcastle, and I sell to all the nationals. Maybe you read my recent story about the MP, Tony Carter-West. It was by me, Peter Challis. All the tabloids followed it up.'

'So what do you want with me?' Hardcastle sounded wary.

Challis didn't reply but stood up and went to a glass frame hanging on the wall. Inside was a certificate from the Pentecostal School of Business in Oregon, USA, stating that the named person had passed his course with honours.

'Cyril Arthur Hardcastle,' Challis repeated the name out loud as he wrote in his notebook. 'You can buy these certificates two a penny in the States. They're not worth the paper they're written on.'

'What kind of story are you doing, Mr Challis?'

Challis sat down again and gave a knowing look.

'Pornography, Cyril. I'm doing a big story on hard core pornography, and the trail's led here.'

'But I'm not involved in that. You've got the wrong man.'

Challis leaned forward and picked up a handful of negatives in their plastic sleeves from a tray. He held up a strip to the bright sunlight from the window.

'Very sexy, Cyril,' he said.

'They're not porn. You can see photos like that in any men's magazine in your local newsagent.'

'What's in those boxes?' Challis pointed to the corner of the room near where Hardcastle was sitting.

Hardcastle pulled a video cassette in a plain cover from the top box.

'It's soft porn, not hard core stuff. I sell these through mail order, all perfectly legal.'

'Where do you keep the hard stuff, Cyril?'

'I'm telling you I'm not involved in that,' Hardcastle exploded. 'I've had enough of this,' and he reached for the telephone. 'I'm calling my solicitor.'

He wondered if the journalist was really interested in Phillips or was that just a moody? He *was* in the hard core business but nothing to do with this person Challis was on about. Just how much did the journalist know? But Hardcastle didn't fancy getting heavy because Challis didn't look the sort of person to mess with. In fact, just the opposite.

'That's okay with me,' Challis replied in a calm voice. 'Why don't you phone the police too? I'll explain how I came to arrive here. I bet they'd love to have a look around your place.

You've got a studio upstairs, haven't you? They'd find that interesting.'

Hardcastle replaced the receiver on its hook as he realised the journalist had called his bluff. Better to co-operate and hope that Challis wasn't interested in him. He was sweating profusely and took off his jacket. He slung it over the boxes and took out a handkerchief to wipe his face. He looked a worried man.

'Well, turn off the tape recorder.'

Challis picked up the recorder, ejected the tape and threw it to Hardcastle.

'Keep it,' he said.

'What do you mean, the trail led here?' Hardcastle asked, after he put the cassette into a drawer.

'Okay Cyril, I'll level with you, and if you play ball with me then I'll see what I can do to keep your name out of the papers.' Challis paused for effect. 'Paul Phillips is the head of a nation wide porn ring. He's also into child pornography, and that carries a lot of bird when you're nicked. I can always have a word with some of the cops in the *dirty squad* at Scotland Yard and I'm sure they'd love to pass it on to your local old bill.'

'Paul Phillips.' Hardcastle quickly opened the ledger. 'And it was six years ago.'

'That's right.'

Hardcastle found what he was looking for and looked quizzically at the journalist.

'If you know so much about this Phillips bloke, then how come you don't know his address? And why are you interested in something that's so old?'

'Cyril, I've gone into Paul Phillips background from the year dot and I'm trying to find out as much as I can about him. I've already got a few addresses but I'd still like the one you've got.' Challis stood. 'However, if you don't want to give it to me, it doesn't matter. I'll just write that the story led here, and you refused to co-operate.'

'No, no, you've got it wrong. I'll co-operate. Here, I'll write out the address for you.'

Challis moved to his side.

'No, I think I'll copy it from the book myself,' and carefully made notes. 'That's very interesting, a London address and telephone number.'

'He was only with us for three months, and only had one letter sent to him. See those initials in the margin, PDNB, it means *photographs do not bend* was written on the envelope.'

Hardcastle looked at Challis as he suddenly realised what he'd said.

'I swear I didn't know what was going on.'

'How did Phillips contact you?'

'I don't know, it's too far back to remember, but it says here he paid three months cash in advance.'

'And this is the address he gave you to send any mail?'

'That's the one.'

'Did you talk to him on the phone?'

'Probably.'

'What did he sound like?'

'Who do you think I am, Mr fucking Memory Man? I can't remember all that time ago.'

'No, I don't expect you can,' Challis agreed.

'So you promise you'll leave me out of the papers then, Mr Challis?' It came out as a whine. 'I've got a wife and kids to think about.'

'Yes, Cyril, you don't have to worry. One more thing though,' and Challis opened his coat. He pointed to a small microphone clipped to his inside pocket. 'Always ask a journalist to turn off *both* his tape recorders.'

126

EIGHTEEN

A quick pub lunch and Challis was on his way back to London. By four pm he was in his flat, greeted by the green flashing light of his answer machine. The message was from a policeman, Chief Inspector Mike Jordan, with reference to Matthew Hardy.

Before Challis left the banker's home Saturday night he made a copy of all the papers Bernie Harris had given him to show the police. The millionaire financier had a well equipped office in his mansion and would have no difficulty operating his affairs from Hertfordshire on a short term basis.

Challis called the policeman's number and a few moments later the chief inspector was explaining the situation. His chief superintendent had told him to contact all the investigating officers in each murder case from the information supplied by Harris. But he should spend as little time as possible following this line of inquiry unless new evidence came to light. And it better be concrete evidence. The idea was far fetched but they should cover their backs because the press was involved.

'And they told me to keep the long distance phone calls as short as possible to save money,' Chief Inspector Jordan said, with a slight chuckle.

Typical, Challis thought.

All the police officers Jordan said he'd spoken to were intrigued by the old soldier's story and promised they'd keep it in mind. The murders were still unsolved and their files kept open, but they all asked the same question.

Who were they looking for?

When Jordan spoke to the Sheffield police they said they'd have a word with Bernie Harris, but that was as much as they could do at this stage.

It was the same concerning Matthew Hardy. Even with his pull with the Chief Constable, there was no chance of getting police protection unless there was proof his life was in immediate danger.

'So don't forget to let me know if you come up with anything else,' the policeman said.

'Yeah, sure,' Challis mumbled as he put the phone down. Bollocks, let the coppers do their own work. He wasn't going to volunteer any more information.

Then Challis had the embarrassing task of calling Bernie Harris and telling him the cavalry wasn't yet on its way to the rescue because the police weren't convinced, although they were looking into it.

'Don't worry,' the old man said, 'and thanks for all the trouble you've gone to.'

Challis sat looking at the telephone feeling guilty. He was supposed to be a hardened hack and shouldn't get personally involved in stories. But somehow he felt he'd let the old soldier down.

The journalist got up and went over to a punch ball on a spring stand in the corner of the room. He started jabbing with his left fist, his bony knuckles hitting hard against the leather, then swinging with his right. Soon he had a fast tempo going which he kept up for several minutes until the perspiration was dripping from him.

It was Challis's way of letting off steam and he'd bought the punch ball during his doomed marriage. Better than beating up the wife, and he'd maintained the habit over the years to release his frustrations.

When his breathing returned to normal Challis got his large A to Z of London from a bookshelf then took out his notebook and looked up the address he'd written down in Hardcastle's office. It was in Ealing, west London.

Challis sat back in his chair wondering whether to telephone or go and look over the property first. He decided to call and picked up the phone, switched on the attached tape recorder and dialled the number.

'The Crescent Health Clinic,' a pleasant sounding female voice answered.

'Could I speak to Mr Phillips please, Paul Phillips.'

There was a slight pause.

'Mr Phillips? I'm sorry sir, but there's no Mr Phillips here. Are you sure you've got the right number?'

'I thought I had. Just let me check,' and Challis repeated the number to her.

'That's correct sir, but there's definitely no Mr Phillips here.'

'Ah, I know what's happened. This is a number I had six years ago, maybe it became a spare line, and now you've got it. That's probably the explanation.'

'It's not, sir. The clinic's been open ten years, and I've been here four.'

'With the same number?'

'Yes sir.'

'Well in that case, *I've* got it wrong. Sorry to have troubled you, and thanks for your help.'

*

The receptionist replaced the receiver slowly and stared thoughtfully at the telephone. Then she picked up the handset again and made a call.

'I just had a man on the phone asking about Paul Phillips,' she said, and listened carefully to the voice on the other end.

'No, he didn't say who he was.'

She listened again.

'Okay, I'll let you know if anything else happens.'

*

The address in Ealing was a converted detached Victorian house in a residential area with the front garden tarmaced over for off street parking. There were two cars parked on the space with room for another two. A big sign above the front door said *Crescent Health Clinic* in scroll lettering with a smaller sign by the side of the entrance, but Challis was parked too far away to read the words.

It was nearly six o'clock and a few minutes later a woman about thirty came out and drove off in one of the cars. Twenty minutes later a middle aged man left the house and walked along the road. After another ten minutes the lights inside went out and a man and woman, both in their forties, left and the man double locked the front door. They both got into the remaining car and drove off. Challis sat patiently for another fifteen minutes before he got out of his car and walked across the road.

He stopped at the front door and saw the smaller sign advertised a list of available services: osteopathy, chiropody, hypnotherapy, aromatherapy and reflexology. There were no names to say who did what but it did state that Mr James Brody was the director of the clinic.

NINETEEN

Keely was dressed and ready to leave when Challis went into the kitchen at six thirty. She had to catch an early flight to Rome to cover a fashion show for her magazine and would be away for two or three days.

'Fresh coffee's on,' she said, and Challis was still half asleep as she gave him a quick hug and goodbye kiss.

An hour later Challis was sitting in his office, checking through his notes. He'd listen to his tape recordings later and see if he'd missed anything and also work out a rough format for the story on his computer.

It was another sunny morning, but already hot and humid, the kind of day that made a person realise global warming was fast becoming fact.

Challis phoned Steve to say he'd pick him up at his studio and by ten o'clock they were driving in the direction of the health clinic in Ealing. During the journey Challis related the previous day's events in Nottingham.

'So who's Paul Phillips? And how does he fit in?'

'Don't know, but that's something I hope to find out soon,' the journalist replied.

After they parked near the clinic Challis walked to the front door by himself while Steve said he'd have a look around and find a good spot to take pics of people coming and going in case they were needed. Also check out the back exit.

A small sign said *please ring the bell* and after Challis did this there was a click and the door slipped free from its safety lock. He stepped inside and followed a sign leading to a brightly lit reception area where several people sat in chairs reading magazines. Challis recognised the woman sitting behind the desk as the one he'd seen leaving by herself yesterday late afternoon. Pretty, with short cut black hair, and when she asked if she could help him, he knew it was the same woman he'd spoken to on the phone.

'I'm the person who called you yesterday asking about Mr Phillips,' he said. 'My name's Challis.'

'Oh yes, I remember,' she said. 'But, as I told you, there's no Mr Phillips here.'

'Are you sure you've never heard of him?'

'I'm positive.'

'What about before you started here?'

'I really can't say,' and she shrugged her shoulders.

'I saw your sign outside and it said James Brody is the director of this place. Is he your boss?'

'Yes, this is his business.'

'Is it possible to have a word with him? I won't take up much of his time.'

James Brody turned out to be the hypnotherapist. He helped people with stress problems, phobias, diet difficulties and people who wanted to give up smoking. He should meet Bernie Harris, Challis thought.

There had been a cancellation and after waiting for about twenty minutes James Brody came into the reception area and shook hands with Challis.

Brody was the man in his forties Challis had seen leave the previous day with a woman. He was stocky with dark brown wavy hair, a charming smile and eyes that were so pale blue, Challis couldn't help staring at them. He wore a three quarter length white coat with half a dozen pens sticking out of the top pocket and had a manner that automatically made a person feel at ease.

'What can I do for you, Mr Challis?'

'I'm trying to locate a man called Paul Phillips,' the journalist replied.

'Sorry, but there's nobody by the name Phillips here. What made you think there would be?'

'I came across some information that suggested he might be at this address. Mind you, it was six years ago, and before your present receptionist's time.'

Brody crossed his arms and sat on one corner of the reception desk.

'This all sounds very mysterious, Mr Challis. What line of business are you in?'

'I'm a freelance journalist, Mr Brody,' and Challis gave him one of his embossed cards, which the hypnotherapist looked at closely then pushed into his top pocket among the jumble of pens.

'Well, you can give us a write-up if you want,' Brody smiled. 'We could do with some publicity.'

Challis smiled back at the remark he'd heard a hundred times before.

'You never know Mr Brody, I *might* be able to do something for you one day.'

James Brody looked thoughtful, trying to remember, but after a minute shook his head. Then suddenly he clicked his fingers.

'What about Pauline Phillips? Could that be the person you want?'

'Could be. Who is she?'

'You remember Pauline Phillips, Miss Quinn. She had the job before you.'

The receptionist looked at Brody and said, 'Of course. It just didn't connect with me when you asked about a man, Mr Challis. I'm sorry.'

'She worked for me for a couple of years,' Brody said. 'Then before she left she showed you the ropes.'

'That's right,' Miss Quinn said. 'I started two weeks before she left and she helped me get the hang of things.'

'Any idea where she is now?' Challis asked.

'I certainly haven't. I never saw her again after she left here,' Miss Quinn replied.

'What about you, Mr Brody?'

'Come with me, Mr Challis.'

The journalist followed Brody along a short corridor and into a tiny office with just enough room for a small desk and a couple of metal filing cabinets.

'This is where I keep all my business papers,' Brody said. 'Patients files are kept separately in the consulting rooms where there's much more space.'

He opened several metal drawers but couldn't find what he was searching for.

'This is really my wife's department,' he explained. 'She does the aromatherapy here and doubles as my private secretary. Wait a minute,' and he left the room.

A couple of minutes later he came back with a woman in a light green overall. She was wiping her hands on a small towel.

'I can't be long because Mrs Tooley is in a hurry,' Challis heard her say as she entered the office.

Brody introduced his wife who went immediately to one of the drawers of a filing cabinet, flicked along the hanging files and pulled one out. She opened it and smiled broadly as she handed it over.

'What would you do without me,' she said to her husband as she left the room.

Brody opened the file on the desk and looked at several papers.

'Yes, this is her address where she was living and also the new place she was starting work at. Funny really, she was a good receptionist and I could have understood if she'd gone to work in an office or something like that, but she went to a shop. Some sort of theatrical costumiers.'

He offered a sheet of paper to Challis who copied the details into his notebook.

*

When Challis got back to the BMW Steve was nearly nodding off in the heat and jumped as the car door shut.

'Any joy?' he asked.

'It seems our man's had a sex change,' Challis replied, and went on to explain.

'The only person who's heard Paul Phillips voice is John Mason, right?' Steve said.

Challis nodded.

'Do you think he could have been mistaken?'

'No, I've met him and he's too shrewd.'

'Maybe Pauline Phillips is very good at imitating male voices. If a person introduces themself over the phone as a man and sounds like a man, then why would you question it? I mean, it's not as though you're looking at the person in the flesh.'

'Yeah, could be,' Challis said. 'So let's find out.'

They decided to try the home address first, which was nearest, not far from Hammersmith Town Hall.

The address was a flat in a large converted house. It seemed all the houses in the street had been converted into flats and the front porches were a mass of tatty name tags and doorbells.

The flat they wanted didn't have the name Phillips on it but Challis rang it anyway. No answer, and after several long presses, rang another. The front door clicked open and as Challis and Steve entered a female voice shouted down from several floors up.

'Who is it?'

135

'We're looking for Pauline Phillips,' Challis shouted back, and started climbing the stairs. The female descended and they met on the first floor.

'Don't know a Pauline Phillips,' the scruffily dressed teenager said, puffing on a cigarette. 'You the old bill?'

Challis grinned. 'Course not. It's a personal matter. She's come into some money and we're trying to trace her. She lived here about four or five years ago.'

'Naw, long before my time.'

'Is there anybody living here who might have known her from those days?'

The girl took a long drag, dropped the cigarette stub on the worn stair carpet and squashed it flat.

'You might try the nosy old cow on the ground floor,' she said, pointing downwards. 'Mrs Weeks, she seems to know everyone's business.'

Challis and Steve turned and walked down as the girl made her way back upstairs. There were three doors on the ground floor so Steve opened the front door, found the bell for Weeks, and kept his finger on the button. Challis heard behind which door the buzzer sounded and moved towards it.

'Alright, alright, I'm coming,' and a woman opened the door into the hallway. She stopped when she saw Challis and Steve. Mrs Weeks was in her fifties, smartly dressed and wearing thick tortoise shell frame glasses.

'Can I help you gentlemen?' she asked in an efficient sounding voice.

'I hope so,' Challis replied. 'We're trying to locate Pauline Phillips. She used to live here.'

'Who are you then?'

The question sounded more like a challenge.

Challis took out his press card and showed it to Mrs Weeks.

'Journalists, eh. So why do you want to find Pauline?'

'You know her then?'

136

'Yes, but you still haven't told me why you want to see her.'

'Well, it's not her we're actually looking for. It's a friend of her's and we think she might be able to help us find this person.'

'What's the story?'

'I'm sorry Mrs Weeks, but that's private.' The woman was living up to her reputation and Challis thought it better to turn on the charm.

'You'll have to wait until it comes out,' he beamed, showing lots of teeth. 'So how about helping the press, then we can have an early night and go home to our wives and kids.'

Mrs Weeks stood looking stonily at the journalist as Challis kept the smile on his face.

'Oh, all right then,' she relented. 'She's not Pauline Phillips anymore, she's married. She got married about three years ago.'

'Do you know what she's called now?'

'Yes. Her name's Mrs Fountain.'

'Do you know her husband's Christian name?'

'It's Michael, his name is Michael Fountain.'

'And have you any idea where they live?'

'No I haven't,' Mrs Weeks sniffed. 'Pauline said she'd keep in touch but I never heard from her after she left. Didn't even invite me to the wedding.'

*

The two men stopped off at a pizza place for a quick meal, and after ordering, Challis got the phone number for the theatrical shop from directory enquiries.

'Hello,' a woman's voice answered after he got through.

'Could I speak to Pauline Fountain, please?'

'I'm sorry, but she's not here, she had to leave early.'

'Will she be at work tomorrow?' Challis asked.

'Yes, she'll be in tomorrow.'

'Thanks,' and Challis clicked off his mobile.

When they'd finished eating Challis dropped Steve back at his studio and carried on home. As soon as he got in he stripped off his clothes down to his underpants and got a cold can of lager from the fridge. He'd just finished his second lager and poured himself a large whisky when the phone rang. It was Nigel Thompson from France.

'How did it go?' Challis asked.

'The locals were more helpful than I'd thought they'd be. My wife's family knew somebody who knew somebody and they gave me a good recommendation.'

'Excellent.'

'I found Giles Faraday's grave and Henri Fabere is buried nearby. Also a younger brother who died on the same day. His name was Edouard Fabere. Neither of the Fabere brothers were married and their parents are dead. There are some cousins about but no closer relatives are alive.'

'What about Faraday, did he have any kids over there?'

'No, nothing like that. Faraday and Henri Fabere were regarded as heroes. I spoke to a couple of old timers who remembered them both from the Nazi occupation days and Faraday was the typical English gentleman. No scandal, just a hard soldier. Killed a lot of Germans and blew up a load of trains. Spoke French like a native and was well liked.'

'So you're sure they died in nineteen forty four?'

'I'm absolutely positive. The graves and headstones look more than fifty to sixty years old and there is a record of their deaths in the local church. I read it myself and it definitely dates from the war.'

'Nigel, you did great.'

'Thanks...don't forget the money.'

TWENTY

The shop he was looking for was near Covent Garden in the heart of London's theatre land. Challis pushed open the door and a bell tinkled over his head. A middle aged woman with a pair of glasses stuck in the hair on top of her head was sorting through small packets of false beards and moustaches. She looked up when the door opened. There was no-one else in the shop.

'Can I help you?' she asked.

'Is Mrs Fountain here?'

'Yes, she is. She's in the back.'

'Is it possible to have a word with her, please?'

The woman pushed open a curtain and called into the rear of the premises.

'Pauline, there's a young man to see you.' She paused, 'He's good looking too.'

Challis's hand self-consciously went to his nose. Only his mother had ever called him good looking. Ruggedly handsome was the best Keely came up with.

The striped curtain was pulled aside and a pretty woman about thirty appeared. She wore a long loose fitting floral dress with a scarf tied around her head Red Indian style and had a holiday tan.

'You want to see me?' she asked.

'That's right,' Challis replied.

'What about?'

'I'm a journalist, Mrs Fountain. My name's Challis. Is it possible to have a word with you in private?'

A quizzical look flashed across Pauline Fountain's face. She glanced at her wrist watch and then at the other woman.

'Well, it's a bit early...,' she started to say but was interrupted by her friend.

'Have an early coffee break, Pauline, we're not busy,' and as they left the shop she added, 'take your time.'

The couple walked to one of the nearby open air cafes in what was once the old fruit market. During the short distance Challis discovered that his companion had returned only last weekend from a very enjoyable holiday with her husband in Cyprus, a place he knew well.

'I tried to get hold of you yesterday,' he said, 'but you had already left.'

'Yes, I had to go to the airport to meet my sister, she's on a visit from Australia.'

When they were seated with two cups of cappuccino in front of them Challis explained he was doing a missing person story. He said her name had cropped up during his investigation and thought she might be able to help him.

'In what way, Mr Challis?'

'I'm interested in the time you used to work for Mr Brody at his health clinic in Ealing.'

Challis noticed the surprise on the face of the woman sitting opposite him.

'That was years ago,' she said. 'It was a boring old job. Mr Brody and his wife were okay but I was just a receptionist. How would that interest you?'

'I wasn't really looking for you. I was looking for a man called Paul Phillips who was connected with that address at the time. Instead, I came up with you. Phillips was your maiden name, wasn't it?'

'Yes, but I still don't see what you're getting at.'

'What about an accommodation address in Nottingham? Does that ring any bells?'

Pauline picked up a small spoon and slowly stirred her coffee, staring at the swirls. After some moments she lifted her eyes.

'Yes, I remember now.' She swirled the spoon some more. 'The bastard's come back to haunt me.'

'What do you mean?'

'Frank Beckett. That's what I mean.'

'Who's Frank Beckett?'

The woman didn't answer and continued staring into her cup.

'Is Paul Phillips really Frank Beckett?'

'Yes,' the reply came out as a whisper and she cleared her throat. 'Yes,' she repeated louder this time. 'They're the same person.'

Challis could clearly see something was bothering the woman sitting opposite him.

'Are you all right? I'm sorry, I didn't mean to upset you.'

'That's okay,' she said. 'It's just brought back a lot of bad memories I thought were gone forever.'

'If you don't mind talking about it, I really would like to know more.'

She nodded her head.

'Okay.'

Challis relaxed. For a moment he'd thought she was going to clam up, or walk away.

'I know the name given to the accommodation address people in Nottingham was Paul and not Pauline because I've been there and talked to the man who runs the business,' he said. 'I know one letter was sent to the address of the health clinic here in London and I've also spoken to someone who talked to Paul Phillips on the phone. And it was a man's voice, not a woman's.'

Pauline Fountain sat looking at the journalist for a long moment before she spoke.

'Frank Beckett was my boyfriend for a couple of years. He was married but separated from his wife and he promised when he got his divorce we would marry, but it never happened, I'm glad to say.'

She finished her coffee.

'Do you think I could have another cup, please?'

Challis queued again for two more cappuccinos and brought them back to the table.

'How did you meet Frank Beckett?' he asked.

'He came to the clinic to see if Mr Brody could help him give up smoking. Mr Brody hypnotises people. Frank became a regular patient and after about a month he asked me out. And I said yes.'

'What about the accommodation address?'

'It was about six months after we started going out together when Frank asked me if I would do him a favour. He said he was trying to find out some information but didn't want to use his real name or address. He said it wasn't illegal or anything like that but it was very personal and would like to keep it secret. He said he was going to use the name Paul Phillips and the clinic's address, and there would probably only be one letter and maybe a couple of phone calls. I checked the post in the mornings and answered the telephone, so there wasn't a problem. Anyway, if Mr Brody had seen the letter addressed to Paul instead of Pauline Phillips he would have assumed it was an error. And Frank was right. There was just one large brown envelope which said it contained photographs, and a couple of phone messages which I passed on to Frank.'

'Did Frank ever tell you what the secret was?'

'No, and I didn't ask. I mean, one letter and a couple of phone calls were soon forgotten.'

Pauline took a sip of her coffee.

'But there was one thing I didn't forget. It was the first time I saw the other side of Frank's character.'

142

'What do you mean?'

'I took the envelope to his flat and I made some joke about it. I said I hoped they weren't dirty photographs and if they were, then I wanted to see them too. But as soon as I said that Frank grabbed me and slapped me across the face. He had this terrible look in his eyes and said I shouldn't insult his family like that. I said I was sorry and didn't realise they were family photos.'

'*Family photos*?' Challis couldn't keep the surprise out of his voice. 'Are you sure?'

'One hundred per cent.'

'Did you ever get to see them?'

'No, never, and after that reaction, I didn't feel like mentioning them again.'

'How old is Frank Beckett?'

'He's seven years older than me, so he's thirty eight. *Just* actually, because my birthday was on the twenty first of July and Frank's a week later, the twenty eighth.'

She finished the remains of her coffee.

'I really must get back, Mr Challis, Betty's on her own and I've been too long already.'

She started to rise.

'But I've got lots more questions to ask you,' Challis said. 'Can I see you at lunchtime, or after you've finished work for the day?'

Pauline stood with her hands resting on the table looking down at Challis.

'Have you been to the clinic?'

'Yes, I was there yesterday,' he replied.

'Is Shirley Quinn still there?'

'Yes, she is. She's the receptionist.'

'You should ask her about Frank.'

'You mean, she's Frank Beckett's girlfriend?'

'She was.'

'Is she still?'

'I've no idea.'

Pauline looked at her watch again. 'Come to the shop at one o'clock and you can take me for lunch. But I must go now,' and she turned and walked away.

Challis hadn't brought his briefcase with him and he took a small notebook from his pocket and began writing down everything the woman had told him. Then he got another cup of coffee and phoned Steve.

'Your holiday's over,' Challis said.

'I thought it was too good to last, what do you want me to do?'

'I want you to go back to the clinic about five thirty today and follow the receptionist, Shirley Quinn, when she finishes work. She parks her car in the front, it's an old Vauxhall, and probably leaves about six.'

Challis gave Steve the receptionist's description and added, 'Better use the motorbike, it will be easier to follow her in the traffic.'

'Okay. What about pics?'

'Don't bother tonight, but find a good place outside her home for you to plot up with the van. I think from tomorrow you'll be on stakeout duty.'

'What about you? Did you find Pauline Fountain?'

'Yes, and it turns out Paul Phillips is really a bloke called Frank Beckett.'

'Who's he?'

'Don't know yet, Steve, I'll speak to you later.'

*

Challis knew the area well and picked out a small restaurant that served excellent food. He reserved a table for two on the way to pick up Pauline and by ten past one they were seated and ordering their meal. Pauline told him she'd be all right for at least an hour and a half and Betty would take a longer lunch break tomorrow.

'I'd like you tell me everything you can about Frank Beckett,' Challis said, as they both sipped gin and tonic.

'What's Frank done?' she asked. 'Don't worry, I'll tell you what I know, but I'm curious to find out if the bastard's in trouble.'

'Pauline, I can truthfully say I've got no idea. The story I'm working on is so involved I couldn't begin to explain. Frank Beckett has only just come into it, and I'm hoping he might lead me to something else. It's a bit like a jigsaw and I'm putting the pieces together.'

'Oh, I thought you might be exposing him as a crook, or something like that.' She sounded disappointed.

'Tell me what you know,' Challis said in a soft voice.

'Well, I've already told you I met Frank when he came to the clinic and then he asked me out.'

'You said he was married.'

'That's right. His wife was French Canadian. Frank said her accent was the sexiest thing about her and marrying her was a big mistake. Frank had been working in Montreal and met her there. Apparently, he only married her because his father thought it might help the family business.'

'And what business is that?'

'Frank's family own a travel agency business with shops all over the country, abroad too. And they're in shipping and property. They own a lot of property here and in Canada, America and France.'

'They sound rich.'

'They're loaded.'

'Frank too?'

'I know his grandfather left him a lot of money and he's got shares in the business. He's got a younger brother who works in the company but Frank didn't do a thing when I knew him. I think his family washed their hands of him, especially after his marriage broke up and his wife went back to Canada.'

'Did you ever meet his ex-wife or his brother?'

'No, and Frank didn't talk very much about them, but I do remember their names.'

Challis jotted down the family names and the name of the company, which the journalist recognised. It *was* big.

They hadn't wanted a starter and the waiter arrived with their main course, and a chilled bottle of white wine.

'What does Frank do with his time?' Challis asked.

'He liked to keep fit and converted a spare room in his flat into a gym,' Pauline replied. 'He played a lot of sport too. Golf was his favourite. He also belonged to a gun club, and then he got interested in acting and the theatre after he met me.'

'Anything else?' Challis asked.

'Towards the end of our relationship he used to go to Paris every now and again,' Pauline replied.

'Any idea why?'

She shook her head.

'No, not really. Frank said he had a good business friend over there. That's all.'

'Do you know this person's name?'

'No, just that it was a man. But Frank never told me his name.'

Pauline paused as she carefully cut into her chicken Kiev.

'He had this beautiful flat in Knightsbridge,' she continued. 'And he drove a Porsche sports car. With all that I really don't know why he asked me out, he could have had anyone.' Pauline grimaced. 'At the time I thought I was lucky.'

'Can you remember his address and phone number?'

She could only remember the address, which Challis wrote in his notebook.

'Any photographs of him?'

She shook her head.

'I tore them up, but I can give you a pretty good description of him.'

Challis wrote again in his book.

'You said something about bad memories. What did you mean by that?' he asked.

'About a month after he first came to the clinic he stopped smoking but still made appointments over the next six weeks or so.'

'Why?'

'He said he wanted to make sure he didn't start again and he found the sessions with Mr Brody so relaxing. And even after he finished his appointments I know he continued to see him because Frank told me they sometimes played golf together. We had a lot of fun in the beginning and were very happy together but about seven or eight months after I met him, he hit me for the first time. Remember I told you about the photographs.'

Challis nodded and took another mouthful of food.

'Then everything was fine for months and I put that incident down to the fact I knew he didn't get on with his family and somehow I'd rubbed him up the wrong way,' Pauline continued. 'I suppose it was eighteen months after we first met that he really started to change. He said he wasn't sleeping very well. He was having bad dreams, nightmares, and so he went to a doctor. And then he started talking about having another family.'

Challis looked at her, his fork poised in mid-air.

'*Another* family, what do you mean by that? Was it anything to do with the photographs?'

'I don't know. He said a few odd things a couple of times but when I questioned him about it he said it was none of my business. Maybe I jumped the gun and got the wrong impression but I remember thinking if he'd suddenly found out he was adopted or something like that, it could have sent him a bit funny. Then he told me he was seeing a psychiatrist...or was it a psychologist? Anyway, some kind of doctor like that.'

'Do you know the names of these doctors?'

'No,' she said, and shook her head, 'I'm sorry but I don't.'

Pauline went quiet and continued eating.

'Carry on,' Challis said, as he sensed she was holding something back, and topped up their glasses of wine.

'I've always been in a drama group and I love amateur theatricals,' she said. 'Frank seemed to get the bug too and used to come with me twice a week. On one occasion he had to play the part of a tramp and he really got into the feel of things. He didn't shave for weeks, and that was fine while the play was on, but for some strange reason he didn't wash and shave for about a month after the play finished. Then he disappeared for a week and the next time I saw him he'd cleaned himself up and carried on with his life as though nothing had happened.'

'Very strange,' Challis commented, as he waited for more. But Pauline stopped talking and Challis could sense her embarrassment.

'This is a getting a bit personal now,' she said.

The journalist smiled reassuringly at the pretty woman sitting opposite him.

'Pauline, don't forget what kind of business I'm in, and I bet I've heard far worse things than you could ever tell me. So don't worry about it.'

'I wouldn't want any of this to get in the papers.'

'All I'm interested in is finding out about Beckett.'

Pauline took another sip of wine.

'He started tying me up before he made love to me. Sometimes he whipped me with his belt and I had to beg him to stop. He seemed to have an anger inside him and took it out on me. He hurt me, but some of the things he did to me I really did try to enjoy, just to please him.'

She didn't elaborate on the *things* done to her and Challis didn't press for details.

'Then he started disappearing for weeks on end, without telling me. I asked him where he went but he said he wasn't seeing another woman, so I had nothing to worry about. But he must have been staying somewhere because he didn't sleep in his flat.'

'Did you live with him?'

'No, I had a small place in Hammersmith, but I did stay a lot of nights with Frank at his home. He never let me have my own key though'

She toyed with the food on her plate.

'Then I had the offer of getting this job where I am now. It was exactly what I wanted so I told Mr Brody and that's when he hired Shirley Quinn.'

'And you stayed an extra two weeks to show her the ropes,' Challis said.

'That's right. And it was about this time Frank seemed to be more like his old self, like when I first met him. But what I didn't realise was that Frank was seeing someone else behind my back.'

'Shirley Quinn?' Challis ventured.

'Yes. He came to pick me up one evening before I left work and I introduced him to Shirley. He must have phoned her up for a date, and it was two months before I found out about them. I knew then he wasn't the man for me, so I suppose it was a good thing I discovered in time what a two timing bastard he was.'

'What happened next?'

'Frank and I had a big bust-up and I walked out on him.'

'And you've never seen him since?'

'Well, I'm not sure. I've got a Mini and about two years ago I was driving through Islington when I thought I saw him walking towards me on the other side of the road. He was dressed rough and I thought he must have had a relapse and was ill again.'

'Was it him?'

Pauline shrugged her shoulders.

'I really can't say for certain,' she replied. 'He had this old, long military style coat on, just like the one he wore when he played the part of a tramp in that play I was telling you about. I was stuck at road works controlled by temporary traffic lights and I was hoping to get a good look at him, but he suddenly went into a block of flats. Then the lights changed and I was on my way.'

'These flats, do you know where they were?'

Pauline's face creased in thought.

'A side street near the Caledonian Road. Yes, I'm sure he was walking from the Liverpool Road direction, which I was heading for. So the flats must have been somewhere between Caledonian Road and Liverpool Road.'

'They're both long roads,' Challis said.

'Yes, but it was nearer the Kings Cross station end, I remember that because I'd picked up a friend there and was giving her a lift to her mother's house.'

Challis nodded and continued scribbling.

'There is one other thing.'

The journalist lifted his head and looked at Pauline.

'Yes?'

'The flats were called Ashley Court. It was written on a wooden board above the middle entrance. All very grotty. The whole place looked as though it could do with a good lick of paint.'

'You're sure of the name?'

'Yes, it's my Father's name, Ashley. That's why it stuck in my mind.'

'When you were with Beckett, did he ever tell you what his illness was?'

'No, but I've never seen a person change as much as Frank did. When I first met him he was a very nice man but two years later he'd become very, very unpredictable. Sometimes he'd be okay for weeks on end then suddenly he'd change and go into violent tempers for no apparent reason. It was frightening. He was like two different people.'

'Sounds like a split personality.'

'Whatever, but I was glad when it was all over.'

'And you're Mrs Fountain now.'

'Yes, thank God.'

TWENTY ONE

The moment Challis returned to his flat he called directory enquiries to check out Frank Beckett's address which Pauline had given him. But the number was ex-directory and the operator couldn't help him. So Challis called the local public library for the Knightsbridge area and they confirmed Beckett was still on the electoral role at that address.

Challis switched on his computer and for the next couple of hours put all the information he'd uncovered over the last ten days on the screen. He only did it in rough form but made sure it was in the right order to use for future reference. Nigel Thompson's fax had arrived from Paris and he added that to his growing pile of paperwork.

Then he made himself a cheese and pickle sandwich and got a can of beer from the fridge. He went into the lounge and switched on Sky news to catch up with the latest events and stretched out on his large sofa.

Seven o'clock the phone rang. It was Steve.

'I followed the Quinn woman and she went to a terraced house in Acton,' he said. 'It will be an easy enough place to use the van and get pictures. Not much traffic and plenty of parking space.'

Challis looked at his watch.

'Give it to about ten thirty and then knock it on the head. And make sure you're not seen. I don't want to blow it at this stage.'

'Don't worry, and I'll only call you if something happens. If not, I'll speak to you tomorrow.'

*

Challis had a quick shower and change of clothes and drove to Beckett's address in Knightsbridge, an exclusive block of flats just off Sloane Street. The street was mainly restricted to residents parking bays with only a few public parking meters. Okay for a stakeout in the evening and overnight, but not an easy place to park during the day without getting bothered by meter maids eager to dish out tickets.

Challis walked past the main entrance to the flats and through the thick plate glass front doors spotted a uniformed porter sitting behind a small desk. Most likely there was somebody on duty twenty four hours a day. The reception area was marble with thick pile carpet and looked impressive.

The journalist took a twenty minute stroll around the area noting there were two pubs close by and a variety of restaurants. He wondered if they were the kind of places Beckett might use.

Challis got back to his car, easing into the traffic heading for home, and as soon as he got in went straight to his answer machine. There was just one message, from Keely, sending her love and saying she wasn't sure what day she'd be returning to London.

Challis picked up the phone and called Steve's mobile. No answer, so he tried his home. Lynn, his wife, answered.

'Steve's not here yet. He said he's working with you at the moment,' she said.

'That's right.'

'Knowing the type of stories you get involved in, then I don't suppose I'll be seeing much of him for a while.'

'Yes, Lynn. But think of all that lovely lolly Steve will be earning. Anyway, it keeps him out of mischief.'

'Not with you around,' she laughed. 'Now, what can I do for you?'

'Steve's using the motorbike this evening and he must have his mobile switched off, so ask him to give me a call as soon as he gets in. No matter what time it is.'

'Okay.'

Lynn had worked as a secretary for several national newspapers before she married and knew the score. The story always came first. Lynn understood - pity Challis's ex hadn't.

The journalist and photographer were the closest of friends and had even been best man at each other's wedding.

When they'd worked together on the same local newspaper they both shared a burning ambition to succeed. And when Challis joined a national daily Steve swiftly got a job on a Sunday tabloid.

But three years ago he too had gone freelance because he wanted to develop a lucrative sideline.

Steve now did a lot of commercial photography and advertising work, as well as freelancing for the nationals, but would usually drop everything to help his friend. Challis appreciated this because Steve was one of the best *snatch* photographers in the business and *always* got a pic. He had a lot of bottle, and Challis never questioned how he sometimes got seemingly impossible photos.

Steve took chances and at times bent the law, Challis knew that. But didn't they all? The thing was not to get caught. That's why, on some sort of stories, a lot of national newspapers preferred to use freelances. Let them take the risk, and not the paper.

It never bothered Challis - as long as the money was right.

The journalist had just finished eating grilled tomatoes on a couple of slices of fried bread and thinking he must improve his diet, as he opened another lager, when Steve phoned to up-date him.

'The Quinn woman didn't leave her house tonight, at least not by the time I left,' he said. 'So what's the next move?'

154

'Stake out the clinic from mid-morning tomorrow. Maybe she'll meet Beckett for lunch, or go to his place in Knightsbridge when she finishes work.'

'Why not stake out his place? We've got a description of him.'

'Come on, Steve,' Challis replied. 'That description Pauline Fountain gave me could fit a dozen men.'

'Yeah, you're right,' Steve said, thinking of past times when he'd spent endless hours waiting to get a photograph.

'At least we know who Shirley Quinn is, and where she is,' Challis said.

'But we don't know if she's still Beckett's girlfriend, do we?'

'True, but if she is then she's got to lead us to Beckett sometime. We'll give it a couple of days and see what happens. Maybe Beckett's away on business, or holiday, or something like that.'

'Okay,' Steve said.

'Besides, I took a look at Beckett's Knightsbridge flat, and it's not the easiest place for a stakeout.'

*

Steve had been sitting in the back of the parked transit van for nearly three hours, his eyes peering through the one way tinted glass windows. His companion in black leather motorcycle gear sat quietly on a small fold-up stool, his young face, with dimpled cheeks, staring intently. Des was also a photographer, at twenty five, ten years junior to Steve, and today he was riding the powerful Yamaha, which was parked a few yards behind the van. The two men swapped transport depending on what the story required, although Steve did prefer the younger man to have the motorbike whenever possible.

There was a ventilation opening in the roof but it was still stifling hot and perspiration dripped from both men's faces.

Steve had a video camera trained on the front door of the *Crescent Health Clinic* catching everyone who went in or out. There was another spare video camera and two Nikon still cameras, each with telescopic lens attached, laying on the floor. There was even a small video camera specially built into one of the headlights which could be operated by remote control. As well as a couple of mobile phones, two walkie talkies and a Nagra tape recorder, there was also a powerful scanner for picking up mobile phone conversations. A brown cardboard box wedged in one corner contained spare films, tapes and batteries and two sleeping bags were neatly rolled up under the seats.

The vehicle contained one other vital piece of equipment - a portable chemical toilet.

Just after one o'clock Shirley Quinn appeared and set off towards some nearby shops with Steve following at a discreet distance on the other side of the road. She bought sandwiches, cakes and drinks, obviously some were for others in the clinic, and then returned the way she'd come.

Steve and Des suffered an uncomfortable and sweaty afternoon until the woman reappeared just after six pm and got in her car. Des followed her on the Yamaha through the busy traffic and kept in touch with Steve via their mobiles.

Shirley Quinn went straight home and didn't venture out again.

The two photographers left at midnight.

TWENTY TWO

The next day went the same as before with Steve and Des continuing their stakeout. But it was Friday and, seeing as Keely was still out of the country, Challis said he'd do an overnight in the van. It would be the beginning of the weekend and something was bound to break soon.

Challis went to bed at five pm but it was too early in the day to be tired and he tossed and turned trying to will himself to sleep. It seemed like hours before he finally dropped off and, of course, when his phone rang at ten he was then in a deep slumber and didn't feel like waking up.

It was Steve.

'Same as yesterday,' he said. 'She left work, went home and has stayed in all evening.'

'See you soon,' and Challis was out of bed and in the shower within a minute.

When he arrived at the transit van Des had already left and Steve and Challis swapped keys. The photographer went home in the BMW and Challis settled down for the night. He had a fair knowledge how to work the equipment and Steve had left the cameras freshly loaded with tapes and film.

He'd brought a flask of coffee and stopped on the way to get some doughnuts and felt fresh after his sleep. Several times during the next six hours Challis left the van and stretched his legs, enjoying the quiet. It was a lovely warm, peaceful night and not long after sunrise the first of the early morning joggers appeared on the streets, which pricked the journalist's conscience. He was getting lazy.

At six thirty Des arrived on the Yamaha with a brown paper bag carefully resting between his legs.

'There was a cafe open just down the road,' he said, handing the bag to Challis. 'Bought us some egg and bacon sarnies and coffee.'

'Good lad,' Challis said.

An hour later Steve drove up in the BMW, found a parking spot about a hundred yards from the van, then rapped gently on the back doors. Traffic was now building up on the road.

After Challis told his photographer the situation hadn't changed he walked to his car and returned home where there was a pleasant surprise waiting for him. Keely had left a message on his answering machine. She'd phoned from Rome and said she would be back in London late morning, and would call as soon as she arrived at her flat.

Challis tumbled straight into bed and slept until his phone rang at two pm.

'Hello,' he answered sleepily.

'Hello, darling, I missed you.'

'Keely, I'm glad you're back,' and Challis sat up against the headboard and stretched, the telephone tucked under his chin.

'You still in bed?'

'Yes, it was a late night.'

'By yourself?'

'No, I've got two Swedish au pairs with me.'

'I hope you're behaving like a proper Englishman, stiff upper cock, and all that.'

'It's *lip*.'

'That too,' she laughed.

Challis sat on the edge of the bed. It was good to hear her voice.

'How did the trip go, Keely?'

'Bloody mayhem. Temperamental Latins and prima donna models. Still, it worked out well in the end, after the proverbial blood, sweat and tears. How's the Sherlock Holmes work getting on?'

'I was on a stakeout all night. Anyway, I'll tell you about it when you get here.'

'Stay in bed, Challis, I'll be over in half an hour.'

Challis had a shower and cold beer, and was back in bed just as Keely arrived. But it was another two hours before he got around to bringing her up to date.

At six o'clock Challis phoned Steve and asked for the latest on Shirley Quinn.

'She went shopping in a supermarket a couple of hours ago and then straight back to her place. Somehow I get the feeling it'll be another poxy quiet night. Still, it has to be done.'

'You sure you don't mind staying the night there?'

'No, Des and I will take it in turns to sleep.'

Steve's wife had gone to her mother's for the weekend and taken their two children, so Steve didn't mind working the extra hours. And Des wanted the overtime. He had an expensive girlfriend.

*

The next morning Challis drove to Acton and once again swapped keys with Steve. But Keely had decided to keep Challis company and organised food and drink for the day.

A couple of hours later the heat in the confined space of the van had sent the temperature soaring and Keely stripped down to a brief white bra and thong knickers.

'I must remember to bring you along on all my jobs,' Challis grinned, and grudgingly put all lustful thoughts on the back burner.

The hours passed tediously and they took it in turns to keep close scrutiny on Shirley Quinn's house. Looking through the telescopic lens attached to a Nikon camera, locked on to a tripod, was the same as using binoculars and brought the front

159

door into sharp relief, even though they were a good fifty yards distance.

A lot of the public were under the impression that a journalist's life was all about meeting glamorous people, drinking in pubs and showbiz parties. For a few that was true, but for the majority it was hard, slogging graft. Door stepping and hours and hours of waiting were par for the course.

Patience is a virtue, certainly applied to journalists.

But the tremendous buzz a reporter got when he stood up a big story made it all worth while. To see that magic word *exclusive* over your by-line was the most elating feeling in the world, and Challis wouldn't trade his occupation for anything else.

*

The two photographers returned at nine o'clock and joined Challis and Keely, now dressed in jeans and baggy shirt, in the back of the van.

'Anything happen?' Steve asked, after he and Des gave Keely a big hello.

'No,' Challis replied, 'still the same. It's beginning to look more and more like Shirley Quinn and Beckett aren't a couple any more. The trouble is, I can't very well phone up and ask her.'

'Have you got any other ideas?'

Challis shook his head.

'No, but give it another twenty four hours and if nothing's happened by then, I'll have to have a rethink.'

'Maybe she does have another boyfriend,' Des said.

'Then where is he?'

Steve slipped through the curtains dividing the van into the driver's seat and dropped off Challis and Keely further up the road near the BMW. Then he turned around and parked the vehicle in a different position.

Challis and Keely got a Chinese takeaway, a couple of bottles of wine and headed back to the journalist's flat. The weekend had passed quietly.

The bombshell would burst tomorrow.

TWENTY THREE

The telephone rang just after seven am and Challis swore as he knocked over a half full glass of wine on the bedside table fumbling for the receiver.

It was Steve.

'Challis, sorry if I woke you, but it's urgent.'

Challis swung his legs on to the floor and blinked the sleep from his eyes. 'What's up?'

'It's Bernie Harris.' Steve paused, 'He's dead.'

'Dead? What do you mean dead? How do you know?' The journalist was now wide awake.

Keely stirred. 'What's the matter?'

Challis turned to her and said, 'Put some coffee on, and get some tissues to wipe up this mess.'

Keely got out of bed and wondered what was up as she saw Challis listening intently to the person on the other end of the phone.

'I had the six thirty news on and it said a man had been shot and killed in his home in Sheffield,' Steve continued. 'That didn't mean anything to me at first but they've just named him on the seven o'clock news as Bernie Harris and said the man's sister, Mrs Sylvia Brown, a widow, was safe but in a state of shock.'

'That's terrible, Steve. It's hard to take in.' There was silence, then Challis continued, 'You know, he was a great old man, a bloody hero. I feel gutted.'

'What are you going to do now?' Steve asked, concern in his voice.

'I'm not too sure, this has really thrown me.' Challis's mind raced. 'You'd better carry on what you're doing and I'll speak to you later.'

Challis was deep in thought when Keely returned with a couple of mugs of freshly percolated coffee and he repeated the conversation he'd just had with Steve.

'I am sorry Challis, from what you told me he sounded like a wonderful old man.' She stopped wiping up the spilt wine and looked at the expression on his face. 'You're really upset, aren't you?'

'Keely, if it wasn't for people like Bernie Harris, you and I wouldn't be walking around with the freedom we've got today. Yes, I am upset. And I'm definitely going to nail the bastard who killed him.'

Challis switched on the television and turned to the early morning news. The old man's death in Sheffield was mentioned but wasn't a main item. A new crisis in the Middle East dominated the headlines but Challis knew it would be different when the whole story broke.

They had breakfast and got dressed, both in a subdued mood. Then a warning thought hit Challis. The police would now definitely get involved and they would want to know all the information he'd unearthed so far.

No way. What he'd started, he'd finish, and the coppers would have to do their own digging.

He picked up the phone and dialled Matthew Hardy's number. It rang only a couple of times before it was answered and Challis heard the banker's voice. He quickly told Hardy the news about Bernie Harris and went on to explain what he was going to do, and swore him to secrecy.

Then he called John Mason in Bristol.

'Who the bloody hell's disturbing my sleep at this hour of the morning?' Mason yelled into the phone before Challis had a chance to speak. 'It had better be good.'

Challis waited a few moments.

'It's me, Challis. Sounds like you had a hard night.'

'Sorry Challis, I must admit I'm not my best first thing in the morning, but it is sodding early for me. What can I do for you?'

'How would you like to go away on holiday?'

'Holiday? What do you mean?'

'Just imagine you've won a competition and you can go anywhere in the world you want, all expenses paid, and given spending money too.'

'Challis, I'm lying in my pit with a terrible hangover and you're phoning, playing silly buggers.'

'John, I've never been more serious in my life,' and Challis went on to explain about the old soldier's death. 'So you see, the police are now going to be involved and they will go and see Giles Faraday's sister, Evelyn.'

'And then they'll find out about me,' Mason said.

'Exactly, and you being an honest, upright member of the community will tell them about Paul Phillips.'

'Well...' Mason started to say before Challis interrupted him.

'I know you'd probably help me and not tell the old bill but I don't want to put you in that position, John. And if you're not around, the police can never blame you.'

'All right then. What do you want me to do?'

'Pack a bag and get a flight anywhere you want as soon as possible. And I mean today.'

'Anywhere? America? India? What about Hawaii? I've always fancied a bird in a grass skirt.'

'Wherever you want John, and stay in the best hotel.'

'This could cost a small fortune, especially with my bar bill. And how long do you want me out of the way?'

'Two weeks should be long enough. By the way, how are you fixed for money? I can get some sent to your bank, or I can arrange for you to pick up travellers cheques from somewhere.'

'No thanks, Challis, I've got a few quid stashed in the bank.' Mason laughed. 'You know what? I think my hangover's getting better.'

'John, there's no need to tell me where you're going, just phone me in a couple of days and let me know how you are.'

'I can tell you that now, Challis. I'll be well and truly pissed.'

Keely left to go home before going on to work and Challis went into his office, turned on his computer and slowly read through everything he'd written so far, hoping he'd spot something he might have missed. He slouched back in his chair, ran every idea he could think of through his head and kept coming back to the same conclusion. He must find out more about Frank Beckett. He contacted a friend of his who worked in a newspaper reference library, but after looking through the cuttings drew a blank.

The ringing of the phone broke into Challis's thoughts and he picked up the receiver.

It was Seton.

'I bet you can guess why I'm phoning you,' he said.

'Bernie Harris.'

'That's right. It appears the old boy was right after all.'

'Yes, and if the police had taken more notice of him he might still be alive today.'

'I know, and I can guess how you're feeling, but you've got to look at it from their point of view.'

Challis snorted.

'They didn't meet him, I did. He was a good old boy, and now he's dead. Murdered.'

'Yes, it is terrible.'

'Seton, I'm glad you called because I wanted to have a word with you. Do you remember the agreement I made with

Matthew, that I would work on the story for two weeks only. Well, the time was up yesterday.'

'But you did say if you made progress then you would carry on. And you have made progress, haven't you?'

'I spoke to Matthew this morning and as far as he's concerned I've finished my investigation. The same goes for you, Seton. I'm working on another story.'

'What are you trying to say, Challis?'

'Now the police are going to be officially involved they will want to talk to me, and I'm not going to tell them anything more than they already know. The one thing I want you and Matthew to do is not mention the name Paul Phillips to the old bill, you understand? Matthew has already given me his word and I expect the same from you.'

'You've found, Paul Phillips, haven't you, Challis?'

'Seton, I'm not going to say another thing, that way you can't let anything accidentally slip.'

'But you are going to continue, aren't you?'

'Don't worry, Seton, I won't let you down.'

TWENTY FOUR

The blue Granada swung off the main street onto the concrete access road leading to the lockup garages. The driver got out and unlocked one of the metal up and over doors, its surface covered in painted graffiti. After the man had driven the car into the garage he opened the boot, got out a long overcoat and put it over his black tracksuit, then carefully locked the garage and started walking at a brisk pace. It was early and the paperboys and milkmen were still making their morning deliveries.

The man pressed the palm of his hand hard against his forehead trying to relieve the pain. A couple of hours ago he'd driven off the motorway to rest for a while, hoping the nagging pangs would disappear, but the attacks seemed to be lasting longer these days. He had pills that helped but didn't take them when he was driving because they made him sleepy. Besides, he had to have all his wits about him when operating in enemy territory.

He walked into Liverpool Road, then ten minutes later changed course towards Caledonian Road. Ten more minutes and he stood outside the block of flats checking that his entrance was clear. He quickly crossed the road, opened the chipped swing doors and listened. It was quiet. His black running shoes were in his overcoat pockets and he took off his heavy boots, ran up the tiled steps in his socks and opened the door to the second floor flat.

He went straight to the bedroom, opened the wardrobe and took out a khaki canvas holdall, unzipped it and placed it on the bed. He took a .22 calibre Ruger Mark 11 handgun from inside his tracksuit top and put the semi-automatic inside the bag, together with his running shoes and binoculars. The bag also contained an Uzi machine pistol and clips of ammunition in another side pocket. He lifted one leg on the bed, pulled up his tracksuit trouser leg and unstrapped the commando knife from his calf. He put the holdall back in the wardrobe, took off his German Army greatcoat and hung it next to the British Army officer's uniform.

Then he reached into a jacket pocket of his civilian suit, took out a small bottle and shook two pills into his hand. He went into the kitchen and swallowed them with a glass of water. By the time he'd taken off his clothes and run a bath the pain was easing, and by the time he'd shaved off his beard, bathed and got into bed there was only a slight throb. He poured a large whisky from the bottle on the bedside table, downed it and was soon in a deep sleep.

*

Shirley Quinn was early starting out for work. The weather was sparkling sunny and the traffic didn't bother her this morning.

She was happy. She was seeing Frank this evening.

He'd been on one of his business trips and they'd been apart for six weeks. Shirley hadn't been sure if he was in England or Paris, where he sometimes went, when she *knew* she had to contact him Fortunately mobile phones worked everywhere in the world.

So she'd spoken to him twice but only because it was an emergency. In fact, it was the first time she'd ever called him when he'd been away in all the years they'd been lovers. But Frank said she'd done the right thing. Especially when she'd rung him the day Challis turned up at the clinic and announced he was a journalist.

From the moment Shirley started going out with boys in her teens she knew she was different from other girls. She was pretty, had a good figure and enjoyed sex. But she wanted more.

She wanted men to physically hurt and abuse her body.

She was bashful when she first asked a boyfriend to take off his trousers belt and whip her. They were both seventeen and on holiday with their parents in Devon and used to sneak off in the evenings to the woods adjoining a golf course. After the second time they made love she got on her hands and knees in the grass and pulled her skirt up over her bare buttocks. She shyly asked him to hit her with his leather belt, then begged to be thrashed harder, something she'd fantasised about for months in her secret thoughts before drifting off to sleep.

But as Shirley progressed through her teens into her twenties she found nearly all the men she went out with wanted to love her, and not hurt her. In fact, many got embarrassed with her suggestions, so she bought contact magazines and delved into the sleazy world of bondage and sado masochism. She went to bizarre sex parties but all the time wished she could meet someone she could be proud to be seen with in the street. Most of the men she played her perverted games with satisfied her lust - but were downright ugly.

Then she met Frank Beckett.

TWENTY FIVE

Chief Inspector Mike Jordan was informed of Bernie Harris's death just before seven am and an hour later was sitting behind his desk in the police station. After making contact with the Sheffield police and discussing the latest developments with his chief superintendent he sat with his lined face deep in thought.

He had just successfully brought to book a team of burglars which had been plaguing the local neighbourhood for the last six months, and was looking forward to having a few days off. God knows, he'd certainly done enough overtime lately.

Now the old soldier had got himself murdered and his leave had been cancelled.

Jordan's wife was a superstitious woman who believed in fortune tellers, read her horoscope every day and was always prattling on about good and bad omens. To see one magpie was sorrow but to see two was joy, and if a bird crapped on you or you stepped in dogs mess it was good luck

So how come he was getting all the shit at the moment, and none of the luck?

The policeman sighed. He felt physically beat and ran a hand through his thinning hair. Then he phoned Challis, apprehensive of his reaction.

'Looks like your information was right,' Jordan said.

'Yes, and I just wish you could have done something to save the old man.'

The policeman could hear the anger in the journalist's voice.

'Mr Challis, I'm sorry about what's happened, but I've not phoned you to have an argument.'

'Did the police in Sheffield go and speak to Bernie Harris? See him personally?'

'They did, and I'm told his house had locks and bars everywhere. They also discovered this morning he slept with a Luger pistol under his pillow.'

'What do you know about the murder so far?'

'Are you still working on this story?' Jordan asked.

'As a matter of fact, I'm not at the moment,' and Challis explained his deal with Matthew Hardy. 'The two weeks were up yesterday, and that's it as far as I'm concerned. From today I'm working on something totally different, a famous TV personality who's cheating on his wife.'

'That's a relief. We were worried you might be going to write something about your meeting with Harris and what you've discovered so far. You see, we don't want to alert the killer that we've linked all the murders together.'

'Well, I do intend writing a story, but not until the police have concluded their investigation. Actually, I thought we might come to a deal.'

'Like what?' Jordan's voice was cautious.

'If I did write a piece now about how the uncaring police attitude cost an old soldier his life, I expect there will be a bit of a public outcry.'

'You try that, Challis, and I'll have your guts for garters. Besides, it's not true.'

'I think you're bluffing.'

There was silence.

'But, like you, I don't want an argument,' Challis continued. 'So, I won't write anything as long as you promise to keep me informed of police progress and I get an exclusive at the end of the day.'

Silence again while the policeman thought.

'I promise I'll talk to you before any other reporter,' Jordan said, 'but I can't keep you informed of police progress until the murders are solved because that's none of your damn business.' The chief inspector paused. 'Take it or leave it.'

'Okay, it's a deal,' Challis said. 'But I would like to know now the details of Bernie Harris's death.'

'Yes, I suppose I owe you that,' Jordan conceded. 'The doctor's report said the cause of death was gunshot wounds to the head. Three in fact. The killer fired three times and every one was a hit.'

'That sounds like marksman shooting. Do you know what kind of gun was used?'

'It was a .22 calibre and the bullets were hollow tipped, made quite a mess of Harris's head. The doctor said any one would have killed him.'

'What was the time of death?'

'About one o'clock this morning. His sister got up about two thirty to make a cup of tea and suddenly had a feeling that something was wrong. She banged on her brother's door but couldn't get an answer. He was a very light sleeper and that made her certain something wasn't right. The door was bolted from the inside so she called the police, and they forced their way in.'

'Didn't she hear the shots?'

'No, and neither did any of the neighbours. But .22's don't make a lot of noise, or the killer could have used a silencer. The .22 gun is a popular weapon with Mafia hit men in the States and interestingly, during World War Two, British agents carried these type of handguns behind enemy lines.'

'You seem well versed on the subject.'

'Bit of a hobby of mine. I've read quite a few books on guns.'

'When I was there the house was like a fortress. So how did the killer get in? '

'He didn't. He used a ladder, propped it up outside Harris's open bedroom window and fired through the iron bars. Don't forget, everybody's sleeping with their windows open in this hot weather. He probably shone a torch into the room and after the first shot it would have just been like target practice. Poor bastard.'

'Where'd the ladder come from?'

'The garage door was forced open and the ladder taken from there. It was padlocked to hooks on the wall, but the chain was cut.'

'How is Harris's sister?'

'Very upset and still in shock. It couldn't have been nice finding her brother shot to pieces like that.'

'No, I don't suppose it was,' Challis said, wondering what would happen now to the timid old woman. She seemed so dependant on her brother.

'What about protection for Matthew Hardy?' Challis asked.

'That's being arranged right now, although we did have a bit of a problem to begin with,' and Jordan went on to explain.

Hardy's son, Ralph, was still in California and would stay there until it was safe, even if it meant missing his start at university, but the banker had insisted on keeping his private minders at his mansion in Hertfordshire.

Finally they'd compromised. Armed police would guard the front entrance, patrol the grounds and at least one would be inside. Hardy could keep three of his security men as *house guests*, but they would be under police control in the event of any trouble.

'And I told Mr Hardy that they'd better not be armed,' Jordan said. 'Besides being against the law I don't want any of our men put in danger.'

'That would never happen,' Challis said, 'most of them are ex-para's and probably seen a lot more action than any of your policemen.'

173

'I suppose so,' Jordan grudgingly agreed, 'but we don't want any Rambo style tactics. The police are in charge.'

'I'm sure you are,' Challis said dryly.

'There is one more thing,' Jordan said, ignoring the reporter's sarcasm. 'I've faxed the Sheffield police copies of everything Bernie Harris gave you, but they said they'd like to go and see Giles Faraday's sister, Evelyn Nash. So, I'd like her address.'

'Are the Sheffield police going to be put in overall charge?'

'I'm not sure at the moment,' Jordan replied. 'Nobody's certain which force will be heading the investigation.'

After Challis read over the address, Jordan said, 'I take it you've told me everything you know about this case.'

'Of course I have.'

'I'd hate to find out at a later stage you've been holding out on me, Mr Challis.'

'No, I've told you everything,' the journalist lied. 'Honest I have.'

TWENTY SIX

The moment Shirley Quinn left work and drove home she was once again followed. But this time she was inside for only half an hour. Then she reappeared carrying a small overnight bag and jumped in a minicab which the photographers followed to Knightsbridge.

Steve immediately phoned Challis and couldn't keep the excitement from his voice.

'They've made contact. Quinn is inside Beckett's flat right this minute.'

Challis felt the adrenalin surge in him too and minutes later was on his way. It seemed the wait had been worthwhile.

But the evening dragged by and when it came to midnight and there was still no sign of her emerging, Des went home on the Yamaha and Steve and Challis settled down for the night in the van, taking it in turns to get some shuteye. Des returned at seven in the morning, once again bringing sandwiches and coffee.

Just after eight am Shirley Quinn appeared in the front entrance of the apartment block and got in a waiting minicab, which took her to work, followed by Des in the busy traffic.

An hour later the three men had a meeting in a small cafe in Ealing, not far from the health clinic.

'She could go back this evening and Beckett still might not show his face,' Challis said.

'He must come out sometime during the day,' Des said.

'Yes, but I was hoping he'd come out with the Quinn woman so we'd have a positive ID.'

'Do you want to give it one more night?' Steve asked, stifling a yawn.

'The main thing I'm worried about is time, and we've wasted enough of that already.' Challis looked serious. 'Now the police are involved I can't be positive what will happen next. Steve, I think the best thing to do, is for you and Des to snatch photos of every male, fitting the description we've got, going in or coming out of Beckett's front entrance. I know it's not going to be easy because of the parking problems but a lot of the time you can be on foot.'

'For how long?' Steve asked.

'Do it for the rest of today and then print what you've got. I'll take them to Pauline Fountain to identify, then if you've got him, we can concentrate on Beckett and not his girlfriend. And we'll stick to that procedure every day until we do get his pic, even if it takes the rest of the week.'

'What are *you* going to do, Challis?'

'Start stirring the shit.'

*

As soon as Challis got back to his flat he went into his office and picked up the phone. Shirley Quinn answered and gave the name of the clinic.

'Hello, this is your friendly neighbourhood journalist calling.'

'Ah yes, Mr Challis, I recognise your voice. What can I do for you?'

'I believe Mr Brody does hypnotherapy, is that right?'

'Yes.'

'Well, I seem to be suffering from a lot of stress lately, difficulty in sleeping and all that kind of thing. Do you think Mr Brody could help me?'

'You looked all right to me when I saw you, Mr Challis. Perfectly healthy.'

'Ah, that was on a good day. You should see me when I'm really stressed out, I look terrible. So, I'd like to make an appointment to see your boss. When can you fit me in ?'

There was silence for a few moments.

'Mr Brody's fully booked for the rest of the week, he's a very busy man. Maybe next week.'

'That's a pity, I was hoping for something today.'

'There is the possibility there might be a cancellation. As a matter of fact there is one appointment today and another for tomorrow I could check on, but I can't promise.'

'Okay then Miss Quinn, I'll phone back in an hour, maybe you'll have something by then.'

The receptionist replaced the receiver and studied James Brody's appointment book. There were several vacant spaces for today and the next few days. She took the phone in her hand and pressed the numbered buttons.

'He's just phoned again,' Shirley said as soon as her call was answered.

'The journalist?' Frank Beckett asked.

'That's right. He wanted an appointment with Mr Brody. Said he was suffering from stress and thought we might be able to help him.'

'What did you say?'

'Said we were fully booked, but there might be a cancellation later today or tomorrow. We do have several spaces free but I thought I'd have a word with you first. He said he'll call me back in an hour.'

'Good thinking, Shirley. Have you any free times for later this afternoon ?'

'One at two fifteen and one at five o'clock.'

Beckett looked at his wristwatch. It was just after mid-day.

'When he phones back tell him you've a cancellation for five,' he said. 'And you're certain you don't know what car he drives?'

177

'No Frank. I told you everything I know last night.' Shirley squirmed in her seat at the memory. Frank had tied her naked to the wall bars in the room he'd converted into a gym and beaten every bit of information from her. She started to get aroused again at the thought of it.

'I'll speak to you later,' he said, before hanging up.

*

Just as Challis drew near the health clinic a car pulled out and left a parking space which he carefully eased into. The journalist waited patiently until there was a gap in the traffic then crossed the tree lined street. Challis looked at his watch as he rang the bell. He was ten minutes early.

Shirley Quinn gave him a warm smile as he entered the empty reception area.

'Mr Brody's running on time so you shouldn't be kept waiting long,' she said.

'That's okay, I'm a bit early,' and Challis matched her smile.

'How was the traffic?'

'Not too bad.'

'Have any trouble parking? Sometimes it can get pretty busy around here.'

'No, I found a space directly opposite.'

The receptionist got up from her desk, walked to a large window and used her fingers to separate the slats of the Venetian blinds.

'Which one is yours?' she asked, as she looked across the small forecourt into the street.

Challis moved to her side. 'The dark green BMW,' he replied, then turned as James Brody appeared.

'Good afternoon Mr Challis,' and the two men shook hands. 'Come this way.'

Brody left the reception area closely followed by the reporter.

As soon as she was alone Shirley Quinn slipped out of the clinic and wrote down the make and registration number of Challis's car. Seated back at her desk she picked up the phone and a moment later was speaking into the mouthpiece. .

*

Frank Beckett relaxed in the driver's seat of his sports car parked a hundred yards from the clinic. A few minutes after five o'clock his mobile phone rang, the high pitched bleep interrupting his thoughts. He listened carefully and started to write in a small notebook, but suddenly stopped in surprise as he recognised the information coming through his earpiece. He flipped back a few pages and looked at the letters already written there.

It was the same number he'd copied from the BMW parked outside Bernie Harris's house in Sheffield over a week ago.

He pressed the off button and sat thinking hard for several minutes then slowly nodded his head in agreement with his thoughts. Circumstances beyond his control had already advanced his mission so it had to be completed without delay.

And now he would have to also eliminate this new threat. As soon as possible.

Beckett got out of his white Porsche, walked towards the clinic and stopped a few yards behind Challis's car, checking he was facing in the same direction. Then he returned to his own vehicle knowing that Shirley would call him as soon as the journalist left.

*

Challis sat in Brody's airy consulting room, the coolness controlled by two large fans switched on full.

'Miss Quinn tells me you're suffering from stress but I must say you look remarkably fit to me,' the hypnotherapist said, his pale blue eyes staring piercingly.

179

Challis knew he was taking a gamble but felt he'd reached the stage where he had to start pushing rather than wait for things to happen.

'No, you're right, I'm not suffering from stress, and I'm glad to say I do feel fit.'

Brody seemed bemused.

'Then why the visit, Mr Challis?'

'I'm looking for information.'

'Information? I don't understand.'

'It's about a former patient of yours, Frank Beckett.'

'Frank Beckett? You mean Miss Quinn's boyfriend?'

'That's right, and I believe you play golf with him.'

'Not for some time. I don't suppose I've seen Frank for over six months.'

'I believe Beckett came to see you because he wanted to give up smoking.'

'That's right, and I get a lot of people come to me for the very same reason.'

'Did he give up smoking?'

'I don't see what business it is of yours.' Brody paused. 'But yes, he did give up smoking.'

'I'm told Beckett had trouble sleeping, and suffered from nightmares.'

'Who told you this?'

'Pauline Phillips,' Challis replied.

'So you located her?'

'Yes, and she told me she was Beckett's girlfriend for about two years, so I imagine they got to know each other pretty well.'

'Of course, I'd nearly forgotten Frank and Pauline used to see each other. I'm so used to him going out with my present receptionist.'

'It must have been serious because they even discussed marriage.'

'What else did Pauline say?'

'That Beckett saw a doctor because he wasn't sleeping very well and later went to see some kind of specialist. Did you ever help Beckett with his sleeping problem?'

'Mr Challis, I'm only a hypnotherapist, not a medical doctor. I just helped Frank conquer his nicotine addiction.'

'How long did it take to cure Beckett?'

Brody took one of the many pens from the top pocket of his white coat and twiddled it between his fingers.

'As a matter of fact, Frank was a very good patient and said he was cured after about a month, and to my knowledge hasn't had a cigarette since.'

'Then why the treatment for another six weeks? That's the extra period of time Pauline told me she booked in Beckett as a patient.'

Brody slowly shook his head.

'I'm afraid it's none of your business, Mr Challis,' he said.

'Was he adopted?'

'Adopted?' Brody sounded genuinely surprised. 'No, Frank never mentioned to me he was adopted.'

'What about another family? Did Beckett ever talk about having another family?'

'Did Pauline tell you this?'

'Yes.'

'What did she say?'

'What do you know about Giles Faraday?' Challis asked.

Brody stared hard at the journalist but didn't answer for a long moment.

'Pauline Phillips didn't tell you about anybody called Faraday,' he finally said. 'And that's for sure.'

'Maybe, but you didn't answer my question. What do *you* know about Giles Faraday?'

'I'm sorry, Mr Challis, but I'm not prepared to say anything more on the subject, there is such a thing called patient confidentiality. I suggest you meet Frank personally and discuss whatever you want to with him. Why don't you speak to Miss Quinn on the way out, I'm sure she'll be only too happy to help you'

'Mr Brody, I hope you're more helpful when the police talk to you.'

'Police? Why the hell would the police want to talk to me?'

'About murder. Several in fact.'

'Murder? Who's been murdered? I certainly don't know anything about any murders, and I'm beginning to resent your attitude. Maybe you are suffering from stress after all.'

'Old soldiers have been murdered, Mr Brody. Three of them very recently, and that's why the police are involved.'

It couldn't have got any warmer in the room because the fans were coping adequately, but Challis noticed several drops of sweat run down Brody's forehead onto his cheek.

Challis stood, rested his hands on the hypnotherapist's desk, and stared unblinking into the pale blue eyes.

'Take my word for it. The police will definitely be paying you a visit. Maybe not for several days yet, but they will definitely be here, and when the story breaks you will be splashed all over the papers. That's why I was hoping you would help *me*, so that maybe I could help *you* when the time came.'

'I don't need your help Mr Challis, and I've got nothing to fear from the police because I haven't done anything.'

Challis crossed the room and turned before opening the door, his hand resting on the knob.

'A bit of advice for you Mr Brody. If I were you I wouldn't repeat this conversation to Frank Beckett...or Miss Quinn. It could be dangerous for you.'

TWENTY SEVEN

Challis slowly accelerated away from his parking spot and joined the stream of cars. As he drove along he contacted Steve who confirmed that he and Des were still taking photographs of all the men coming and going from Beckett's apartment building. They would talk again later in the evening.

Challis looked at his watch and decided he didn't have enough time to go home before meeting Keely so headed in the direction of Pimlico. Keely lived in a small stylish terrace house, bought after her divorce, and treasured as her symbol of female independence. Something she wasn't prepared to give up. Anyway, not yet.

She was having a party for friends and colleagues from her magazine and Challis was under strict instructions to attend. He'd forgotten all about her invite until she called him in the morning to remind him, with the warning that a *no nookie* ban would go into immediate effect if he didn't show. Too many times he'd been absent because of job commitments and he had to admit it had been some time since he'd stayed the night at her place.

It seemed to be Challis's lucky day for parking and he found a vacant meter almost outside Keely's front door, it was after six thirty as well, so no money was necessary. Challis got out of his car and didn't notice he was being watched as he walked towards the blue painted door, tossing his key ring in the air. He was surprised to find the deadlock on as well and had to use two keys to gain entry.

The driver of the slow moving Porsche stopped, quickly wrote down the address and then sped off in the direction of Knightsbridge to wait for Shirley.

*

When Challis walked into the small kitchen he found a note from Keely saying she'd just popped out to get some more shopping and within fifteen minutes she came bursting into the house with two carrier bags.

'Sorry, but I suddenly thought of a few more things I needed,' she said. Keely always bought too much but she had a generous nature and couldn't bear the thought of there not being enough for her guests.

Half an hour later two of Keely's girlfriends arrived to give a helping hand with the food while Challis looked after the drinks. A couple of hours later the downstairs of the house was packed with people, with the overflow spreading out through the lounge French windows. Keely had done a clever job with the small back garden, turning it into a stone paved courtyard filled with large potted plants.

Before he had too much of a skinful Challis went upstairs to Keely's bedroom to escape from the loud music and called Steve. It was ten o'clock.

'I left Des outside Beckett's flat and came back to the studio to print what we've got so far,' the photographer said. 'I'm dividing the prints into two lots. One, the obvious tradesmen and there were several workmen as well, and two, the men who looked as though they lived there and fitted Beckett's age group. I'm numbering them on the back and doing two sets, one for you and one for me.

'Did you see Shirley Quinn?'

'Yes, she arrived round about eight thirty and I left Des by himself ten minutes later. I told him to phone me if she appeared again, but he hasn't called so far. He said he would stay until about midnight and go back there about seven tomorrow morning.'

'When will I be able to get my set of pics?'

'I'm at the studio now and I'll be working late so I think I'll put my head down here for the night. You can pick them up first thing in the morning.'

'I'll try and get there by about half eight and then take them to Pauline Fountain's place.'

'I'll probably be gone by then but there will be somebody here,' Steve said, then laughed. 'It's typical, me working and you enjoying yourself. So how's it going?'

'The usual thing,' Challis replied. 'Everybody getting pissed, including me.'

'As soon as this story is finished I'm taking a week off to do the same thing.'

But Challis knew he wouldn't. Steve would probably take a few days off, but it would be to spend more time with his family, and not get boozed. The photographer had a good marriage.

*

As soon as the alarm went off the hangover hit Challis and he sat on the edge of the bed holding his head in his hands. He was in good company. Keely was doing a Greta Garbo groaning *she wanted to be left alone.* Not that she was in a hurry to get up because she had wisely arranged to take the day off.

Challis walked barefoot down the narrow stairs and went into the kitchen hoping to find some fresh orange juice in the refrigerator, but had to settle for cold tap water instead. The downstairs looked as though a bomb had hit it, with bottles, glasses and beer cans littered everywhere. He bolted shut the French windows Keely had carelessly left open all night, noting that the empties in the small courtyard would probably

185

fill a couple of dustbin bags. Keely was going to have a busy day when she decided to surface.

Challis kept a spare razor and toothbrush, as well as clean underwear and shirts in the house, and by eight o'clock had quietly closed the front door behind him.

The sun was already bright in a cloudless blue sky and seemed to bounce off the pavement straight at him. He wore a lightweight jacket and trousers but his tongue was dressed for winter. He scraped the offending organ against his teeth trying to get the fur off.

Challis slipped behind the wheel of his car, switched on, and cursed out loud as the engine whined but failed to catch, then went dead altogether. He tried several more times but the motor remained silent. He didn't bother looking under the bonnet because turning a key in the ignition was the limit of his mechanical ability. Challis shoved some pound coins in the parking meter and went back into the house, knowing his request wouldn't go down too well.

'Keely, I'm sorry to wake you,' he said, shaking her bare shoulder.

'What is it? What's the matter?' she mumbled, and sat up in bed. Challis pulled up the pillow between her and the headboard and quickly explained he was going to have to contact his garage to come and fix his car.

'So is it okay if I tell them to ring your bell and you'll give them the car key?' he asked.

'Yeah, sure,' she replied, yawning widely.

Challis used the bedside telephone and gave the garage Keely's address. Challis was a regular customer, they'd serviced his cars for years, and were only too happy to oblige.

'But they won't be able to make it until late this morning, or possibly lunch-time,' he told her. 'They said they'd take it back to the garage and hopefully I can pick it up from there later today. However,' and Challis nuzzled her face, 'I'll need you to feed the meter outside so I don't get clamped and have the car towed away.'

'That means I've got to get dressed, and I'm feeling like death this morning,' Keely moaned.

'Teach you to drink too much.' Challis dug his hand in his trouser pocket, took out his loose change and dumped it on the bedside table. 'I'm not sure if that'll be enough.'

'Don't worry,' Keely said. 'I've got loads of change in my glass jar.'

'Let me know when they pick up the car.' Challis said, and gave her a peck on the cheek before he stood. 'I'll switch on the kettle on my way out, some black coffee will do you the world of good.'

*

Shirley Quinn was bathed, dressed and waiting for the minicab firm to phone and say her cab was waiting outside to take her to work. She never used her own car when visiting Frank, parking was too much hassle.

She'd enjoyed her night of rough sex even when Frank tied her legs so wide apart she thought she'd split in two. It had been great to have Frank all to herself for two nights in a row but later today he was going away again and wouldn't be back for at least a week.

Shirley was worried about Frank. He was ill, and getting worse. They'd been together for over four years and his symptoms had gradually worsened. In the beginning it had been mood swings. Calm and ordinary for weeks on end then a sudden eruption of rage and anger, seemingly for no apparent reason. But after they had been seeing each other for about a year Frank slowly confided some of his problems to her and said he was seeing a psychologist.

He was having family troubles but Shirley never could quite get to the bottom of it. It was a mystery, and Shirley had learned to listen and not probe for answers or else Frank would go into one of his terrible moods and refuse to see her for days, sometimes weeks. Their weeks apart, due to his business trips every summer, were bad enough.

And now there was this strange episode with her boss after the reporter left the clinic yesterday. James Brody seemed casual enough as he sat with her in reception and talked warmly about her boyfriend, but then he asked if Frank had ever mentioned anything about the murder of old soldiers, recently or maybe years ago.

Why on earth would she know anything about murders? When she told Frank he just laughed and said Brody ought to go and see a shrink. But Shirley sensed there was something wrong.

However, her main concern was his headaches. They had started about a year ago and definitely got a lot worse over the last few months. Frank was seeing a specialist and said there was nothing to worry about but Shirley had seen the tablets he took. Very strong pain killers, exactly the same type as one of her aunties had been taking before she died of a brain tumour.

She looked around the large lounge, so expensively and tastefully furnished. She loved Frank's home but never thought she would become a part of it. She didn't think Frank would ever ask her to marry him, and didn't really mind, just so long as she remained his girlfriend. She was quite willing to be his slave because she wanted Frank no matter what the conditions.

The telephone rang, breaking into her thoughts, but she didn't answer it, Frank did in the other room, and shouted through that her minicab was waiting outside. Shirley went to kiss Frank goodbye but as she entered the bedroom he slid the silk sheet from his naked body, pulled her head down, and she placed her mouth over his erection instead.

TWENTY EIGHT

Challis had no trouble getting a taxi and when they arrived at the studio address in Paddington he told the driver to wait. Steve had already left to continue the stakeout in Knightsbridge and Mandy, the young secretary come general dogsbody, handed Challis a folder of photographs. With a quick wave of thanks he was back in the cab and on his way.

Betty was serving a customer as Challis entered the theatrical shop.

'I take it you've come to see Pauline again,' she said.

'That's right.'

'She'll be back in a minute, she's just gone to get some croissants and coffee.' As she finished speaking the door tinkled open and Pauline Fountain entered carrying a large paper bag.

'Hi, nice to see you again,' she said.

'You too.'

'Are you after more information?' Pauline put the bag on the counter.

'I've got some photographs for you to look at.'

Challis pulled two large brown envelopes from the folder and showed Pauline the pics of the men he felt most likely to be Beckett. And he was right.

Pauline handed back four photos to Challis without comment but stopped at the fifth and looked up.

'That's him, that's Frank.'

Challis took the photograph from her and stared at the man caught in mid-stride as he left the front entrance of the block of flats in Knightsbridge. He looked lithe and athletic and when the photograph was enlarged it would give a much clearer view of his face.

'What's he done?' Pauline enquired. 'I'm intrigued, and I know you're not going to all this trouble for nothing, so it's got to be something important.'

'Don't you worry about it,' Challis said. 'I'll ring you and let you know when the story is coming out.' He put the photographs back in the folder. 'Thanks for all your help,' and he was out of the door into the street.

A few minutes later he was in another taxi. He called Steve and gave him the identifying number of the photograph Pauline had picked out.

'Hang on a minute and I'll sort out the right one.' There was a moment's silence. 'So that's who he is,' Challis heard him mutter. 'I'll show Des this picture then go back to the studio and start doing some blow-ups.'

'Have you seen Beckett this morning, now you know what he looks like?'

'No, I don't think so, but Des saw the Quinn woman leave in a minicab earlier.'

'My car's up the creek and I'm in a taxi on my way to Knightsbridge,' Challis said. 'I'll join up with Des and let you know if Beckett leaves.'

Challis had the cab drop him off several hundred yards from his destination and walked the rest of the way. Des was astride his motorcycle studying a clipboard as though he was a messenger biker. His crash helmet was on the pavement, with one steel capped boot resting on top.

'You look hot.' Challis spoke softly as he walked up behind him.

'That's for sure,' and Des looked enviously at Challis dressed in lightweight clothes. 'I've put my camera in here.' He patted the tough plastic pannier fixed to the bike. 'There's no need to get any more pics at the moment. Steve said he'd be able to get some good blow-ups with what he's got.'

'You might as well shove this in there as well,' and Challis handed Des the folder, then motioned to the entrance of the block of flats about fifty yards away.

'Have you seen him today?'

'No. Shirley Quinn left about eight and that's all. But at least we know what he looks like now.'

Des got off the Yamaha, picked up his crash helmet and crossed the road with Challis.

'It's not been too bad with the bike, the parking wardens don't worry so much about them. It's the cars they ticket. And Steve was on foot all the time.'

They walked past the front of Beckett's block, then crossed the road again back towards the gleaming black motorcycle, glancing over their shoulders every few strides, careful not to miss anyone.

Challis looked at his watch, it was ten twenty. 'I'll wander around for a bit.'

Challis strolled past the entrance again to the end of the short street and lounged against some black iron railings. An elderly man and woman came out of the flats and walked in the opposite direction to Challis, who was wondering how long he'd have to wait before his quarry appeared. Suddenly the journalist stiffened and brought a hand to his eyes, shading them from the sun.

It was Beckett. Challis was sure he was the man in the photograph. The man, dressed in a grey suit and collar and tie, stood on the front steps and looked up and down the street. Then he starting walking in the direction of Challis who, fortunately, was on the other side. Challis turned his back until he was sure Beckett was past him and started to follow. Five minutes later they were in Sloane Street where Beckett suddenly stopped and flagged down a taxi. Challis desperately looked around for another then breathed a sigh of relief as Des drew up beside him.

'I didn't know if you'd spotted him.'

'I wasn't sure, but then I saw you take off, so I followed. I'd better tail the cab and I'll contact you later,' Des said, as Beckett's taxi started to move.

'I'm coming,' and Challis swung a leg over the pillion seat.

'But I haven't got a spare crash helmet,' Des said.

'Well then, let's hope we don't get nicked,' Challis replied. 'Now let's get going.'

The taxi drove through Knightsbridge into Brompton Road, along by Harrods department store, then started weaving through side streets in the direction of King's Road, finally stopping outside Sloane Square tube station, not far from where the journey began. Surely he didn't suspect he was being followed? Beckett must have paid the driver inside the cab because as soon as he got out he dashed straight into the station.

'I'll keep in touch,' Challis said as he leapt off the motorbike. 'You go back to Beckett's place.'

Challis pushed past people thronging the entrance just in time to see Becket go through the automatic ticket barrier and walk in the direction of the stairs leading to the westbound trains. Challis pulled out his loose money, thankful for the change from his taxi journeys, inserted two pound coins into the ticket machine and swiftly followed in the direction of Beckett. Just as he ran down the stairs he heard a train entering the platform, saw Beckett board and hurled himself forward as the doors started to close.

Challis moved towards the other end of the carriage straining his eyes into the next one but couldn't spot his man. He must be in the carriage further up. The train drew into South Kensington station packed with young tourists carrying large backpacks. As the doors opened they surged through the opening jostling Challis as he kept his eyes peeled. Then he saw Beckett on the platform among a crowd of people walking towards the down stairs signposted the Piccadilly Line and Challis jumped off.

Beckett went to the platform heading north and after a couple of minutes a Cockfosters train noisily shuddered to a stop. Challis entered the carriage next to the one Beckett got into, with a clear view through the glass communicating doors. The train wasn't very full and Beckett had his back to him as he stood at the far end leaning against a door, one hand casually gripping an overhead support bar.

The next stop was Hyde Park Corner and Challis saw Beckett turn towards the door as the train entered the station. When the doors opened Challis stuck his head out and saw only about a dozen people alight. Then he saw Beckett suddenly step out onto the platform and pulled his head back in. He looked out again, getting ready to leave, and was just in time to see Beckett jump back into the carriage, the door sliding shut behind him. Challis frowned, it was as though Beckett was taking evasive action, but the journalist was sure he hadn't been spotted. He was an old hand at following and had now taken off his jacket to alter his appearance.

Green Park was the next stop and this platform *was* busy, being a connecting station for two other tube lines. Challis stepped off to let passengers inside but couldn't see Beckett, so got back on. Then he saw Beckett on the platform and Challis gripped his door to stop it closing, but relaxed as Beckett stepped back on the train and a split second later the doors closed.

But as the train picked up speed Challis saw Beckett standing on the platform. He'd jumped off again. Challis clenched his teeth, angry with himself.

Bollocks.

He'd lost him.

TWENTY NINE

Keely got up about half an hour after Challis left, had a shower, then bravely turned the water to an ice cold spray. She dressed in brief shorts and T-shirt, sat in her courtyard and towel dried her hair, before going into the kitchen. Three cups of coffee and a couple of slices of toast later she was beginning to feel ready to face the world again.

She spent the next few hours cleaning up the debris of the party, only stopping to go outside and feed the parking meter. By mid-day her house was once more in order and she was longing for a drink of fruit juice. The garage men hadn't yet arrived to take away the car but she took a chance and went to the pub at the end of the road and bought half a dozen small bottles of orange. Then she went back to the courtyard, unfolded a sun bed, and stretched out.

*

Frank Beckett boarded the next Piccadilly line train and travelled as far as King's Cross. He'd kept to his usual elusive routine and was positive he hadn't been followed. Not that he suspected he would be, it was just a natural, instinctive precaution.

As he left the busy station he avoided the taxi rank queue and walked for a good ten minutes crisscrossing the road before hailing a cab. He changed cabs once more, deliberately directing the driver in a roundabout route, before reaching his destination, satisfied this journey had been as thoroughly executed as all the others he'd made over the years.

194

But today, for the first time, there was a difference as he arrived at the lockup garage. It was the first time Beckett had driven the blue Granada dressed smartly in a suit and not the long shabby military coat.

Beckett found a convenient place in the next street to his other flat and a few minutes later clicked shut the front door behind him. He went straight to the bedroom, opened the large wardrobe and pulled out the canvas holdall. He unzipped the bag, checked the contents, then reached into the back of the wardrobe and took out a long narrow wooden case painted camouflage green and brown. He laid the case on the bed, flicked open two metal latches, and swung back the top on its hinges. Inside, nestling on egg crate foam was a Dragunov Soviet Army sniper rifle, fitted with an image intensifying night sight. The weapon was semi-automatic with a ten round detachable box magazine. Beckett snapped shut the case, pulled open the bottom drawer of the wardrobe, and took out a small khaki bag. He undid the drawstring and placed two hand grenades on the bed.

Beckett quickly undressed, strapped his commando knife to his calf, and put on his black tracksuit and heavy boots, his running shoes were already in the holdall. He shrugged on the familiar long German greatcoat and pulled up the collar.

He was in a bad mood. The threat of his discovery had greatly increased because of that meddlesome journalist, and Challis would have to pay for his interference.

Next he took the .22 Ruger semi-automatic from the large bag, checked the magazine clip, and slid the gun into the holster stitched inside his tracksuit top. He picked up one of the grenades and one piece face mask and put them in separate side pockets of his long coat then put his mobile phone in an inside pocket. Finally, he placed the other grenade in the holdall, along with the Uzi machine pistol. He was ready.

195

As Beckett went to close the wardrobe doors his face wrinkled in pain and he put a hand to his head. He blinked his eyes, drew in large breaths of fresh air, and reached into his suit jacket pocket hanging on the rail. He took out his bottle of pills and looked at them. He'd never taken them on operations before - he'd learned to live with the pain instead.

But Beckett knew this would probably be his last mission. The war was coming to an end.

He turned, opened the bedside cabinet door, took out a full bottle of Johnny Walker and shoved the pills and whisky in a side pocket of the holdall.

He picked up the khaki bag and wooden case, walked into the lounge, pausing in front of the group of photographs to give a brief salute, then left the flat and hurried to his car. When Beckett arrived in Pimlico he noted with satisfaction that Challis's BMW was still parked in the same spot.

*

Keely must have dozed off and the insistent ringing of the doorbell made her sit up with a start. She blinked her eyes and walked back into the house through the lounge leading to the hallway and front door. She looked at her small wristwatch, it must be the mechanics, she thought, as she opened the front door.

It all happened so quickly Keely only had a glimpse of the man on her doorstep. But she felt instant pain as a fist struck her a fierce blow in the face and she fell backwards to the floor.

She dimly heard the door kicked shut and felt another blow to the back of her head. She lost consciousness immediately and didn't feel herself being dragged into the lounge.

THIRTY

Challis caught a train back to Sloane Square underground station and emerged into the bright sunshine, furious with himself for losing Beckett.

When he arrived at the Knightsbridge address Des told him Steve had just parked the surveillance van several streets away and Challis immediately called him. Challis explained Beckett had given him the slip and the only thing to do was to continue the stakeout.

'Strange really,' he told the photographer. 'It was as though Beckett suspected someone might be following him. But I'm sure he didn't see me.'

'Don't worry about it,' Steve said. 'It could happen to anyone. He'll probably be back soon.'

Maybe, but Challis was still annoyed, and added a few choice swear words to his thoughts.

Ten minutes later Steve joined them and produced the enlarged head shots of Beckett. Challis studied his face. He was good looking with a strong jaw line and dark brown wavy hair but somehow Challis got the impression that the eyes were tinged with bitterness. Or pain.

The three men took it in turns to have a snack and cold drink in one of the nearby pubs and by two o'clock Challis was wondering why Keely hadn't phoned to say his car had been picked up.

Half an hour later he was just going to call her when his mobile rang. But it wasn't Keely - it was Chief Inspector Jordan.

'I've just had a call from the Sheffield police,' he said. 'A couple of their men went and saw Evelyn Nash and found out something very interesting.'

'Oh yes, and what was that?' Challis asked innocently.

'You know bloody well what it was. You've been holding out on us.'

'I have?'

'John Mason, another freelance reporter like yourself. You went and saw him after you visited Mrs Nash ten days ago, didn't you?'

'Only very briefly.'

'So why didn't you mention it to me the last time we spoke?'

'Because I didn't think it was important. He didn't tell me anything that was of any help.'

'Then I wonder why he's gone on the missing list?'

'He has?'

'Mrs Nash gave us the same address she said she'd given you, but when we tried to contact him one of his neighbours said he'd suddenly gone on holiday. Unfortunately, they didn't know where.'

'Well, *I* don't know where he's gone,' Challis said truthfully.

'Didn't you ask him why he went and saw Mrs Nash all those years ago?'

'Yes, and he said it was something to do with an article for a magazine. But it was so long ago he'd forgotten what it was all about. Not a very helpful bloke at all.'

'And that's it?'

'Chief Inspector, I told you I'm not involved any more. At the moment I'm trying to find the estranged husband of the woman who's having an affair with a famous TV personality. And that's keeping me busy.'

'Why do I get the feeling I don't believe you Challis?'

'Is it because all coppers are disbelieving sods?'

The policeman chuckled.

'No more than newspaper reporters,' he said, and added in a harder tone. 'I do hope you're telling me everything.'

Chief Inspector Jordan disconnected and Challis stared at his phone. 'Nearly everything,' he mouthed silently.

Challis called Keely. He let the phone ring about ten times then tried again. Still no answer. Maybe she'd tried phoning him before she went out and he'd been engaged. He swiftly pressed the small buttons to connect him to his garage.

He spoke to one of the mechanics who told him the BMW would be ready in about an hour and a half. It was something to do with the electrics, the details of the explanation were lost on Challis, but it wasn't too serious.

'And don't forget to bring your car key, Mr Challis, there wasn't any answer from that address you gave us, so we had to tow your car back to the garage.'

'Yeah, sure. Sorry about that.'

Challis was puzzled. It wasn't like Keely to let him down. In fact, this was the first time. Challis called her number again and let it ring and ring - but nothing. In case there was an intermittent fault on his mobile, or Keely's phone, he walked to a nearby call box and checked her number through the BT operator who told him it was in working order.

So why hadn't Keely called him? Even if she'd had an emergency and had to go out she would have called him.

For some reason which Challis couldn't explain he began to feel increasingly uneasy and had an overwhelming urge to go to Keely's house.

He walked to where Des was seated on his motorbike. 'Is there a spare crash helmet in the van?'

'Yes,' Des replied.

'Go and get it and come back here,' Challis said, then walked off to the other end of the street where Steve was keeping vigil.

'I'm getting Des to take me to Keely's place.'

'Is there anything wrong, Challis?'

'I'm not sure, I'll let you know. And if Beckett returns, call me straight away.'

Challis spun round as Des came to a stop and he put on the spare crash helmet, swung on to the pillion seat and held on tight as Des opened the throttle and roared off. He sensed Challis's urgency and weaved swiftly in and out of the traffic.

THIRTY ONE

As soon as the Yamaha's engine died both men were off the motorbike and outside Keely's front door, Challis fumbling for his key ring. The door opened as he turned the Yale lock, which instantly made Challis cautious. The Chubb deadlock wasn't on and Keely always double locked her front door whenever she went out.

Challis carefully opened the door wider and listened. Silence except for the noise of the passing traffic in the street behind him.

'Keely,' he shouted and moved further down the hallway, Des closing the door behind them. The first opening on the left was the lounge and Challis put his head into the room.

'Oh my God,' he muttered, and quickly took off his crash helmet.

Keely was bound hand and foot with kitchen string. Her hands behind her and her ankles tied to the short wooden legs of a gold velvet Victorian chair. String tightly wound around her waist and chest, also encircling the chair prevented her from moving. A tea towel had been cut into strips and used as a gag.

One eye looked pleadingly at Challis. The other one was swollen shut, the skin starting to turn purple. And in that split second Challis realised just how much he really cared for her.

'Get a knife or scissors.'

Challis barked the order to Des as he gently eased the gag from Keely's lips down over her chin. He pulled bits of cloth from her mouth and she gratefully sucked in air.

'Oh Challis,' she gasped, but didn't cry. He clenched his fists tight and wanted to hit someone. Hard.

Des came back into the room with a pair of kitchen scissors and passed them to his friend.

'I'll go and have a look at the rest of the house,' he said.

'It's okay, there's nobody here now. He's gone.' But Des had already left the room and didn't hear Keely.

Challis cut the string holding her to the chair then carefully snipped the thin white cord from her ankles. Keely moved herself sideways and Challis cut the last of the bonds from her wrists. She moaned a little as the circulation once again flowed freely.

'Oh Challis,' she repeated, then whimpered in a little girl's voice. 'My lovely hair.'

Challis looked down at her lovely long blonde hair. It was scattered on the floor. The bastard had scalped her!

Des confirmed the house was empty and then made Keely a mug of tea with plenty of sugar. She drank with remarkably steady hands and said, although she'd been frightened, the man told her he wasn't going to kill her.

'He wants to kill *you*, Challis,' Keely said. 'It's you he's after...he thought you lived here. He said he was going to kill you like all the others because you were the enemy.'

Keely's head looked red and stubbly with several nicks where the razor had cut her. There was a nasty bruise behind her right ear caused by the blow which had knocked her unconscious. Challis wanted to take Keely straight to a hospital but she insisted on having a shower and changing her clothes.

'I don't feel too bad, really. Not now you're here.'

Challis felt helpless. He wanted to hug her tight but was scared he might hurt her.

While Keely was in the bathroom Challis phoned Steve and told him what had happened. The photographer's reaction was one of shock and concern for Keely. She was well loved by all her friends.

There was one other feeling the three men shared. Immense anger.

It had to be Frank Beckett. All agreed on that.

After Keely had changed she wound a towel around her head and they sat in the kitchen, but she couldn't identify Beckett from the photographs Des brought in from the Yamaha's pannier.

'He wore a woollen mask over his face,' she said, and went on to describe his clothes. The black track suit was the same description as the Southampton woman had given, and when Keely described the long coat something jarred in Challis's memory. But he couldn't place it.

Keely said when she regained consciousness she was tied to the chair and heard the intruder searching the place. She wasn't gagged at first but when the doorbell rang she shouted and the man rushed back into the lounge and clamped a hand over her mouth.

'It must have been the people to take your car away. They rang the bell and knocked for a few minutes, then they left.'

The man kept asking her where Challis was and why was his BMW still parked outside? It was then Keely explained about the doorbell ringing and that the car had broken down and needed fixing.

'He went to the front windows, must have seen them taking your car, and started swearing. The funny thing is, nearly all the time he was here, he kept talking to himself. In English, French and German. Really weird he sounded. And when he spoke in English it seemed as though he was speaking in two different voices. Strange...'

'Did he mention Giles Faraday or Henri Fabere?'

'Not Faraday, but he said people had to pay for Henri Fabere's death, you included.'

Challis gently questioned her but Keely said most of the man's ramblings didn't make much sense to her.

'He talked about killing the enemy and said lots of Englishmen were traitors.'

Keely assured Challis the man hadn't sexually assaulted her, or hurt her, other than from when he first entered the house.

'He said I was a collaborator and should be punished. I told him I didn't know what he was talking about.' Keely lowered her voice. 'Then he cut off my hair.'

Challis cupped her hands in his on the kitchen table and squeezed gently.

'Where is my car key?'

'It's on one of those hooks under that shelf.' Keely replied, pointing in the direction where she kept an assortment of keys.

Challis found the key and put it in his pocket

'There are some of my business cards here,' he said.

'That's right,' Keely said, 'there are some in one of the bedside drawers.'

'Well, when I was up there I saw all the drawers had been turned out.' Des sounded grave.

'So now he knows where I really live,' Challis said.

'What made him think you lived here in the first place?'

Challis looked at Keely. 'That's a good point,' and his face creased in thought. Then he clicked his fingers. 'Of course...I went and saw James Brody yesterday. But before that I phoned to make an appointment and spoke to Shirley Quinn.'

'And she must have phoned Beckett,' Des said.

'Yes, and after I left he followed me here.' Challis paused. 'I remember something else too, Keely. You had gone out to get some shopping and I had to let myself in. Beckett must have been watching and saw me use a key to open the front door.'

'And assumed you lived here,' she added.

'That's right. And when he saw my car still parked outside today he thought I was at home.'

'Shouldn't we tell the police?' Keely asked.

'No,' Challis's reply was immediate. 'This is personal now, and besides, what proof have we got? On the surface Beckett appears to be a respectable wealthy man and if he's got an alibi what could the police do? Beckett would probably come under suspicion and that's about all at this stage.'

'But *you're* sure it's Beckett who did this to me?'

'I can't see it being anyone else.'

'Then he's going to try again to get you, Challis,' Des said.

'Maybe, but at least I'll be ready for him.'

'That's what Bernie Harris thought, but it didn't do him much good in the end.'

Challis shrugged his shoulders but didn't say anything.

'So what are you going to do next?' Keely asked.

'Find a safe place for you, just in case he comes back here looking for me. However, I do think you should go to the hospital, Keely. You were knocked unconscious, after all.'

'No Challis, I feel fine.'

'Okay then,' he said slowly, 'you know best.'

It was decided Keely would go and stay with Steve's family in Highgate, north London. She and Lynn got on well and Steve called back to say his wife was only too happy with the arrangement.

Then Challis contacted the security company supplying Matthew Hardy's bodyguards and spoke to Gerry Cassidy. He related what had happened at Keely's and stressed the fact that having just failed, the killer might have the millionaire lined up next. Challis said that because of certain circumstances he wasn't informing the police so Cassidy had better make sure his men were extra vigilant. The journalist was careful not to mention Beckett by name.

Challis phoned his garage and told them to leave his car outside if they were closed before he arrived and put their bill in the post.

Keely packed a suitcase and came back into the lounge looking an entirely different person, wearing a short blonde wig and dark glasses.

'That looks much better,' Challis said, and kissed her gently on the tip of her nose.

'Luckily, I've got several wigs which I borrowed from fashion shows.'

'And forgot to return,' he teased.

Challis picked up the phone again and ordered two minicabs from a local firm, then dialled one more number.

*

James Brody had just shown out a patient and was in the reception area when Shirley Quinn answered the phone.

'Yes Mr Challis, Mr Brody is here.' She put a hand over the receiver. 'It's that reporter again. Do you want to take it here or shall I put him through to your room?'

Brody frowned and extended his arm.

'Mr Challis, what do you want now?'

'Frank Beckett attacked my girlfriend today and told her he wants to kill me.' Challis's tone was terse and bluntly to the point.

'He did what? I don't believe you...why would he want to kill you?'

'Brody, as far as I'm concerned you're in it up to your eyeballs, and I've got the proof. The reason I'm calling now is to give you one last chance before I give your name to the police. It's entirely up to you. Co-operate and I'll leave you out of it or you can take your chances with the police. It's only information I'm after.' Challis paused. 'I don't think the publicity would do your business much good.'

Brody's body sagged and he sat on the corner of the reception desk.

'I must tell you about the tapes,' he said.

'Tapes? What tapes are you talking about?'

'I haven't got them - but I can tell you what's on them.'

'Tell me now.'

'No,' and Brody straightened as the front doorbell rang. 'I can't speak now, I've got a client just come in.'

'When can I see you?'

'Come to my home about seven thirty. My wife's going to the theatre with a friend straight from work, so we'll be able to talk then.'

Brody gave Challis his address and put down the phone. He suddenly felt drained.

THIRTY TWO

When the minicabs arrived Challis got one to take him to the nearest bank cash point to withdraw some money, then return to Keely, where he gave both drivers enough to cover their fares, plus twenty pounds tip each to follow his instructions.

Keely set off in the first minicab with the second car close behind. Des and Challis cruised in the rear.

They drove to the Embankment, following the river Thames to Westminster Bridge, then along Whitehall and past Trafalgar Square, heading in the direction of Soho. About ten minutes later the leading driver put his right arm out of the window, waved a signal and accelerated as he entered a narrow one way street. The second minicab immediately slammed on its brakes and slid sideways completely blocking entry to the road. Challis swung off the back of the motorcycle as cars behind honked their horns in frustration. The driver got out, lifted up the bonnet and gave a slight smile as Challis came into view.

'It'll take a few minutes to fix. Is that okay?'

'That's fine,' and Challis walked back to the Yamaha satisfied nobody had been able to follow Keely.

The powerful machine moved swiftly through the traffic until the two men reached Challis's address. The journalist opened the front door from the street with his key and Des followed Challis across the small lobby where they got in the lift to the second floor. Challis walked along the carpeted hall, stopped outside his flat door and knelt down. He looked closely at both locks but they didn't appear to have been tampered with. He unlocked the door and cautiously went inside, Des close as a shadow.

A few minutes later both men felt easier when they made sure the flat was empty. There was one message on his answering machine from John Mason which said he was happily ensconced on a tropical island.

'But I'm not saying where. I'll send you a postcard.'

Challis erased the message and quickly packed a small holdall. He'd decided to stay in a hotel for the next couple of nights. Better to be safe than sorry.

Challis poured them both a large scotch then called Steve.

'Keely's on her way to your home and Des is with me in my flat.'

'What are your plans now?' Steve asked.

'I'm going to get Des to drop me off at my car then I've got an appointment to see James Brody at his house.' Challis looked at his watch. 'Looks like I'll be a bit late.'

'I'm still outside Beckett's place. Shall I stay here?'

'No, I don't think there's much point, we've got his pics and know where he lives. I think maybe we should use a different kind of approach now, perhaps do a face to face showdown.'

'For chrisake Challis, that could be dangerous. I know you can handle yourself but the man's a murderer, and if he has killed all these people, then he's got to be some kind of raving lunatic.'

'Yes, and something terrible must have happened to him which sent him crazy. That's the crux of the matter, where the story is.'

'If you say so...anyway, you reckon I should leave?'

'Yes Steve, have an early night. Besides, Keely will feel safer with you there. And give your wife a big kiss from me. Tell her I appreciate it.'

'No problem,' Steve said, 'you know she thinks the world of Keely.'

The dark green BMW was parked in the road to the side of the garage and Challis told Des he'd see him tomorrow.

'I'm not sure what time, depends on what happens tonight. Either Steve or I will give you a bell.'

Challis put his bag in the boot then opened the driver's door, but before turning the key in the ignition phoned Keely.

'I'm all right, Challis,' she said, 'Lynn's making a fuss over me.'

'Okay kid, make sure you get plenty of rest, and I'll call you tomorrow...I love you'

'I love you too, Challis.'

Words they hardly ever spoke to each other simply because their feelings said it for them.

It was nearly eight o'clock when Challis drew up outside Brody's house, a semi-detached, about fifteen minutes drive from his clinic. Challis walked up the crazy paved path and rang the doorbell. He waited a minute then rang again, keeping his finger on the button. He could hear the musical chimes from inside the house, but nobody came to the front door.

Challis looked through the letter box but his view was obstructed by an inner flap. He rapped hard on the brass knocker. Still no joy. He moved to the front windows and tried looking in but it was difficult to see much because of the white net curtains, and it was still sunny so there was no need for lights to be on.

The wrought iron gate between the house and the brick garage was locked preventing access to the rear garden so Challis walked back down the path to his car. Maybe Brody had gone out for a while, perhaps for a takeaway seeing his wife had gone to the theatre, or maybe to the local off licence. Challis returned to his car.

Half an hour later he went back and rang the doorbell again just in case there was a back entrance from an alley and Brody had returned unseen. But the front door remained closed and still no sound from inside.

Challis drove to a small parade of shops a couple of streets away, bought fish and chips and returned to eat them outside the house. He called directory enquiries and Brody's number was listed. He rang it several times. No answer.

*

The souped up Ford Granada kept well within the speed limit as it left the A1 motorway and followed the signs for Hatfield. It was nine o'clock, two hours since Beckett had left James Brody's house. Road works had held him up. Fortunately there hadn't been any on the southbound carriageway when he'd had to dash back to London late that afternoon after receiving the phone call.

He picked up his mobile from the passenger seat and moments later was speaking with Shirley.

She felt flattered when he said he needed her help, a request that had never occurred in their relationship before. Frank said he wanted her to take a few days off and he'd spoken to her boss just minutes before this call. Mr Brody had said it was fine by him and hoped she enjoyed the break.

Frank wanted her to go to his home, stay the night, then early next morning pick up his sports car and meet him in Hatfield in Hertfordshire. He said he'd already phoned the porter to let her in his flat, and told her where he kept the garage and car keys. Frank told her to dress casual, trousers and trainers, because they would be out in the country.

Shirley quickly changed and packed an overnight bag. Then she scribbled a note to the girl she shared the house with, a

British Airways air hostess who'd been on holiday for a week and should be returning home about midnight, and said she'd be away for a couple of days.

Beckett clicked off his phone just as he drove past the Galleria shopping mall heading in the direction of the lockup garage he'd paid six months rent in advance for. He'd rented the garage a week after Colonel Hardy's funeral and used it as a base while he made plans for the banker's execution.

The area was deserted and quiet as Beckett stopped in front of the shabby wooden doors. Black paint was peeling off with hardboard nailed over several of the broken frosted glass panes. He unlocked the new padlock, drove in and secured the doors from inside.

Beckett went to the boot, removed the wooden case containing the sniper rifle, took it to one corner of the garage and squatted on a sleeping bag. He switched on a large powerful flashlight, opened the case and spent the next five minutes checking over the deadly weapon, finally slipping the magazine back in place. Then he ate a chocolate bar, had a drink of bottled water and lightly dozed.

*

It was beginning to get dark and the street lights came on but not in the house. Challis's thoughts returned to Keely. If only his car had started or if he hadn't lost Beckett on the underground system then maybe nothing would have happened to her. He shrugged his shoulders, it was bad enough with what *had* happened, no need to make it worse by feeling guilty.

Keely was safe now - and that's what mattered.

Lights began to go out in the other houses and Challis looked at his watch. Just gone eleven. Ten minutes later a Nissan Micra drew up with two women inside. One got out and leaned back inside the car to give a cheery goodnight then

212

walked up the paved pathway. Challis recognised Mrs Brody but thought he'd give her a couple of minutes inside before ringing the bell.

He had just opened his door and was standing when he heard a terrible scream. Silence, then the hideous sound was repeated several more times, echoing in the quiet suburban street. The front door opened and Mrs Brody staggered out. She clung to the front of the house, climbed over the small brick dividing wall to her next door neighbours, and bashed hard on their door knocker.

'Help me, help me,' she screeched.

Lights came on in the house quickly followed by several others in the street. Curtains were opened and Challis saw people trying to focus on the cause of the commotion. The journalist decided to fade into the background and as he drove off saw Mrs Brody slump on the step as her neighbours door opened. Challis drove to the end of the road, turned around and parked about seventy five yards away from his original spot.

Minutes later the flashing lights of a police car passed by and stopped outside Brody's. Within fifteen minutes there was another patrol car and ambulance, closely followed by several unmarked police vehicles.

About a dozen people were gathered on the pavement. Challis left his car and joined the curious throng of onlookers, some in their dressing gowns.

'What's going on?' he asked.

'Not sure, mate,' a stubbly faced man replied.

'I think it's murder,' an elderly woman said. 'Did you hear those screams?'

After a further twenty minutes word filtered through from the next door neighbours that Mrs Brody had found her husband dead when she returned home from the theatre.

'He was stabbed to death.'

Challis saw a couple of plain clothes detectives talking to a uniformed PC and wandered over.

'I hear someone's been murdered,' he said.

The policemen looked at him.

'Who are you, sir?'

'I'm a journalist,' and Challis showed his press card.

'Blimey, you were quick off the mark,' one of the CID men said.

'Just a coincidence. I was passing and saw all the lights. One old lady over there said a James Brody has been murdered, stabbed to death.'

The policemen were slow to react but one finally said, 'Yes, that's just about correct.'

Challis fought hard not to show emotion on his face but his heart was pounding. Another murder, and he had called Brody to make an appointment. Shirley Quinn had answered the phone…she must have told Beckett. If he hadn't phoned then Brody would probably still be alive. More guilt? Maybe it *was* time to let the police have all his information.

'Any idea who did it, or when?' he asked in a calm voice.

'Now, you know as well as me we can't say any more. You'll have to wait for a press statement. Anyway, it's too early to know anything for definite.'

'Okay then, I'll be off to my bed. Thanks.'

Challis turned and walked to his car. Bed? He'd forgotten all about that. He had to find a hotel first.

THIRTY THREE

Just after midnight Frank Beckett drove through the outskirts of Hatfield on the way to Matthew Hardy's mansion which lay between the villages of Wheathampstead and Sandridge. He left the main road, cut through the country lanes he was getting to know well, and fifteen minutes later the car headlights picked out the iron railings leading to the brick pillars and front entrance of the estate. The Range Rover and large saloon were now gone, replaced by just one white patrol car and police motorcycle. Beckett carefully kept to a steady thirty miles an hour as he drove past, his gaze fixed straight ahead.

He knew, by the police presence, they suspected someone wanted to kill Matthew Hardy, but it was obvious they didn't know his identity, otherwise he'd have been under arrest by now. Even so, Beckett wondered how they'd latched on to his plans. That damned journalist must be behind it. The puzzling thing was the private security guards had appeared before he'd killed Corporal Harris.

He'd been in two minds whether to take out the old man first or the colonel's son. The sudden appearance of the guards had made up his mind for him.

Now the police involvement made the completion of his mission a real challenge.

The Granada kept going for another quarter of a mile then pulled off the narrow road and reversed behind two large trees next to a hedgerow, a spot he'd used several times before, making his car hidden from view to any passing traffic.

Beckett went to the boot, took off his long overcoat and put on his black running shoes, then took out the camouflaged case. He slipped on his woollen face mask, silently crossed the road and disappeared into the darkness.

Two minutes later the black clad figure emerged from a clump of trees and ran swiftly across the farmer's field backing onto the rear of Hardy's property. Beckett reached the particular spot of the thick perimeter hedge he was looking for, near a solitary oak tree, reached up and placed the case on top of the seven foot high hedge. Then he knelt and carefully extracted a nylon rope hidden in the base. He stood and threw the looped end over a broken branch about ten feet above his head and pulled himself up, his feet aided by the tree trunk. He swung himself onto the branch, pulled up the rope, freed it and transferred to another thick bough which extended over the thorny hedge. Beckett lowered himself onto Hardy's land then pulled the end of the dangling rope over to the hedge and wedged it among the prickles. Next, he removed the rifle case from the hedge, then dropped to his knees as the moon broke through the clouds. A few minutes later it darkened and he quickly crossed the paddock leading to the small woods which lay directly behind the banker's mansion.

Once in the safety of the trees Beckett slowed, took his bearings and moved cautiously forward. After a hundred yards he found the rotten tree trunk laying on the ground among brambles and tall grass and carefully pushed the long case in the hollow opening at one end. The case disappeared from view and Beckett moved a broken branch and twigs over the open end.

He left the tree trunk and made his way silently through the woods until he came to the edge and could see clearly across the flower gardens and neatly trimmed lawns. Lights were on in several of the rooms and floodlights strategically mounted on the outside walls brightly lit the immediate area.

Beckett could make out people in the house then moved his head as he heard a noise and saw a policeman on patrol, carrying a sub-machine gun, move towards the trees. Beckett turned and silently returned the way he'd come.

*

Dead on six am Shirley left Frank's Knightsbridge flat and cut across Sloane Street in the direction of Belgravia where he'd rented a mews garage for years. At ten past she reached the garage and five minutes later was threading her way through the traffic. It was another lovely morning, although a couple of days ago the long range weather forecast had predicted storms were heading across Europe towards the UK.

Shirley loved the feeling of power as the white Porsche sped along the roads, so different from her old Vauxhall. As the miles flashed by she wondered what kind of day she'd have with Frank, but it didn't really matter as long as they were together. His phone call had been a wonderful surprise because she hadn't expected to see him for a week.

When she'd called Frank yesterday, after Challis had rang and spoken to Mr Brody, she related everything she'd heard then told him the reporter was meeting her boss later at his house.

That phone call from the newspaper man had certainly unsettled Mr Brody. Who wanted to kill Challis? And what was that about tapes? It was a pity she'd only heard one side of the conversation.

Frank had thanked her but hadn't given any indication he would be contacting her again so soon. Shirley wondered what had happened in the space of a few hours that suddenly made him want to see her.

Shirley stopped at the first telephone box she saw as she entered Hatfield and called Frank. She listened closely to his voice and ten minutes later was stationed in McDonalds car park in the Galleria. A few minutes went by then she heard a tap on the roof of the car and saw Frank.

She was immediately surprised by his unshaven face and black tracksuit, so different from his usual well groomed appearance.

He smiled as she got out of the car and kissed her on the lips.

'You need a shave, Frank.'

He ignored the remark, instead gave further instructions, and told her to get back in the car. A minute later a blue Ford Granada, with badly chipped paintwork drew alongside, and Shirley put the Porsche in gear and followed. After fifteen minutes the two cars stopped outside a small cafe, Frank went in, and ten minutes later emerged holding a plastic carrier bag. The two cars moved off again until they reached the lockup garage where Frank unlocked the padlock, pulled open the double doors and Shirley drove inside. Frank closed the doors nearly shut and parked the Granada sideways in front of them. He squeezed in through the opening, bolted the doors firmly closed, and took the Porsche key from Shirley.

'Thanks,' he said, and kissed her again. Shirley responded but then pushed away from him.

'What are we going to do today?' she asked.

'I thought we'd have a picnic in the country this afternoon but this morning we could spend in here.'

'In here?'

'I'll make sure you enjoy yourself,' he said, and bent Shirley face down over the Porsche. He spread-eagled her arms and pulled her brown tracksuit bottom down and over her ankles, the elasticated waist slipping easily off her body. He reached forward, gripped her black nylon briefs, and gave a quick jerk. The flimsy material tore at the crotch and Frank pulled down his own tracksuit, kicked her legs apart and positioned himself behind her.

The hotel's early morning alarm call woke Challis at seven thirty.

It wasn't easy getting a room in London with the type of glorious weather the capital was experiencing this summer but the journalist had stopped at a nightclub in the West End last night. The owner owed him a favour and after a few phone calls found a vacancy in a small hotel off Edgware Road. He booked in for three nights.

Challis got out of bed and made himself a cup of coffee from the self service tray in the room. He called Keely but she was still in bed so he told Lynn not to disturb her, then Steve came on the line and Challis gave him the news about Brody's murder.

'Bloody hell,' was the photographer's reaction. 'But you said you were seeing him last night.'

Challis explained in detail the events of the previous evening.

'He must have been dead all the time you were waiting outside the house,' Steve said.

'That's right.'

'And when you called the clinic, Shirley Quinn answered before you spoke to Brody?'

'Yes, and you can bet your bottom dollar she got hold of Beckett, just like when I phoned and was followed to Keely's.'

'You know something, Challis?'

'What's that?'

'It seems every bugger involved with this story is ending up dead. If you're not careful there won't be anyone left to get quotes from.'

'Ha, ha, very funny.'

'Well, it's true.'

'How was Keely last night?'

'Much better than I expected, she's a tough little lady. She's still in bed but I can take the phone to her if you like.'

'No, let her know I called and tell her I'll speak to her later.'

'What are you going to do now, Challis?'

'I'm going to knock on Frank Beckett's front door.'

'You're what?'

'You heard me.'

'You must be bloody mad.'

'Thanks,' Challis replied dryly. 'But, frankly, I don't give a fuck. Anyway, I shouldn't think he'd try anything on with me in his own apartment. And if he does, well, I owe him one for Keely.'

'I still say you're crazy.'

Challis showered, quickly dressed then had breakfast in the small dining room downstairs. Back in his room he phoned his British Telecommunications contact but was told he was off sick, so Challis called Lucy Barnes husband, Mark, at his detective agency and told him what he wanted.

He took his mobile phone from its charger, grabbed his briefcase and left the hotel. His BMW was in a nearby car park about ten minutes walk away and forty five minutes later was parked on a yellow line outside Beckett's block of flats. He sat and waited patiently for his mobile to ring. A quarter of an hour later Mark got back to him, with Beckett's ex-directory number.

Challis tried it three times but only got an answer machine. The man's voice was, *educated but not lah de dah*. Challis remembered John Mason's description.

Challis saw a traffic warden approaching so drove around for ten minutes then parked back in the same spot. He crossed the road and entered through the open heavy glass front doors. The uniformed porter, a pleasant looking man in his fifties, looked up as the journalist stopped in front of his desk.

'Can I help you, sir?'

'I've got an appointment with Frank Beckett, he told me to come here this morning.'

'Right sir,' and the porter looked in a lined book on the desk top and reached for the phone. 'I'll just give him a ring on the internal phone to make sure he's in.'

He dialled, let the phone ring, then replaced the receiver.

'Sorry, sir, but Mr Beckett doesn't appear to be at home. Are you sure he said this morning?'

'Positive,' Challis replied.

The porter looked in his book again and reached for another phone.

'I'll try his outside line,' he said, but moments later shook his head. 'His answer machine is on.'

'Maybe he's forgotten to turn the machine off, and he is in,' Challis said.' I know he's expecting me, and he did say it was urgent. Is there some other way you can check?'

The porter reached behind him and pressed a bell. Moments later a door in the corner of the lobby opened and a young man about twenty, wearing a long green apron, appeared.

'Bruno, will you go upstairs and ring Mr Beckett's bell to see if he's in. It's number thirty two, on the third floor.'

'Yes, Mr Martin.'

Five minutes later the pony tailed young man was back with the news that Beckett was definitely not in his flat.

'That's strange,' Challis said, 'I'm sure he said this morning. Did you see Mr Beckett go out?'

'No, but I do know Mr Beckett is away a lot on business trips. Sometimes weeks on end.'

'Do you know his girlfriend, Shirley Quinn?'

The porter smiled.

'Oh yes sir, Miss Quinn is a regular visitor, she's been coming here for years. Nice looking woman.'

'When was the last time you saw her?'

Mr Martin thought for a moment.

'Yesterday, or the day before is the last time *I* saw her...but,' and the porter opened another book, 'yes here it is. Mr Beckett phoned up yesterday evening and told us that he wanted Miss Quinn let into his flat. I had already left by then and Fred Hughes was on duty, he does the four to midnight shift. This is his writing.'

'She must have left by now, any idea what time she went?'

'As a matter of fact I do. George Pearson does the twelve to eight and I relieved him this morning. He told me Miss Quinn left real early this morning, about six o'clock.'

'By cab?'

'I'm sorry, but that I don't know.'

'That's okay, she's probably at work by now. I'll give her a call there, she'll know where Frank is.'

'If Mr Beckett returns soon who shall I say called?'

'Tell him Challis called, he'll know who it is.'

'Of course, Mr Challis,' and the porter carefully wrote the name in the book.

The journalist left and gave a wry smile as he took a parking ticket from underneath his windshield wiper. Once behind the steering wheel he got out his mobile and phoned Brody's health clinic.

'Can I help you?' a woman's voice, but not Shirley Quinn.

'Have I got the right number, is that the clinic?'

'Yes it is, how can I help you?'

'Is Miss Quinn there?'

'No, I'm afraid the clinic is closed for the time being.'

'Closed, why's that?'

'A family bereavement.'

'Oh, I see. It doesn't matter, I'll phone back in a few days to make an appointment,' and Challis broke the connection.

The voice probably belonged to a policewoman. Had they sent Shirley home or hadn't she turned up for work?

Challis gave a quick call to Steve then eased away from the kerb and drove to meet the Paddington paparazzi.

THIRTY FOUR

When Challis arrived at the studio he explained to Des about Brody's murder and told him to go to Shirley Quinn's home address.

'And do what?'

'If she's there, sit on her and don't let her move. Call me or Steve and we'll be straight over, but be very careful, just in case Beckett's around.' Challis playfully punched the young photographer on his shoulder. 'Look after yourself.'

'Don't worry, I can,' Des grinned cockily.

As soon as the young man left Challis looked around Steve's cluttered office.

'Have you got an A to Z here?'

Steve went to a shelf behind his small desk, lifted up a pile of large brown envelopes and produced a stiff backed copy of the London street guide.

Challis took it, looked in the index and began turning pages.

'What are you looking for?' Steve asked.

'Ever since I lost Beckett on the underground I've been trying to work out where he might have got a train to,' Challis replied.

'And?'

'Well, when I first spoke to Pauline Fountain, she said she thought she saw someone like him enter a block of flats somewhere between the Caledonian Road and Liverpool Road.'

'They're in the Islington, Camden area, aren't they?'

As soon as Steve mentioned *Islington* Challis remembered what had been bothering him. 'Of course,' he said, clicking his fingers.

'Of course what?'

'You remember when Keely described her attacker and said he was wearing a long coat?'

'Yes.'

'Pauline said when she saw this man she thought was Beckett, he was wearing an old, long military style coat. And she said she was driving through *Islington.*'

'Then it's got to be the same man,' Steve said.

'Beckett was travelling on the Piccadilly line, which stops at Kings Cross, and from there it's only a short cab ride to the area Pauline described. All he had to do was jump on the next train.'

'Have you got an exact address?' Steve asked.

'No, but it's a rundown block of flats called Ashley Court, and Pauline narrowed it down. She said it was the King Cross end of the two roads.' Challis looked at the A to Z. 'The Pentonville area, I suppose.'

Steve did several enlarged photocopies of the relevant page, and the two men worked out a grid system to drive through the streets and find the flats.

The phone rang, breaking their concentration. It was Des.

'Shirley Quinn isn't at home,' he said. 'She's gone away.'

'How do you know?' Challis asked.

'She shares the house with a woman called, Diana, nice looker too.'

'So how come we didn't see her when we staked out the house?' Challis interrupted.

'She's an air hostess and has been on holiday for a week. She only returned late last night. Anyway, she said Shirley has gone away for a few days and doesn't know where. Her Vauxhall car's still parked outside the house so Diana reckons

Shirley is with her boyfriend, Frank.' Des paused. 'One other thing.'

'Yes?'

'The police have been here looking for Shirley. It was about her boss's death.'

'I see.'

'So what shall I do now?'

'You'd better meet up with Steve and me, we're going flat hunting.'

*

It took a couple of hours of driving around and asking people but with the BMW, transit van and Des on the Yamaha, it enabled them to cover the area with a fine toothcomb. Finally they found Ashley Court, its name in faded black letters on a lop-sided wooden board, and parked their vehicles.

'A bit different from Beckett's place in Knightsbridge,' Challis observed.

'But does Beckett live here? He might only have been visiting someone,' Steve said. 'And if he does live here, which flat is his?'

'There are three entrances,' Challis said. 'So if we each take one and show the tenants Beckett's photograph, then we might find out. And make a note of the people who answer, and those who are out, in case we have to come back.'

Steve got the photographs from his van and the three men started door knocking. Challis and Steve took the two end entrances and Des the middle one.

Challis pushed open the front swing door, his footsteps loud on the stone tiles, but only one of the two ground floor flats Challis tried answered. An old lady, who had to go back inside to fetch her glasses, had a long scrutiny of the two pics of Beckett, one of them a close-up, but failed to recognise him.

Both tenants were in on the next floor and one of them thought Beckett's face looked familiar, but wasn't certain. Challis trudged up the next flight of stairs and rang the bell of one of the two doors, but it didn't seem to be working so he bashed hard on the knocker. Nobody came to the door so he rang the bell of the flat opposite. It didn't look as though there would be an answer there either but finally the door was opened by an old man in his eighties. Challis noticed a hearing aid behind the man's ear and spoke loudly.

'Could you have a look at these photographs, please,' and Challis shoved the pics into the pensioner's gnarled hands.

'Who are you?' the old man asked.

'I work for a solicitor and the man in this photograph might have been a witness to a car accident involving one of our clients. He's not in any trouble and, as a matter of fact, we'll pay him for his time if he can help us. We were told he lived in these flats, but I haven't got the exact number.' Challis paused. 'Do you know him?'

The old man slowly nodded his head.

'Yes. He lives in there,' he said, and pointed in the direction of the opposite door. 'But I don't see much of them.'

'*Them*? How many live there?'

'Two I think...brothers...anyway they look alike. Though one is much better dressed than the other.'

But other than that the old boy didn't know much, and had no idea of the names of the occupiers of the flat or when they would be back. Challis thanked him and went back outside. He crossed to his car and stood with his back against the BMW looking at the flats and couple of old cars parked in the pot-holed private road.

A few minutes later Steve and Des walked towards him and he gave them the thumbs up sign. When they reached him he told them what the old man had said.

'Do you think two people live in the flat?' Des asked.

'No, I think it's just Beckett, and for some reason uses this place to change his clothes and disguise his appearance,' Challis replied, then added. 'I've got to get inside that flat.'

'What, break in?' Steve asked.

'If necessary.'

'What's the front door like?'

'It's got two locks and I think if we tried to go in that way we'd make a lot of noise. The old boy opposite is deaf but he still might see us, and he's the type who'd call the police straight away. So let's have a look at the back,' and the three men walked towards the rear of the block.

There was a small balcony outside every flat for hanging washing but Beckett's was on the second floor and a long ladder would be needed, Challis thought, as he pinpointed the flat.

But it gave him an idea and he used his mobile to phone Gerry Cassidy. They spoke for several minutes.

'And you reckon you can have someone here in about an hour?'

'Yes, Challis, and it's only because you've put a nice bit of business my way that I'm doing it,' Cassidy said. 'We are really busy and I've got two of my regular men off sick, but don't worry, I know a couple of blokes who'll be ideal for what you want.' He laughed. 'Just don't ask them what they do for a living.'

THIRTY FIVE

Frank Beckett left the Porsche in the garage and he and Shirley drove off in the Granada. She'd hoped they would be going in the sports car but Frank only drove it to a nearby petrol station, filled up and returned it to the lockup. He said he wanted her to drive the Porsche tonight because he had something special on. Shirley tried to wheedle more out of him - but he wouldn't elaborate.

During the time they made love that morning he kept impressing on her she must do as she was told and ask no questions. Seeing he was more insistent just as she reached one of her many orgasms, Shirley obediently agreed, but she wondered what he had in mind for her. She'd enjoyed the morning, the grim surroundings of the garage adding to her sexual excitement, but the sandwiches Frank bought earlier in the day hadn't been very tasty so they stopped at a small supermarket and bought utensils and ingredients, including wine and sparkling water, for a picnic. Shirley felt like a teenager going on a lovers date.

The Ford cut off the country road and Frank Beckett guided the car along the tree lined lanes. He made no comment to Shirley as he drove past the police car prominently parked in Matthew Hardy's entrance, nor when he drove past the spot where he'd hidden the Granada last night. He followed the lane until he came to a crossroad and turned right. This lane swung in a large loop, running into a minor road, which was on the other side of the merchant banker's estate. Beckett pulled off the road into a small clearing and reversed the car between bushy trees until the branches and leaves sprang back in place, hiding the vehicle.

'This is where I will want you to park the Porsche this evening,' he said. 'And don't worry about finding it again, I'll show you.'

'Why, Frank? There's nothing here.'

Beckett didn't answer.

'You're not a burglar, are you? You're not going to rob a country mansion?' Shirley's voice held a trace of laughter.

Frank turned and looked at her.

'No, I'm not a burglar.'

Shirley noted Frank's serious expression and didn't try another flippant remark.

'Somebody, who lives very close to where we are now, owes me something much more than money can buy, and if everything goes according to plan, I will be paid in full.'

He softened his face and smiled.

'Now let's get the picnic stuff, I'm hungry.'

Frank got a red plaid blanket from the boot while Shirley emptied the back seat of food and drink. After a meal of chicken legs, beef and salad, washed down with a mixture of wine and sparkling water they both relaxed in the shady undergrowth.

'Who is this person who owes you, Frank?'

Beckett didn't reply straight away. His head was laying in Shirley's lap and he was enjoying the feel of her hand as she gently stroked his brow. The pain had returned. It was getting worse.

'Shirley, what I'm talking about is a debt of honour.'

He tilted his head back and looked deep into her eyes.

'It's a family debt, and today should be the final settlement. Then it will be over.'

Shirley stared at him but stopped herself asking another question as a tortured expression flashed across his face.

230

'Oh God,' Beckett groaned, as an intense stab of pain exploded in his head and his whole body went into a cold sweat. He felt too weak to stand and rolled over on to his hands and knees. He managed to crawl a few feet from the blanket before being violently sick.

'Frank,' Shirley cried out, and was instantly beside him.

'I'm all right,' he said, taking deep breaths. 'Get me some water,' and rose shakily to his feet. Shirley gave him a half full bottle of Perrier and he rinsed out his mouth, then took a swig. He walked slowly to the car boot and took a bottle of pills from the pocket of his army coat. He shoved two into his mouth and downed them with another drink.

Shirley moved the blanket further away from where Beckett had vomited and he lay down.

'I'm going to try and get some sleep.' He looked at his watch. 'Wake me in an hour, no longer.' Beckett gripped her wrist tightly. 'Understand?'

Shirley nodded her head docilely. A few minutes later he was asleep and she quietly tidied the remains of the picnic, putting the rubbish into carrier bags. She hoped Frank was getting proper medical advice because she knew his throwing up had nothing to do with the food. They had eaten the same and she felt okay. Besides, he'd taken those painkillers, so it had to be his headaches.

Shirley sat quietly looking at him, wishing him better. Exactly on time she gently shook him awake.

'You've been asleep for an hour, Frank.'

Beckett blinked his eyes, sat up, and put his arms around her. He held her like this for a few minutes before he spoke, and when he did, Shirley was startled, scared even, and felt a shiver run down her spine.

Frank was speaking in another man's voice.

'Everything will be finished tonight, Henri,' he said. 'You will be avenged in full, I promise you that...so will I.'

Shirley slowly pushed Frank away from her.

But somehow it wasn't her Frank anymore.

'It's all right, darling,' she said in a caring voice. 'Who's Henri? Who are you talking about?'

'It wasn't fair.' Beckett's glazed eyes bored into hers, and Shirley saw tears running down his cheeks, and he put his arms around her again, rocking them both back and forth. They stayed like this for several more minutes then Beckett relaxed his grip and stood up.

'Who's Henri?' she asked again.

Beckett's eyes were now clear and his cheeks dried.

'None of your damn business,' he answered harshly, his voice back to normal. 'It was a long time ago, Shirley, and soon it will all be dead and buried.'

Beckett went to the glove compartment of the car and pulled out his binoculars.

'I won't be long,' he said.

'Where are you going, Frank? You still don't look so good.'

'I'll be about an hour. You finish the wine while I'm gone and don't let anyone see you.'

Beckett pushed his way through the trees until he reached the road. It was empty and he quickly crossed over and climbed the five bar gate into a field where a dozen cows were grazing. He moved sideways, knelt down in the shadow of the hedge, and scanned the area through his binoculars. No sign of human life, the same as the other times he'd been here. Beckett ran about sixty yards until he came to another hedge which he followed for about the same distance then stopped. This would be his exit point from Matthew Hardy's estate.

Beckett dropped to his knees and carefully tugged at a clump of turf about twelve inches long by six inches wide. It came up in one piece and Beckett did the same with another clump, revealing a twenty four inch opening six inches deep in the ground. Nestling in the bottom was a powerful sharp saw, with two spare blades wrapped in strong plastic, a pair of long-handled secateurs and heavy duty gardening gloves. Beckett pulled on the gloves and set to work cutting through the base of the hawthorn hedge.

He wasn't worried about being seen on the other side because that part of the hedge was hidden by half a dozen conifer trees. The hedge was about two feet thick but it only took about forty five minutes to cut an opening two feet wide. Then he meticulously rebuilt both sides of the hedge, leaving the centre hollow, and carefully laid a latticework over the top.

It looked solid again but Beckett knew he could run straight through it without any problem. It was essential he had an escape route just in case he didn't succeed tonight and had to try again.

Beckett realised he probably wouldn't be able to kill Matthew Hardy's son as well, and wasn't too bothered at this stage. If he survived, then he would worry about that tomorrow, but the father *had* to die. He was the direct offspring of Colonel Hardy who had been responsible for everything.

Before returning to the car Beckett distributed the remainder of the cut hawthorn along the base of the hedge.

THIRTY SIX

Just over an hour after Challis spoke with Gerry Cassidy a small white van, with adjustable ladders on its roof rack, arrived and parked behind the BMW.

Two burly men in white overalls got out. One got a couple of buckets and a tool bag from the rear of the van and the other walked towards the journalist and two photographers.

'Mr Challis?'

'That's right.'

'We're the special window cleaning service,' the man said with a grin. 'Gerry told us what you want doing. Which flat is it?'

The man returned to the van to help his mate untie the ladders then Challis showed them to the rear of the flats, pointed out Beckett's balcony, and returned to the front.

Twenty minutes later one of the men walked out the front entrance.

'I got in through a window and drilled and chiselled the deadlock from the inside. I've left the Yale on the latch so all you've got to do is push the front door open,' he said, and went to the back of the van.

'Nice work,' and Challis watched with interest as the man took out a pane of glass and tin of putty.

'I'll cut this to size and replace the one I broke,' he said. 'Then we'll wait around until you're finished.'

It was decided that Des would stay outside just in case Beckett returned and he would be able to warn them on his mobile.

'Or if you see the old bill,' Steve said. 'We don't want to get nicked for breaking and entering.'

*

Challis pushed open the front door of the flat and walked into the narrow hallway with its dark patterned wallpaper and even darker brown painted woodwork. Steve followed him and closed the front door. Two bedrooms led off the left of the hall, the bathroom and kitchen were on the right and the lounge at the end.

What immediately struck the intruders was the style, furniture and decoration of the interior. Everything was an exact replica of the nineteen forties. It was as though they had stepped back in time and the air seemed uncannily still and quiet like the atmosphere of a shrine.

Challis told Steve to take pictures of all the rooms before they disturbed anything. Then the two men searched thoroughly but it quickly became apparent that there were few personal belongings in the flat. And what they did find was surprising, to say the least.

Hanging in the mahogany wardrobe of the larger bedroom was an army officer's uniform, a grey lightweight suit and a shirt with a tie looped around the metal hanger. Challis was positive it was the suit Beckett was wearing when he lost him on the tube train.

But who did the uniform belong to?

The journalist opened the bottom drawers but except for two pairs of shoes the rest of the wardrobe was empty. In a chest of drawers were two neatly folded khaki shirts, a regimental tie, underwear and several pairs of socks. There was a half drunk bottle of Johnny Walker whisky on a bedside table and a used crystal tumbler.

The small bedroom was furnished but completely empty of anything personal. The kitchen had a limited stock of tinned

235

foods and a tea caddy. The contents of the bathroom consisted of two hand towels, a bath towel and a few toiletries. Challis picked up a shaving brush and flicked the bristles. He'd never used one. Nor anything like the lethal looking cut-throat razor and leather strop next to it.

The biggest surprise of all was waiting in the lounge. As soon as Challis opened the door his eyes were riveted to a group of silver framed photographs on the dark wood sideboard. They were of Giles Faraday and his family, a couple of them identical to the photographs Challis had borrowed from Evelyn Nash.

These were obviously the copies John Mason had sent to the accommodation address in Nottingham years ago which were forwarded on to Brody's clinic. Challis recalled Beckett had claimed they were *family photographs* when Pauline had given the envelope to him.

Challis looked at the framed pictures again. How the hell could they be *family*?

A search of the sideboard revealed another three bottles of whisky, a bottle of sherry and an assortment of glasses. Challis crossed to a small writing table and picked up several tape cassettes. Glenn Miller, Vera Lynn, Bing Crosby, Benny Carter, names from the thirties and forties. Challis opened the middle drawer and saw more tapes, but these were different. These weren't music cassettes. He picked one up and saw three sets of initials, J. B./ F.B./ G. F. and a date which was over six years old written in biro on the white label. There were half a dozen tapes, recorded, judging by the dates, over a period of six weeks.

Also in the drawer were several letters and medical appointment cards. Challis picked up the letters and glanced through them, a puzzled look forming on his face.

Then he went back to the tapes, picked out the earliest date and inserted it in the radio cassette player on top of the desk.

He switched on and immediately recognised Brody's smooth voice.

And then everything fell into place.

'My name is James Brody and I am an hypnotherapist. For just over a month I have been treating Frank Beckett for his smoking addiction and he now appears cured. However, during the last session while Frank was under hypnosis he suddenly started talking about having a previous life, that he had lived before as someone else.'

There was a short pause and another man's voice came on the tape, a voice Challis had heard before...on a telephone answer machine.

'My name is Frank Beckett and I give my full permission to be hypnotised by James Brody. But I wish to retain control of the tape recordings and they will be my sole property, and because of this I am paying James Brody an agreed fee.'

Then the hypnotherapist's voice again.

'Although hypnosis is not an exact science I firmly believe in reincarnation and have regressed several people before with varying degrees of success. Frank is curious and has agreed to participate in my attempt to discover anything about a past life he might have had. This is tape recording number one.'

There was a longer silence this time then Brody's voice was heard, speaking in a lulling tone.

'Relax, just relax and breathe easily. Relax and send your mind drifting back through time. You're looking for memories...memories that happened in times before you were born.'

The hypnotherapist's voice droned on.

'You're in a long dark tunnel...drifting...drifting. Drift through it until you come out into the light.'

Brody's persuasive voice repeated to Beckett that he was beginning a journey into the past, a familiar journey with many memories.

'Go back to before you were born...go back one hundred years to eighteen ninety seven...remember...remember. Who are you?'

Silence.

'Come forward twenty five years...to nineteen twenty two...release those memories.'

Silence again.

'I can tell by your face you're remembering something. Hello, who are you?'

Then a different voice...a child's voice.

'Gi...Giles...' the voice faltered.

'Did you say your name is Giles?' Brody asked.

'Yes.'

'How old are you Giles?'

'I'm five.'

'Are you at school?'

'No, but Mummy says I'll go soon.'

'What's your mummy's name?'

'Mummy.'

'What's mummy's name...her first name?'

'Don't be silly, it's Mummy.'

'Do you have another name besides Giles?'

'Philip.'

'What's your last name? You're Giles Philip...what?'

'Far...Fara...Faraday.'

Challis saw Steve looking at him and shrugged his shoulders and shook his head in bewilderment. There was a weird atmosphere in the room.

Over the next fifteen minutes Challis fast forwarded the tape, stopping every now and again to listen as Brody coaxed the *child's* background from him. Gently at times, then with authority, even firmly when the *child* seemed to be hesitant in replying. Just as a parent or teacher might talk to a five-year-old.

238

He only brought Giles up to the age of twelve and kept asking the same questions as though trying to trap the *boy.* Brody darted from year to year back and forth, even to when Giles was a *baby,* but the answers were always the same. He described his parents, the house he lived in and the childish jealousy he felt when his younger sister, Evelyn, was born.

Challis noted that Giles's voice became more mature as he got older and was amazed at the change in speaking patterns as the *child* jumped from year to year.

The journalist inserted the next tape in sequence.

'Not everyone can be hypnotised, and those who enter a deep trance are a minority, but Frank responds well.'

Challis fast forwarded from Brody's intro and listened to segments of the tape. It still dealt with Giles early life and slowly moved into his teens.

Challis ejected the tape, inserted tape number five and felt a tingle of excitement as he listened to the adult voice of Giles Faraday in his twenties. It sounded nothing like Frank Beckett's and the journalist fast forwarded the tape halfway.

'It is now nineteen thirty nine...September nineteen thirty nine. What does that mean to you?' Brody asked.

'War. Britain and Germany are at war.'

'How did that affect you? Were you in the war?'

'Yes.'

'You fought in the war?'

'Yes.'

'Which branch of the services were you in?'

'The army.'

'When did you join?'

'I volunteered in October nineteen thirty nine and joined the Royal Fusiliers.'

Challis kept forwarding and listening to the tape and from what he gathered it covered Giles Faraday's army career through the evacuation of Dunkirk in nineteen forty, then when he transferred to the Special Operations Executive a year later, the Christmas of nineteen forty three, which Evelyn Nash had described, until he parachuted into northern France in March nineteen forty four, three months before the D-Day landings.

Challis quickly inserted the last tape.

'Where are you now?' Brody asked.

'In a bar.'

'What are you doing?'

'Drinking cognac.'

'Where is this bar?'

'In the village of Roujan, in northern France.'

'Are you drinking by yourself?'

'No, I'm with a friend.'

'What is your friend's name?'

'Henri Fabere.'

'How are you dressed?'

'Like a Frenchmen, in civilian clothes.'

'What are you talking about with your friend?'

'Henri is in the Resistance and we're talking about tomorrow.'

'What's happening tomorrow?'

'I will be impersonating a German officer and two Frenchmen will be dressed as German soldiers. One of the men is Henri's younger brother.'

'Why will you be dressed like this?'

'I will be arresting three men and a woman who live in the next village. They'll think they're safe because they have been helping the Germans for two years and will be able to get someone to vouch for them. But they are collaborators and when I bring them back here they will be executed as traitors. They will be shot.'

'What is tomorrow's date?'

'July the twenty eighth, nineteen forty four.'

Challis forwarded the tape. Then he heard Faraday's voice talking in French...a minute later he was speaking fluent German.

'Stop, stop a moment...relax and don't get agitated,' Brody said.

There was silence then Brody continued.

'You speak French and German...any other languages?'

'Some Italian and a little Russian.'

'Well, I only speak English, so when I ask you questions you must only reply in English...understand?'

'Yes.'

Challis fast forwarded a little more.

'Where are you now?'

'We are walking from a small orchard into a field. There is a ruined farmhouse nearby...we have prisoners...but now we're being shot at...Edouard is down...Henri's brother is dead. The collaborators are escaping...Claude, shoot them. You've got two of the men...shoot the traitors. The woman's down...but one of the men has escaped. Claude is hit in the chest and bleeding badly. Two British soldiers are walking towards me...but I'm dressed as a German and they'll think I'm the enemy.'

Challis was mesmerised as he listened to the voice describe, almost word for word, the same skirmish Bernie Harris had related to him before he was murdered.

Suddenly the voice gasped out in pain.

'What's the matter?' Brody asked anxiously.

'I've been stabbed with a bayonet.'

'Where?'

'In my right shoulder.'

'Does it hurt much?'

'It's not too bad. The bayonet went through the fleshy part...didn't hit a bone.'

'Who did it?'

241

'Private Woodcock...that's what the British captain called him. Somebody else called him Woody.'

Challis remembered the recent horrific death of Ronald Woodcock in Southampton, and the murders of his son and grandson. The motive for the killings now seemingly clear, if unbelievable, and the journalist and photographer stood spellbound as the words hung in the stillness of the room.

'Can you remember any other soldiers names?'

'Private Kemp...Corporal Harris...Johnson's dead'

'No more?'

'Not by name...but I can see their faces.'

Giles Faraday then explained the arrival of Henri Fabere and the difficulty he was having in convincing the British soldiers he was English.

'If only they would come with us to Henri's village' Then the voice became louder with urgency. 'We're being shelled...a direct hit on top...we're being shoved up the cellar stairs into the open. The Germans are shelling us...now we're running across a field...there's a flare in the sky...it's like day. The British soldiers are running towards a hedge...another flare, and machine guns are firing at us. Mortar shells exploded just in front of us. Henri and I must make a dash for it...away from the soldiers. Bullets are flying everywhere...Henri's hit...so am I...we're both down.'

The voice became louder with pain and anger.

'I've been shot by my own troops. I'm not sure if Henri's dead...I'm on my feet trying to drag him to safety.'

The voice paused briefly and there was the sound of a deep breath.

'Bastards!'

The one word echoed through the room, followed by a gasp of agonising pain, then deathly silence.

THIRTY SEVEN

The breeze ruffled her hair through the open passenger window but it was still hot inside the car. The kind of muggy day that was never going to cool down, the one glimmer of hope being the forecast of storms heading from France and due tonight, bringing cooling rain.

Shirley glanced sideways at Frank as he steered the Granada back towards Hatfield and wondered what was wrong with him. The experience she'd just had with Frank had been disturbing.

Who was Henri? Not Henry - but the French pronunciation.

He'd definitely been speaking in another voice! But why? How? It hadn't sounded false as though Frank was trying to impersonate someone else. It had sounded natural, as though he really *was* someone else.

It had sounded eerie.

And what was going to happen tonight? Shirley had a feeling of dread.

They were just approaching the town suburbs when Beckett drove into a large service station.

'I want to top up with petrol,' he said.

'That's okay, I'd like to get some peppermints,' she said, moving her handbag onto her lap.

'No, stay in the car,' he commanded.

Shirley looked at him as he got out and unscrewed the Granada's petrol cap. She opened her door, swung her feet on to the concrete and quietly stood as Beckett shoved a petrol hose into the tank. His back was towards her and she walked to the large glass plated doors of the shop about twenty yards away.

'Shirley, come back,' Beckett shouted.

She turned and smiled at him.

'I want to get some peppermints,' she repeated.

Beckett beckoned furiously with his hand to return but Shirley walked through the automatic glass doors. She selected two packets of mints, walked over to the newspaper shelves and picked up a copy of the London Evening Standard, a paper she bought every day. She was pleasantly surprised they delivered this far out from the capital and started flicking through the pages as she joined the short queue behind the cashier's counter.

Just as she took her change Beckett walked in behind a muscular young man in a T-shirt.

'Wait for me, Shirley,' he said, and in the next breath shouted to the cashier, 'number six,' holding up his money and trying to push past the young man.

'Do you mind,' the young man growled. 'Take your turn.'

'Sorry,' Beckett said, and apprehensively watched Shirley go outside.

Suddenly she stopped, held the newspaper wide open with both hands and gasped, her heart thudding. Then she turned and stared at Beckett through the glass. Slowly her eyes returned to the inside page lead story and small photograph of James Brody. He was dead. Her boss had been murdered. The police said he had been stabbed to death about seven o'clock yesterday evening, but the body hadn't been discovered until his wife came home over four hours later.

Shirley looked again at Frank. He had now paid and followed the young man through the automatic doors on to the forecourt.

'Mr Brody's dead, Frank,' she said, thrusting the paper in front of his face. 'He's been murdered. You told me you spoke to Mr Brody last night, just before you phoned me, but you couldn't have. He was already dead.'

'What are you saying, Shirley?' and he grabbed hold of her arm, trying to move her in the direction of the Granada.

'You knew he was meeting that journalist at his home at seven thirty because I told you.'

'Come on, Shirley, don't talk so stupid, get in the car.' Beckett gripped her arm tighter and started pushing her.

'All this talk about murders, and tapes. Mr Brody knew something, didn't he?' Shirley wrenched her arm free and tried to push Beckett away. 'And you went to his house before the journalist arrived.'

Shirley placed the palms of both her hands against Beckett's chest trying to gain more distance from him.

'*You* killed Mr Brody, didn't you, Frank? Are you going to kill someone else tonight?'

He didn't reply but grabbed Shirley in both arms, lifting her off the ground.

'Oi, you, what's your trouble then?'

Beckett swung his head round and saw the muscular young man jump down from the driving seat of a white transit van. He leant back inside and pulled out a shiny black metal baseball bat.

'Leave the lady alone,' he said, walking menacingly towards the couple, and slapping the end of the bat into his left hand.

'Do you want him to leave you alone, miss?'

'Yes, please.'

The young man was about two yards from them when Beckett violently thrust Shirley away from him. She stumbled backwards and the young man grabbed hold of her to stop her falling.

Several other drivers had inquisitively turned their heads at the commotion and saw Beckett jump into the Ford, slam the door and rev the engine hard.

Beckett had no hesitation about what he was going to do next. He looked through the windscreen just as Shirley and the young man broke apart and aimed the heavy vehicle straight at them. The man leapt backwards but Shirley wasn't so fortunate and the car hit her in the back, tossing her in the air, her limp body thudding into another car pulling away from a pump.

Beckett cursed as he saw a driver speaking on his mobile phone. Was he talking to the police? Beckett swore again as he smashed against the wing of a car driving into the service station. But he mustn't panic. Think like a soldier. He started to calm down, even though his head had started to throb.

As he entered a built up area he slowed his speed to thirty miles an hour. Should he abandon his car and walk, or take a chance and head for his garage? He had his bag and coat in the boot which he needed and would be too conspicuous carrying, so decided to try for the garage about fifteen minutes drive away.

He reckoned he was just five minutes from his goal when he spotted a white patrol car three vehicles in front of him. As usual, whenever the public saw a police car, they immediately slowed to a crawl. This time Beckett was very much in favour because he had no intention of overtaking and kept his foot light on the accelerator.

*

PC Teddy Lawson sat in the passenger seat with his head turned looking through the rear window at the traffic behind him.

'Slow down a bit,' he said to the driver, as the road started an inward crescent shape, and stuck his head out of the passenger window.

'There's an old blue Ford Granada three cars behind us,' he said.

Only minutes ago an urgent message had come over the radio for all patrol cars to be on the lookout for this type of Granada. The voice had said not to try and arrest the driver or alert him, only to report his whereabouts and follow. The man was dangerous and had tried to kill a woman.

'What do you think I should do?' the driver asked his partner.

'Take the next turning, do a U-turn, and then follow the bugger.'

The driver nodded in agreement.

*

A minute later Beckett saw the police car turn left and as he drove past the turning saw the car do a three point turn. Beckett knew then he'd been recognised and swiftly overtook the two cars in front, causing the second to slam on its brakes. He pressed hard on the pedal and was surprised not to hear the piercing sound of a siren. He went past the next two turnings on the left and suddenly swung right as a road close to his garage came into view. He spun left a few hundred yards further on, came to a crossing and went the wrong way down a one way street, then a minute later entered the wide alley in front of the six lockup garages. He quickly got out the car and looked both ways. No sign of the police. Within a few minutes he'd driven the Porsche out of the garage, stashed everything he needed in the passenger seat, and put the Granada in its place. Then he drove the sports car out the other end of the alley and parked. He put his hand in one of the army overcoat pockets, took out a small round object and returned to the lockup. He was inside no more than five minutes.

*

'We've lost him,' PC Lawson reported back to his control room. 'He just seemed to vanish.'

The controller said to keep looking and was sending more police cars into the area to help with the search.

The patrol car cruised the area slowly, its two occupants diligently hunting for the blue Granada, and didn't pay any attention to the white Porsche as it sped past them.

THIRTY EIGHT

Before he left Beckett's flat Challis called Joe Steiner on his mobile and explained he wanted half a dozen tapes copied as soon as possible. Steiner ran a small electronics business in Cricklewood and the journalist had been buying highly sensitive microphones, among other devices, from him for years. His company was one of the leading specialists in bugging equipment and his hand-built video camera briefcases were a must for every top photographer.

Steiner moaned a little at the short notice but said he'd do it after Challis told him to double the bill because it really was urgent.

When he got outside Challis told Cassidy's men to wait while he found a local newsagent with a photocopier machine and copied the letters and medical appointment cards he'd found with the cassettes. Then Challis gave the tapes and Steiner's address, with the letters, to Cassidy's men. He told them the tapes would be copied straight away and he wanted the originals and the letters put back in the desk drawer of Beckett's flat as soon as possible.

'Otherwise, a certain copper I know will have me banged up for taking police evidence,' Challis said.

'No problem, we'll go in the same way as before,' one of the men said. 'But what do you want done with the copies?'

'Deliver them to my flat in Victoria,' Challis replied, and scribbled his address on a piece of paper from his notebook. 'Put them in a large envelope, there's a letterbox in the front entrance that's big enough to take them.'

Challis could hardly contain his excitement which felt like a powerful stimulant inside him. He knew he'd stumbled across a story any journalist would give his eye teeth for. And to think less than two weeks ago he was bored out of his skull. You could never tell what's around the corner in this business.

When the two men had driven off in their van Challis and the photographers drove to a nearby pub with a car park and went inside. They found a quiet space and, as Steve went to the bar, Challis told Des what they'd discovered inside the flat.

'What do you think, eh?' Steve grinned at the younger man as he placed a tray with three pints of lager on the table.

'It's a fantastic story,' Des said. 'But it just doesn't seem possible. In fact, it's near enough unbelievable.'

'Yeah, think of our picture by-lines,' Steve said, and raised his glass. 'Challis, you'll be able to syndicate this all over the world.'

'I know.'

'And make a lot of money.'

'That's for sure.'

'So this is the motive for all these murders?' Des looked questioningly at Challis. 'Beckett thinks he's Giles Faraday...or was, in a previous life? He got killed in France all those years ago and now he's murdering the people who were responsible for his death to get even?' Des paused. 'I know it sounds daft, but my Mother's into all this. She believes in the supernatural...clairvoyants, mediums and all that. She's convinced they've got psychic powers and often goes to meetings.'

'Yeah, one of my uncles died ten years ago and my auntie's convinced he's sent her messages from the spirit world,' Steve said. 'Poor old dear's being conned.'

'Do you believe in reincarnation?' Des asked.

'Up until today I'd have said no, but now I'm not so sure,' Challis replied. 'It's nice to think when we die we'll come back on Earth as someone else, but I suppose it's a bit like flying saucers. You either believe - or you don't.'

Challis took a swig of his beer and looked at his friend over the rim of the glass.

'The thing is, Steve, we both heard the tapes.'

'I know,' the photographer said, 'but I think the answer is a lot simpler than that. I think Beckett is a walking nutcase and that was Beckett's subconscious we heard. The insane side of him, voices in his head and all that sort of thing. I've read about people in institutions who think they're Napoleon or Julius Caesar.'

'So why Giles Faraday? A nobody. Anyway, how could Beckett have known about Faraday in the first place?'

'That's true,' Steve said thoughtfully.

'Have you ever read about the Bridey Murphy case?' Challis asked.

'Sounds vaguely familiar...'

'It was an American housewife in the fifties who for fun agreed to be hypnotised as an experiment. Under hypnosis she claimed to have lived as Bridey Murphy in Ireland nearly two hundred years ago. Her tape recordings contained masses of detail that checked out, and the truth about her story has never been resolved, one way or the other. Hers was the first famous case of reincarnation that gained worldwide attention. There was even a film made about it.'

'That may be so,' Steve said. 'But where's the physical proof? I bet nobody's ever come up with that. No, I'm sorry, I don't believe in reincarnation. There must be some other explanation, don't you think so?'

Challis thought for a long while before answering.

'Yes, maybe you're right,' he replied hesitantly. 'But there is another intriguing thing. When I first spoke to Pauline Fountain she told me Beckett's birthday was on the twenty eighth of July. That's the date Faraday died in France.'

'So what's that supposed to mean?'

'I don't know. Probably just a strange coincidence. But I'm going to write the story as it happened...and the public can make up its own mind. But whatever way it works out, the story is dynamite.'

'Are you going to tell the police about the tapes?'

'No, not yet anyway. The police are looking for Shirley Quinn and they will now know about Beckett. But at the moment they've no reason to suspect that he's the killer. As far as they're concerned he's just a boyfriend with no connection to the murders. It's Quinn they want to speak to.'

'And maybe they'll only find out about Beckett's flat in Knightsbridge. She might not know about his other place,' Steve said.

'That's right, and in that case they will have to read about the tapes in the paper, the same as everyone else.'

'The old bill won't be happy.'

'Who gives a shit.'

'But suppose the police do suspect Beckett and arrest him before your story comes out, then that's going to make it *sub judice*,' Des said.

'Yes, that would screw up everything because nothing could appear in print until after the court case. So let's hope he stays free. You see, I'm not going to accuse Beckett of being the murderer. I can't, I've got no proof. The way I'm going to write it is base the story on Bernie Harris's interview before he was killed. Then I can bring in the other murders, the attack on Keely, and then the tapes. Don't forget, Beckett doesn't admit killing anyone on those tapes, just that he claims he lived before as Giles Faraday. And that's what I'll say.'

'I don't suppose he'll sue you,' Des chuckled. 'Maybe he'll do a Lord Lucan and disappear.'

'What was in those letters you took from the drawer?' Steve asked.

'Beckett was seeing a couple of doctors,' Challis replied. 'One in particular I'm going to try and get hold of.'

'What do you want me and Des to do now?'

'I don't think there's much you can do,' Challis replied, 'so you might as well have an early finish for a change. I'll keep phoning Beckett's place the rest of the day and if I don't get any joy then we'll start the stakeouts again tomorrow.'

'Shirley Quinn's as well?'

'Yes.'

Des decided to take the opportunity to head straight home and then go and surprise his girlfriend. Lately she'd been demanding he take some time off, or start looking for someone else. 'Stuff the overtime,' she'd said.

Steve said he'd go back to his studio to develop the photographs and he also had a backlog of work to catch up with.

Outside the pub the three men said their goodbyes and Challis got in his car. He took the copies of the letters from his inside coat pocket, read through them again then dialled the number of psychologist, John Andrews. A brisk sounding woman informed Challis that the consultant was busy with a patient and couldn't be disturbed.

'What's it about?' she demanded.

'It's private,' the journalist replied. 'What about if I came to your office when Mr Andrews has finished with his patients for today?'

'I'm sorry, but nobody sees Mr Andrews without an appointment. Besides, Mr Andrews has an important dinner with several colleagues this evening.'

Challis was beginning to dislike the unhelpful tone of the woman's voice.

'Listen, whoever you are, I'm only going to say this once so make sure you get it correct,' he said. 'My name is Challis and I'm a freelance journalist. One of your boss's patients is a mass murderer and I've reason to believe John Andrews knows all about it. I haven't yet told the police because I thought I'd give him a chance first to explain. Have you got that?'

There was silence.

'I hope you pass this message on immediately,' Challis continued, 'because if you don't I'm sure you'll get fired when his name and photograph is splashed all over the papers. And I'll make sure he knows how unhelpful you were. Now, I'm going to give you my mobile phone number, and you can tell John Andrews I'll wait ten minutes for him to call me.' Challis paused. 'Understand?'

'Yes...I understand,' the woman replied in a stunned voice.

Challis timed it. The call came back in just over five minutes.

'Mr Challis?'

'Yes, and you must be John Andrews.'

'That's correct. Now what's this all about? You've frightened and upset my receptionist and if you don't give me a satisfactory answer then it will be *me* going to the police, to report *you*.'

'I can understand how you feel but I had to be pretty dramatic to be able to speak to you.'

'That's not the answer I want, Mr Challis.'

'Frank Beckett is one of your patients and I have every reason to believe he's murdered half a dozen men this summer, and as many again over the last few years.'

'What?'

'Murder, Mr Andrews, and it will take some convincing to make me believe you didn't know anything about it.'

'Mr Challis, this is preposterous. You must be a madman.'

'What about tape recordings? Tape recordings between Frank Beckett and a hypnotist called James Brody. Have you ever listened to them, Mr Andrews?'

The silence answered Challis's question.

'Beckett murdered Brody yesterday.'

'He *what*?'

'I said, Beckett murdered James Brody.'

'I don't believe you.'

'It's in today's newspaper.'

'I've been too busy to read the papers.'

'Take my word for it. He stabbed him to death.'

'What do you want, Mr Challis?'

'A meeting, that's all, so I can clarify some points with you. I'll tell you everything I know if you'll be just as open with me.'

'I can't promise that, but...,' and Andrews gave a nervous cough, 'all right, I'll see you.'

'Your receptionist said you were busy tonight.'

'Yes, and that's an engagement I can't break. What about tomorrow?'

'What time?'

'Six thirty will suit me fine. I will have seen my last patient by then.'

'Okay,' the journalist replied, 'see you tomorrow.'

THIRTY NINE

The banker pushed the papers to one side and rubbed his eyes. He was tired and offered a weak smile to his secretary, a well dressed woman in her middle thirties. Tessa Seddon had been employed by the merchant bank for ten years and being divorced and childless had eagerly volunteered to work in Matthew Hardy's mansion. Promotion always in the forefront of her mind.

'I think you should call it a day, Tessa,' he said. 'I've just one more phone call to make and I'll be finished in about five minutes.'

Hardy's personal secretary at his London office was married and he'd thought it too much of an imposition to ask her to move into his home, but Tessa fitted the bill perfectly. He'd taken her into his confidence and explained that an attempt might be made on his life but assured her his house would have the best possible protection.

Obviously, the revelation had shocked her but once she'd got over that feeling, Tessa realised she could turn the opportunity to her advantage.

Tessa was sleeping in Hardy's son's bedroom who was in California. The private bodyguards her boss had engaged were housed in the spare rooms and the secretary had soon become acquainted with one of them.

Tom Varney, just a couple of years older and also unmarried, had eagerly returned her smiles and pleasant hellos. They soon realised they were on the same wavelength and he visited her bedroom on only the third day of her arrival. The hint of danger in her new surroundings excited and aroused her feelings towards the rugged ex-para.

Tessa left the office as Hardy picked up the phone and was connected to his bank in London. The directors had decided to expand their commercial interests in Boston, Massachusetts, in the States, and were launching a new holding company. After a few minutes agreeing with most of the proposals Hardy replaced the receiver, walked to one of the large windows, and stood looking out.

The late afternoon sun was still wonderfully warm, time for his regular swim to freshen up.

*

Tessa headed straight for the kitchen. She tried to keep to a diet and had come to an amicable agreement with the cook that she would prepare most of her own meals, which were mainly salads. Mrs Peters didn't mind at all and was glad to have one less to look after. Ever since the security men moved in she'd been run off her feet. Even though most of them had now left, policemen had taken their place, so it ended up near enough the same. Thankfully, her husband, Jim, was a diamond and helped her cope through the busy times.

Tessa ate in the breakfast room adjoining the kitchen. When she'd finished she went back and put her plate and cutlery in the dishwasher. Then she opened the large fridge and took out four cans of beer and a bottle of white wine.

'Bit of a thirst on, eh,' Mrs Peters commented with a smile, as the younger woman put the drinks on a tray and started to leave.

Tessa looked at the cook who was dicing a large onion and winked.

'Won't do your diet much good,' the cook added, as Tessa pushed open the kitchen door. Mrs Peters was no fool and knew Mr Hardy's secretary had found herself a man. Good luck to her, she thought, get as much of it as you can while you're young.

*

Shirley Quinn lay ashen face in the hospital bed with plastic tubes protruding from her nose, a drip in her arm and wires running from her body to a monitoring machine. Bandages covered the top part of her head. She was stable but unconscious.

The only other person in the small room was a uniformed policewoman who sat patiently watching for any sign of wakening. The WPC's notepad and pen rested on the edge of the bed.

Outside in the corridor a white coated doctor explained his patient's condition to plainclothes detective, Chief Inspector Mike Jordan.

'She's got a fractured skull and pelvis, and her left leg's broken. There doesn't appear to be any internal bleeding and hopefully there's no brain damage. She's very lucky not to have been killed. A hit and run accident, I believe.'

'Yes, something like that,' the policeman hurried his words. 'When do you think we'll be able to talk with her? It's important.'

'That's hard to say. She kept drifting in and out of consciousness when she was brought in and she's been heavily sedated since then. A couple of hours, maybe more.'

The doctor's bleeper made an interrupting noise.

'Sorry, I must go now, I've got to get back to casualty.'

Chief Inspector Jordan watched the white coat disappear from view then looked down at the ladies handbag he held in one hand.

Shirley Quinn was the name of the woman in the bed and it hadn't been an accident. Someone in a blue Ford Granada had cold bloodedly tried to kill her and a good description of the driver had been obtained from a young man who'd witnessed the murder attempt.

The Granada had been spotted by a patrol car, but given them the slip before they managed to get the number. Now other cars had been drafted into the area to help in the search. The driver had to be caught before he *did* kill someone.

There was only one thing for it, Jordan would have to go back to his office and get on the phone. He'd contact the local police in London and they could go round to the address on the woman's driving licence to inform next of kin, or friends about the accident. Then he'd do some digging of his own. The handbag contained an address book with a lot of numbers neatly written in it. Somebody would know something. That was for sure.

He poked his head into the room and whispered to the young policewoman.

'I'm going back to the station now. Let me know the moment she comes to, and make sure you write down everything she says.'

*

After his swim Matthew Hardy once again decided to have a light meal on the raised terrace overlooking the pool, then spend the evening relaxing by the water, a routine which was now becoming a habit after nearly two weeks of virtual seclusion from the outside world. Still, it *was* restful, and the banker promised to remind himself in future to take it easier when he returned to the City.

The swimming pool was mostly under glass attached to the house but the side facing the gardens could be folded back, concertina style.

Karen, the merchant banker's attractive blonde wife, walked up the dozen terrace steps carefully carrying a tray of iced gin and tonics. She was dressed in an emerald green one piece bathing suit and was going to share the meal and outdoor evening with her husband. It was too hot indoors.

A lone security guard, his eyes never still for a moment, sat in a canvas backed director's chair in the open near the far end of the pool. A small leather bag within easy reach on the ground.

*

Tessa stepped from the shower and dried herself with a large bath sheet. Then she pulled on a white towelling robe and walked into the bedroom. Matthew Hardy's son was no doubt used to the luxury of a bathroom en suite but it brought into focus the contrast of her own upbringing on a tough council estate in Liverpool.

There was even a small refrigerator in the room which now contained the drinks she'd brought from the kitchen.

She sighed at her reflection as she vigorously brushed her hair in front of a mirror. Money...what a difference it made to a person's lifestyle.

Tessa stopped and turned as she heard a gentle tap. She crossed to the door and Tom Varney slipped inside.

She gently nuzzled his lips.

'Would you like a beer?' she asked, and went to the fridge when he nodded. He placed a small leather bag on a chest of drawers, snapped the ring-pull of the can open and took a swallow.

'Is everything arranged for tonight?' she eagerly asked.

'Yes,' he replied. 'I'm working to midnight, mainly checking the inside of the house and the roof, and I'm taking my break at nine o'clock.'

FORTY

The chief inspector gave one of his CID sergeants Shirley Quinn's details and told him to inform her local police station about the accident. Then he took the woman's address book from her handbag.

There was no reply from the first phone number Jordan tried. But the second made up for it.

'You're joking,' he said seriously, as the information sent his mind whirling. 'Thank you, thank you very much,' and he replaced the receiver in slow motion, thinking hard.

He left his cluttered office and hurried to the canteen. It was half empty and his eyes darted around the tables until he found what he was looking for.

'Do you mind?' the chief inspector said, and took the London newspaper from the PC before he'd time to answer.

Jordan quickly turned the pages, then spread the paper on the table and tore out the lead story he wanted.

'Sorry about that.'

'That's okay, sir,' the startled PC said.

Jordan read the article on the way back to his office and once inside picked up the phone again.

It looked as though the driver of the blue Granada *had* already killed before.

*

'Pull over,' PC Lawson said, and the driver pulled into the kerb, near where they'd lost the Granada. So far none of the police cars in the area had reported any sighting of the Ford and the two policemen, after widening their search, had decided to go back to square one.

'He can't have disappeared into thin air, so there's only one other answer, he must have a garage nearby. The only trouble is, where?'

'There's not many private houses around here,' the driver said. 'It's mostly commercial.'

'That means there are quite a few lockup garages in this area.'

'And one of them could be his,' the driver nodded.

'Right, so let's concentrate on any in this immediate locality.'

They drove slowly, trying to imagine the route the Granada might have taken. They stopped when they reached a crossroads.

'Left or right?' PC Lawson asked, turning his head. The road ahead was a one way street with a no entry sign facing them.

'What about straight over?'

'But it's a one way street,' PC Lawson replied.

'Exactly.'

They drove carefully along the street until they were faced with a T-junction. They turned left and kept going until they reached another road junction, then went back the way they'd came. A few hundred yards past the T-junction they spotted the wide alley and half a dozen lockup garages. A man in oil stained blue overalls was tinkering with the engine of an old MGB but straightened when he heard the police car come to a stop behind him.

'Can I help you?' he asked, wiping his greasy hands on a piece of rag.

'How long have you been here?' PC Lawson asked.

'About fifteen minutes.'

'Do you know who uses these garages?'

'I've got three of them,' the man replied, pointing them out with his finger. 'The one at that end is empty, and the other two are let.'

'Any idea who to?' the police driver asked.

'A mate of mine's got one, but I've no idea who rents the other.'

'Do you own a blue Ford Granada?'

The man shook his head. 'No.'

'What about the other two?'

'My mate drives a red Rover, but there was an old blue Granada parked outside the other garage this morning.'

'Do you know if it's in the garage now?'

The man shrugged his shoulders.

PC Lawson walked towards the garage and tried looking through the head high windows, but those that weren't nailed over with hardboard, were painted black on the inside. The policeman borrowed a large spanner from the mechanic and smashed one of the panes. He looked inside, turned his head and gave the thumbs up sign.

'The Granada's here, better let the station know.'

The driver returned to the patrol car while PC Lawson had another word with the mechanic who produced a pair of heavy-duty bolt cutters and a minute later the padlock lay on the ground with the garage doors wide open.

PC Lawson checked there was no-one hiding inside, then peered through the windows of the Granada. It was empty. The car had been parked with the driver's side close to the garage wall and he cautiously gripped the front passenger door handle. It was unlocked and as the door swung open PC Lawson noticed too late the length of string tied from the inside of the door to the safety pin of the hand grenade wedged between the front seats.

The confined explosion ignited an open jerrycan of petrol and hurled the policeman's body back against the door, bouncing it on to the brick garage wall. There was a searing sheet of flame followed by another explosion and then the petrol tank erupted in a mass of flames.

The other policeman had just finished his call and stood by the patrol car transfixed, horror staring from his eyes as the interior of the garage became an inferno.

'Oh no,' he groaned.

*

As soon as he'd swapped cars Frank Beckett headed for Stevenage and bought a white tracksuit top in a sports store which was still open. The young man in the petrol station would have given the police his description so he also stopped at a chemist and bought some shaving gear.

Beckett knew it was only a matter of time before the police found out about him, and the Porsche. If they did discover the Granada, the booby-trap might delay them identifying the owner for a while, but they had Shirley. And it didn't matter if she was dead because they would have found her handbag. Could even be checking the contents right now.

Beckett drove back to the A1 motorway and headed north. The first service station and restaurant he came to he stopped, had a shave, changed tops and watched the cars arriving. Fifteen minutes later the car he was waiting for parked about ten spaces from him, a new four door green Ford Mondeo, with just one occupant.

The lone driver, a small middle aged man, got out, pressed his key and the central locking system snapped shut. The man walked towards the restaurant and Beckett drove the Porsche to the furthest corner of the large car park.

He took out the holdall and army greatcoat and moved to a wood bench near the restaurant exit. He discreetly slid the commando knife from the sheath strapped to his calf and held it underneath the coat draped over his right arm.

Half an hour later the man left the restaurant and as he approached his car pressed his key to open the doors. Beckett quickly moved towards him.

'Excuse me, sir.'

The small man turned, his back against the car, and shaded his eyes against the bright early evening sun.

'Yes?' he queried.

Beckett dropped his bag, slid back the army coat and pressed the knife hard against the man's stomach, the sharp point pricking him painfully. The man looked down and saw the lethal weapon.

'You're hurting me,' he gasped, fear showing in his eyes.

Beckett pushed the man towards the rear door.

'Get in the back and I'll stop hurting you,' he said.

The man did as he was told and sat on the seat. Beckett leant down and pulled open the man's suit jacket, picked his spot, and thrust hard. A dumbfounded expression replaced the man's look of fear as he gurgled and died.

Beckett quickly scanned the area but nobody had noticed anything. He wedged his holdall against the man, closed the staring eyes and got behind the wheel of his new transport.

Once again on the motorway he headed back south in the direction of the banker's mansion.

FORTY ONE

It was hard to believe it was only yesterday Keely had suffered her brutal attack. It wasn't just the clever makeup or wig that made the difference, it was her resilient attitude. Her stamina.

Steve was right. She *was* a tough little lady.

'I've put it out of my mind, Challis. As far as I'm concerned it's best to treat it as though I've been lucky. It could have been a lot worse, and losing my hair was the most harmful part of it. Fortunately, that will grow again.'

They sat on a white painted wooden seat under the shade of an apple tree in Steve's back garden and Challis brought Keely up to date. The photographer had already told her of Brody's murder so Challis didn't go into the gory details and concentrated more on his discoveries, the tapes and letters, in Beckett's other flat.

'It's unbelievable to think that Frank Beckett is the reincarnation of Giles Faraday,' Keely said. 'But now you've told me I can understand the way he acted after he attacked me. The different voices and speaking in French and German. Revenge for Henri Fabere...and for himself too, I suppose. It's all so bizarre.'

'Do you believe in life after death?' Challis asked.

Keely paused before replying.

'I'm not sure. Do you?'

The reporter shrugged his shoulders.

'I feel the same as you,' he replied. 'Great story, though.'

'Have you any idea when it will be finished?' Keely asked.

'As soon as it is I'll take you on holiday,' and he bent forward and kissed her on the cheek. 'I can't see it taking much longer now.'

Prophetic words, if only Challis had realised it then.

*

Mike Jordan stood by the hospital bed quietly talking to the woman police constable. Shirley Quinn's eyes flickered open every now and then, and the chief inspector gave her a sympathetic smile.

He'd already spoken to the London police handling James Brody's murder and informed them of the attempt on Quinn's life. The police had been anxious to talk to the woman now lying in the bed, and Jordan said he'd let them know when she regained consciousness. They'd spoken to the air hostess Shirley Quinn shared the house with and come up with a man's name. Frank Beckett.

The only trouble was, he drove a distinctive white Porsche sports car.

Jordan was absolutely seething inside. Before he left for the hospital word had reached him of the horrific death of PC Lawson.

Did this man Beckett own two cars? He hoped he'd now find out the answer.

The WPC had written down the words Shirley had spoken since coming to. She'd said Frank Beckett had tried to kill her. He'd killed her boss, Mr Brody, and she must speak to someone called, *Challis.*

'But she's been rambling a bit, sir,' the policewoman said.

Jordan nodded his thanks. *Challis.* So the journalist hadn't been telling him everything after all. He should have known better than to trust the press.

The policeman sat in the chair by the side of the bed and leant forward.

'My name's Chief Inspector Mike Jordan and I'd like to ask you a few questions,' he said in a gentle voice. 'I hope you feel up to it.'

Shirley Quinn moved her head on the pillow and looked at the policeman.

'Feel sleepy,' she said in a soft voice.

'Who's Frank Beckett?' Jordan asked.

'My boyfriend.'

'And he tried to kill you?'

'Yes.'

'Why?'

'Because he killed Mr Brody.'

'And Mr Brody was the man you worked for?'

'Yes.'

'Where does Frank Beckett live?'

The policeman wrote down the Knightsbridge address and telephone number.

'The car your boyfriend tried to run you down with was a blue Granada, is that right?'

'Yes, an old one.'

'And he also drives a white Porsche sports car?'

'Yes.'

'Where is the Porsche now?'

'In Hatfield...I drove it there...it's in a garage now.' Shirley's voice sounded feeble.

'Where's the garage?'

'I don't know.'

'How do you know Challis?'

'He's a reporter...he came to see Mr Brody...I'm tired.'

'Just a couple of more questions, Shirley.'

She smiled weakly.

'Why is Beckett in Hatfield?' Jordan asked.

'I think he's going to kill someone.'

'Who Shirley, who's he going to kill?'

'Don't know...someone in the country...we had a picnic.'

'Where? Where did you have a picnic?'

'Not sure...drove from Hatfield into the country. He wants revenge.'

'Try and remember. Where did you drive to? Shirley, Shirley...'

But Shirley was asleep.

Mike Jordan's thoughts were spinning like a tumble drier. Beckett was going to kill somebody else. Someone in the country. Jordan sat there thinking, the WPC watching him.

Suddenly he smiled and slapped his knee as the obvious hit him. Matthew Hardy, the millionaire whose life was in danger. The case that had been bugging him since he'd got involved.

And some of the men from the Tactical Firearms Unit at his station were on duty at the merchant banker's mansion in the country.

Then that meant this Frank Beckett must be the killer of all those old soldiers!

As the full realisation of his discovery sank in the chief inspector's smile broadened. Did this mean he'd solved the murder mystery?

Of course it did.

But the policeman was under no delusions and knew he'd been lucky enough to be in the right place at the right time. Maybe his wife was right about her superstitions after all.

And he'd probably get a commendation, especially after saving the tax payer a fortune.

Might get promotion as well.

*

Beckett's mind was back on track by the time he drove past Matthew Hardy's main entrance heading for his hiding place where he'd previously parked the Granada that afternoon and

269

had the picnic. Because, he thought rationally, his plans hadn't altered all that much.

Originally, he was just going to use the Ford, and he'd only included Shirley at the last minute to stop her finding out about James Brody. He knew he'd have to dispose of her sometime once he killed her boss and blamed himself for not having done it in the garage this morning.

But he'd still succeed.

He dragged the dead body from the back of the Mondeo and dumped it in the undergrowth. Then he changed back into his black tracksuit top and emptied the contents of the khaki holdall onto his overcoat.

He checked the Ruger semi-automatic and Uzi and decided he'd take just one spare clip for the handgun and three for the machine pistol. Beckett tossed the one remaining hand grenade in his hand and thought maybe he should have brought more from his reserve armoury. But they were in his London lockup garage. He shrugged his shoulders. Too late now.

He pulled a full bottle of whisky from the bag and took a swig, then looked at his watch and settled back against the front wheel of the car. It was starting to get dark earlier than usual and Beckett thought he heard a distant rumble of thunder.

Storm clouds were gathering.

FORTY TWO

Challis arrived outside his flat and had just killed the engine when his mobile rang.

'I didn't know whether to phone or send a patrol car for you,' Mike Jordan said.

Was the policeman being sarcastic? Or was he serious? Challis wasn't sure.

'Who is this?' Don't you know it's an offence to make threatening phone calls? If you don't stop, I'll call the police.'

'Right, Challis, that's it. We haven't met yet, but when we do, I'll have you nicked.'

'Oh, it's you, Chief Inspector. I'm sorry, but I didn't recognise your voice.'

'Don't wind me up, Challis. I know you've not been levelling with me and withholding evidence in a murder inquiry is a serious matter.'

'What do you mean?'

'Shirley Quinn...Frank Beckett...James Brody. How's that for starters?'

'What about them?'

'Brody is dead and the Quinn woman is seriously injured in a hospital near Hatfield. Beckett tried to kill her. She's been asking for you.'

The journalist's thoughts were jumping ahead of his words, but managed to keep his voice calm.

'Hatfield,' he said, 'Mathew Hardy lives out that way.'

'That's right, and I believe this man, Frank Beckett, is going to try and kill him tonight. What do you know about Beckett?'

'I've never met him.'

'I didn't ask that, Challis. I asked what do you *know* about him?'

'I think he's Shirley Quinn's boyfriend.'

'I could have told you that. What else do you know?'

'He could possibly be the murderer you're looking for.'

'Why didn't you tell me about him before?'

'Because I wasn't sure and didn't want to give the police wrong information.'

'I thought you were finished with this story,' Jordan said. 'You told me you were chasing some big TV star.'

'I am, but I suddenly got involved again.'

'What are you trying to wriggle out of, Challis?'

The journalist ignored the question.

'Are you over at Hardy's place now?' he asked.

'That's none of your business.'

'Well, that's where I'm going.'

'The police won't let you in.'

'Matthew Hardy will, so I don't see how you can stop me.'

'Okay,' Jordan said in a resigned voice. 'I'm on my way there. I'll leave word at the front entrance that you're coming.'

'And my photographer, Steve White. He'll be arriving after me.'

'Okay,' Jordan said, and abruptly broke the connection.

You didn't have to be a mind reader to know Mike Jordan was not a happy policeman. So what was going to happen when the full story appeared? He'd probably have a coronary, and Challis immediately knew it would be a good idea if he went on the missing list as soon as the headlines hit the streets. Anyway, he'd promised Keely a holiday.

Challis phoned Steve's number and quickly repeated what Jordan had told him.

'Drop everything and find out what hospital Shirley Quinn's in. It'll be a local one. And then go and photograph her in bed.

If she's conscious say I'll see her as soon as possible. Tell her she can't avoid being in the story so she might as well earn some money out of it. She mustn't talk to any other reporters, only me, and if she co-operates I'll go easy on her...give her the usual spiel.'

'Yes Challis, don't worry, I know the routine.'

'Do you think you can get hold of Des?'

'He'll be with his girlfriend.'

'Well, try, and if you do, tell him there's a lot of dosh in it for him. But if you can't contact him make sure another photographer meets me at Mathew Hardy's, and tell whoever's coming to mention my name or the police won't let them in. Also, when you've finished at the hospital get over to Hardy's place and join me as soon as possible.'

Challis gave Steve the banker's full address and phone number then restarted his motor and headed north towards the motorway.

He felt the same excitement running through him he used to get when he stepped into the ring for a fight.

The journalist wondered how Beckett felt.

*

Tessa poured two glasses of chilled wine and handed one to the security guard. Then she turned off the bedside light, drew back the heavy curtains and stood looking out at the floodlit gardens and beyond to the small copse shrouded in shadow. Varney joined her, his left hand gently running up and down her back.

'Do you know something, Tom,' she said.

'Know what?'

'I'm really looking forward to later.'

Their plan had been hatched yesterday evening when Tessa had told Varney she'd always wanted to make love in the open air but never had the opportunity.

'It's something I've always wanted to try, doing it on the grass.' She turned facing him, her hand softly rubbing his groin.

'You'll enjoy it,' he said, feeling himself stiffen at her tender touch. He grabbed her hand and pulled it from him. 'I've still got work to do.'

They had decided to satisfy Tessa's fantasy in the trees she was now staring at through the window. Although the estate was under tight security Varney had done several stints patrolling the grounds before the police arrived, and knew of at least one spot where he could get from the back of the house to the small woods without too much difficulty. He'd had a word with the guard by the pool, but other than him, nobody would see their route.

'Give her one for me,' his friend had said, and with that assurance Varney had arranged to have a later meal break.

He knew how enthusiastic Tessa was about her idea and didn't want to disappoint her but he had a nagging feeling something was up. Just before he'd visited Tessa's room, John Conway, Cassidy's right hand man, had been in urgent conversation with the inspector in charge of the police. Years of training had given the ex-para a nose for trouble, but he didn't want to mention his fears to her.

'You won't let me down, will you?' she asked, her hand wandering again.

'As long as there's no emergency tonight, you're on,' he said, and cupped her chin in his hand. 'I won't be able to be away for more than an hour, so just wear a skirt and top, no underwear,' he grinned cheekily. 'It'll save time.'

'My thoughts entirely.'

*

It had suddenly got pitch black and the air was oppressive as Challis hurtled along the motorway at ninety miles an hour.

The impending storm was badly needed. The humidity was unbearable.

The BMW began to slow and, just as the turnoff sign the journalist wanted appeared, his mobile rang. It was Steve.

'I managed to get hold of Des and we're both on our way,' he said.

'Where are you now?'

'I've been on the A1 for about five minutes, I'm in the van.'

'That's means you're not all that far behind me. Did you find out which hospital Shirley Quinn's in?'

'Yes, and I've got my white coat with me.'

'You make a good doctor,' Challis said.

*

It had taken the black clad figure twenty five minutes to jog from his hiding place along the country lanes to the farmer's field and his point of entry to the banker's estate. The run was uneventful and only once had to duck into a dry ditch as car headlights appeared.

Beckett found the oak tree and hauled himself up the nylon rope, his running shoes gripping the tree trunk. When he reached the thick branch on the other side of the hedge he adjusted the Uzi tucked inside his tracksuit top before lowering his weight to the ground.

The sound of thunder was getting louder, and moving closer.

FORTY THREE

The unmarked car stopped by the police guards for a moment then crunched its way up the long driveway. As soon as it came to a halt Chief Inspector Mike Jordan was out of the passenger seat and running up the steps to the banker's mansion. The front door opened and he was greeted by Inspector Gordon Weller, the uniformed officer in charge of police security.

They'd spoken on the phone not long ago and hurriedly made arrangements for more armed men to be sent to Hardy's estate.

'They should be here in about half an hour,' Weller said.

'Good,' and the two policemen went looking for Matthew Hardy.

*

John Conway was annoyed. The police had told him about Beckett but given instructions that once reinforcements arrived neither of his men, or Conway himself, were to be involved and they must stay in their rooms until further notice.

'Mind you, this Beckett fellow must know we're on to him, so these extra men will probably be a waste of manpower,' Inspector Weller had told him. 'I doubt very much if he will show his face around here now.'

Conway tended to agree and passed on the instructions to Tom Varney and Bill Reece, the only men he'd been allowed to keep on once the police had taken over after Bernie Harris's death.

Then he'd complained to Matthew Hardy about the police interference, and their latest orders.

'Don't worry about it,' the banker had replied. 'You're doing a great job and I believe the same as the police. I think Beckett will have been frightened off, and now they know who he is, it won't be long before they catch him.'

This was the view he still held and was repeating to Chief Inspector Jordan on the terrace.

'No, I'm not going in the house yet. I'm quite satisfied with your protection and I really don't think anything will happen tonight, tomorrow night, or any other night. If the man has got any sense then he will be long gone from here and trying to think of a way to avoid arrest. He could even be out of the country by now.'

That was the problem, Jordan thought, Beckett didn't seem to have any sense. Only a madman could have killed all those people.

'And besides,' Hardy continued, 'it's too hot indoors. There's a storm brewing and I promise you as soon as it starts to rain my wife and I will go inside. How's that?'

The policeman wasn't happy, but if the millionaire had made up his mind, there wasn't much he could do about it.

'Right you are, sir.'

*

Once Tom Varney got Conway's news he went straight to Tessa's room. Ironically, it was nine o'clock, the time she was expecting him.

'I'm sorry, but things have altered,' he said.

'What do you mean, Tom?'

'It looks as though we won't be going for our walk in the woods after all.'

'Oh, don't say that,' she said, her face crestfallen. 'I've been looking forward to it all day.'

277

'I know,' he said, and told her the reason for the change of plan.

'Well then, it seems there's hardly any chance at all this man will try anything tonight,' she said, sounding relieved. 'Does it mean you're free now?'

'Yes, but I'm supposed to stay in my room.'

'Like a good little boy? Tom, you're a grown man, nobody can tell you what to do. I'm willing to take a chance, so why not you? Look...'

Tessa pulled her tight black sweater up over her full breasts then did the same to her stretch black mini, which was so short, she only had to hike it up a few inches to reveal her pubic area. Why she'd ever packed this skirt in the first place she never knew - but was now glad she had.

'...no knickers or bra, just like you wanted.'

Varney knew he shouldn't but, like many a good man before him, lust won over logic. His friend was still on duty by the pool so there was no problem there, and when he was replaced by a policeman Tom figured it would be easy enough to make an excuse for him and Tessa on their way back. But...he was disobeying orders...and that bothered him.

Varney tried to reassure himself that Beckett wouldn't show anyway and made an instant decision.

'Okay, Tessa, we'll go. You know your way to the pool?'

'Yes,' she nodded, and rearranged her clothes.

'You go first, take your time and wait underneath the brick terrace. Your boss is on the top but he won't see you. I'll only be a couple of minutes after you and then I'll lead the way.'

Varney picked up his small leather bag before he left the room.

*

Beckett moved cautiously to the rotten tree trunk on the ground and retrieved the long camouflaged case. He took out the Soviet sniper rifle, put the case back in its hiding place, then moved towards the house.

Just before he reached the spot where the copse ended and the neatly trimmed lawns began he changed direction, stopping in front of a large conifer tree. He'd climbed the tree before and knew exactly the best vantage point. Beckett slung the rifle over his shoulder and began his ascent.

He reached the place which enabled him to stand on a thick branch with his back firm against the trunk of the tree and gave him a clear view of the rear of the house and swimming pool. He lifted the weapon to his shoulder, looked through the image intensifying night sight, and moved the rifle slowly in a sweeping arc. He rested the barrel on another branch, slightly adjusted the sight and gave a grunt of satisfaction as the images on a green background came into focus. Perfect.

Two men, one in police uniform, had just walked away from the two figures seated at a table on the terrace overlooking the swimming pool. One was Matthew Hardy and, Beckett presumed, the woman sitting opposite was his wife.

The marksman sighted on Hardy's head and his finger started to gently squeeze the trigger, then stopped and relaxed. The financier had suddenly moved forward and laughed, then quickly ran down the terrace steps. His wife swiftly followed and they both dived in the pool.

Beckett kept his eye firmly fixed to the night scope. He would wait until they got back to the table.

*

The couple had reached the trees without being seen and made their way through the small woods. The police hardly went into the copse at night, preferring to patrol the open grounds, the possibility of an ambush only too obvious. Any intruder wishing to gain access to the large country house

279

would have to cross the floodlit gardens anyway, and the police had concentrated on that area.

Tom Varney was well aware of this as he led Tessa by the hand and wasn't worried about any clumsy copper stumbling over them. He reached a spot where there was a large patch of grass in a slight hollow, stopped and gently pushed the eager woman to the ground.

*

Challis slowed down as his headlights picked out the police car and motorcycle. Jordan had left word that the journalist should be let through but the two armed policemen, wearing bullet proof vests, wouldn't let the BMW pass until they'd double checked. Challis reminded them about Steve and added Des's name to the sheet of paper on a clipboard one of them was holding.

He arrived at the house and a policeman sporting a holstered pistol opened the front door to Challis. He told him Jordan was in the drawing room and Matthew Hardy was on the terrace with his wife. The journalist decided to see the policeman first. Get it over and done with.

Challis opened the door to the large room and saw two men, one in uniform, deep in conversation. They looked up at the interruption.

'Who are you?'

Challis grinned, and stuck out his right hand as he introduced himself. Jordan completed the handshake and allowed the flicker of a smile to cross his face. He didn't have a lot to do with the press but was well aware of their influence. This Challis bloke looked all right, but he *had* withheld information. The policeman was wary.

'We finally meet in person,' he said.

'Chief Inspector,' Challis paused. 'Are you still going to arrest me?'

Jordan shook his head and gave the journalist a hard look.

'I must say you're a cheeky bastard, but you're lucky today. I've got too much else on my mind at the moment. Don't forget though, I'm in charge. I don't want any heroes trying to make a name for themselves.'

'You don't have to worry about that.'

Jordan introduced his uniformed colleague who said he was going to have to leave because he was expecting more of his men to arrive any minute.

'Have you met Matthew Hardy?' Challis asked.

'Yes, just a little while ago,' Jordan replied.

'Well, I'd like to have a word with him. I believe he's on the terrace. Do you know where it is?'

'Sure, I'll take you.'

They left the drawing room and headed for the terrace, the policeman showing the way.

As Challis and Jordan went through the glass doors leading to the marble tiled swimming pool they saw a man and woman laughing and splashing each other. The journalist walked to the side near the terrace steps out into the open air. After a few moments Hardy saw him and swam over.

'Hello, I suppose you've heard the news,' he said, his arms supporting him on the edge of the pool. His wife joined him and they both climbed out of the water, grabbing their brightly coloured robes lying on the bottom steps.

'Sorry,' he continued,' you never met my wife the last time you were here.'

Challis shook Karen's hand. She was a good looking woman.

'Let's go and sit down,' Hardy said, 'and then I'll get some drinks.' A sudden roll of thunder, the closest yet, resounded through the still night air. 'Before it rains,' the banker added, as a distant flash of white lightning split the black heavens.

The group started to climb the steps.

Des arrived on the Yamaha just as the patrol car and motorcycle moved to one side allowing another unmarked police car to ease through the entrance.

After gaining clearance the photographer followed the vehicle up the driveway and when it stopped made himself known to the four policemen wearing body armour and carrying Heckler and Koch submachine guns.

'Wouldn't like to get shot by mistake,' he said.

The remark fell flat on the grim faced men as they slipped ballistic helmets on their heads.

One of the armed men immediately started patrolling the front gardens and the remaining three filed round the side towards the rear of the property. Des grabbed his camera equipment from the plastic pannier on the bike and followed.

Inspector Weller was waiting by an open pair of French windows at the back and gave instructions to the leader of the armed policemen. Two of the men began searching amongst the shrubbery and flower beds nearest the rear of the mansion, and the remaining policeman accompanied the inspector in the direction of the swimming pool, the replacement for Bill Reece.

They walked past the back of the high raised terrace until they came to the end and saw the security guard staring intently in front of him. Weller followed his gaze just in time to see the banker, his wife, Mike Jordan and the reporter he'd just met start to climb the steps.

Frank Beckett's eyes had also been busy since the high powered sound of the Yamaha alerted his ears, and he dimly saw figures suddenly appear, moving in and out of the floodlit area and shadows cast by large shrubs. He'd already spotted the lone policeman patrolling the gardens and realised these other men were reinforcements.

He returned his attention to the night scope and stiffened as he saw images slowly walking up the terrace steps towards the large wrought iron table and chairs.

The figures began to come into focus and Beckett picked out the banker and kept the scope on him until the four people were grouped by the table.

He was perspiring heavily under the black woollen face mask, the sweat trickling into his eyes, and pulled it off his head in one quick movement. He sighted once again.

Another man, now talking to the banker, was partly obscured as Beckett lined up the cross hairs on the back of Hardy's head, his finger resting gently against the trigger. Suddenly, the other man's face came into view. It was *Challis*, and an incredulous look of anger flashed into Beckett's eyes, making him snatch at the trigger. The bullet missed its intended spot and caught Matthew Hardy high in the right shoulder slamming him into the journalist, sending them both crashing onto the paved ground.

The reason Jordan and the banker's wife immediately dropped to their knees was an instant reflex to discover what had happened to the fallen men. Neither of them realised Hardy had been shot, the multi coloured robe hiding any sign of blood, but that response undoubtedly saved their lives as several more bullets ricocheted off the metal table smashing drinking glasses.

Bill Reece had seen enough action in the first Gulf War to realise from the initial shot what was happening. The security guard instantly jumped up from his chair and shouted to the two policemen walking towards him.

'Over there, someone is firing from the trees over there,' and then ran along the side of the pool and up the terrace steps.

By the time Reece arrived at the top Challis had freed himself from the weight of Hardy and in doing so realised the stickiness on his hands was blood. Hardy groaned but was still conscious.

'You'll be all right, so don't worry,' Chief Inspector Jordan said, as he carefully pulled away the robe.

Reece looked over the policeman's shoulder and saw the wound wasn't life threatening but knew the banker would be a lot safer inside the house. He unzipped his small leather bag and withdrew a .32 Browning automatic.

'Can you walk?' he asked.

'Yes,' Hardy nodded, and gritted his teeth.

'Once I start firing all of you get down the steps and into the house as quick as you can,' Reece said, and pulled the heavy table on to its side.

'Ready?' he asked, then steadying the gun in both hands crouched behind the table and aimed in the direction he thought the sniper had fired from. He quickly emptied the eight shot magazine, ejected the clip and pulled a spare from the leather bag. By the time he'd fired the other eight shots the three men and woman were safely out of sight.

Reece slipped the remaining clip into the Browning and followed them.

FORTY FOUR

Even when Beckett saw the banker fall he knew he'd only wounded him and fired three more times in quick succession. The sudden shock of seeing Challis's face appear in the night sight had momentarily distracted his aim.

Maybe he should have switched targets and killed the journalist. But Beckett knew that was stupid thinking, and forced his feelings under control. He had a job to do, a mission to complete, and military discipline to adhere to. He inhaled deeply and let his breath out slowly.

Then the sound of returning fire from the terrace instantly made him realise he had a fight on his hands. Different from the other times.

He tilted the rifle downwards and saw two men running towards the trees. He sighted on the uniformed policeman, not wearing body protection, pulled the trigger and saw him stop in his tracks and flip sideways as the heavy calibre bullet struck him in the chest. The man running behind immediately threw himself on the ground and Beckett heard the rapid sound of gunfire. Bullets ripped into the branches of the next tree but didn't deter the sniper as he calmly aimed at the four floodlights mounted on the brickwork at the rear of the house. He took them out one by one, plunging the lawns and gardens into near darkness, the only light now coming from the swimming pool and rooms in the mansion.

There was just one more bullet left in the ten round magazine of the Dragunov rifle and Beckett concentrated on the shrubbery where he'd seen the reinforcements. Movement caught his eye as he looked through the image intensifying sight and saw the man was wearing body armour and a hard helmet. Beckett lowered the sight and took careful aim. He squeezed the trigger and saw the policeman fall clutching his thigh.

Beckett wedged the sniper rifle between branches, nimbly climbed down and as soon as his feet touched the ground removed the Uzi from inside his tracksuit. He slipped the mask back on and took his bearings.

*

Tom Varney quickly withdrew from Tessa as the first shots reached his ears and placed two fingers over her lips before she could speak.

'Shush,' he whispered, his mouth pressed against her ear. 'Stay here, and don't make a sound.'

The security guard adjusted himself and buttoned up the front of his black jeans. Then he unzipped his small leather bag, removed the Browning automatic and put the two spare clips in his jeans back pockets.

He leant down again close to Tessa.

'I won't be long,' he said, 'but make sure you don't move. I'll come back for you as soon as I can.'

Tessa didn't say a word but managed a small nod as Varney disappeared in the darkness.

By the time he reached the edge of the trees the floodlights had been extinguished.

Varney crouched there waiting and listening between the sounds of thunder, every now and then the landscape illuminated by sheet lightning.

*

They helped Matthew Hardy to his office and laid him on a leather couch. The banker's wife produced a first aid box from the kitchen and, after her husband's smiling assurance he would live, went looking for the rest of their family, a worried look on her face.

Mike Jordan took control of the situation and ordered an ambulance, not that it would do Inspector Weller much good. He was dead - and another policeman had just been brought into the room suffering from a leg wound.

Des had been just feet away from the man when he was shot and dragged him through the open French windows into the house. He assisted the policeman through the drawing room into the hall where another policeman showed him to the banker's office.

As soon as John Conway entered the room Bill Reece, who had discreetly returned his gun to the leather pouch, informed him of the incident by the pool. Conway listened intently, then asked, 'Where's Tom?'

'I don't know,' Reece lied. 'Maybe he's outside seeing what's happening. I'm sure he'll be here soon.'

Challis was standing next to Jordan as he came off the phone, but had to wait while he had a word with the policeman who'd been on guard at the front door when the journalist first arrived.

'What are you going to do now?' Challis asked.

'Wait,' was the terse reply, and the two men stood looking at each other.

'More people are getting killed.'

'No need to rub it in.'

Then the policeman Jordan had given instructions to came back into the room.

'The entrance is clear for the ambulance to come straight in and the motorcyclist will escort it to the front door,' he said. 'The other man is coming to the house now.'

'That means there will be nobody on guard at the entrance,' Challis said.

'No need,' Jordan said. 'Beckett's already in the grounds, so I've ordered all my men to group in the house. He's already killed one and wounded another. I think we'll be safer inside.'

Jordan looked at the uniformed policeman.

'How many men will that be?'

'Seven, with your driver, but that's not including the wounded one, or the policeman on the motorbike.'

Jordan called John Conway to him.

'Could you, and your man over there,' Jordan motioned to Bill Reece, 'go with one of my men and make sure all the doors and windows are secure. You know the layout of the house better than most of us.'

Chief Inspector Jordan then delegated one of his men to guard the rest of Matthew Hardy's family and servants, and the others to patrol the ground floor.

'And when the ambulance arrives I want two of you on the front door.'

Challis went over to Des.

'Let's have a look around the rest of the house,' he said, and the two men slipped out of the room.

*

Beckett knew an ambulance would have to be called for the wounded men and made his way through the trees to the point where they ended closest to the side of the house nearest the driveway.

He then laid flat on his stomach and wriggled his way across the smoothly cut lawn towards a large Rhododendron bush, stopping motionless several times when streaks of lightning split the darkness.

He reached the five foot high bush and crouched, the Uzi machine pistol in his left hand and a grenade in his other. Minutes later he heard the strident sound of the siren gradually getting closer.

288

*

As soon as Varney heard the sound of the approaching ambulance he immediately guessed what the gunman would do and raced across the lawn to a rose bed near the house. He dropped on the ground and moved closer to the building, edging towards the gravel drive, only stopping when the steps leading to the white painted front door came into view. Moments later the ambulance arrived, escorted by a police motorcycle, and crunched to a halt. Two ambulance men jumped out the front, opened the back doors, grabbed a stretcher and, as they ran up the front steps, the heavy panelled door was opened by an armed policeman.

After a couple of minutes they reappeared carrying the man with the leg wound, a policeman with a submachine leading the way, another following behind the stretcher. When they reached the bottom of the steps Matthew Hardy was helped into the doorway by Mike Jordan and Challis.

Varney raised himself to his knees and looked around him, his eyes straining in the darkness. Suddenly, a bolt of lightning zigzagging across the sky briefly turned night into day and the security guard saw a shadowy shape move from the cover of a large bush. Varney quickly lifted the Browning automatic and loosed off two shots, then stood and yelled towards the ambulance.

'Get back inside...get back.'

He fired twice more, steadying the gun with both hands, and saw the black clad figure slightly stumble and turn in his direction, then had to dive for cover as a spray of bullets thudded into the earth by his feet.

Beckett gave another spurt from the Uzi then continued running towards the brightly lit front of the house. He'd felt the bullet nick his side but it was the shock more than anything that had made him falter in his stride.

289

There were bursts of shots now coming from the police by the stretcher as Beckett weaved from side to side narrowing the distance. Forty yards...thirty yards...at twenty Beckett pulled the pin from the fragmentation grenade and lobbed the small pineapple shape in the direction of the ambulance. It seemed to curl in slow motion before it plunged to the gravel and exploded, sending pieces of shrapnel in all directions. Both the ambulance men were blown off their feet, blood pouring from ripped uniforms. The armed policeman at the front was hurled several feet on to the rough driveway, groaning and holding his legs, while the policeman strapped to the stretcher stared lifelessly upwards, blood pumping from a neck wound. The motorcycle cop stood rigid by his bike, untouched, but momentarily in a state of shock.

Beckett dropped to his knees, emptied the remainder of the clip in the Uzi, then snapped another magazine in the pistol grip and sprayed more bullets at the front steps.

The group standing in the doorway staggered back to safety as bullets tore chunks out of the wood surround and smashed the glass panes on either side of the door. The policeman who'd been walking behind the stretcher just made it back to the top of the steps when a burst from the Uzi caught him. He fell through the doorway, his left arm hanging uselessly, blood dripping on the floor. Two policemen rushed forward and fired through the shattered panes towards the flashes coming from the garden.

'Get another fucking ambulance here,' Jordan shouted to Challis, making himself heard over the gunfire, 'no, make it two.'

The journalist hurried away, sensibly switching off the front and hall lights.

One of the policemen stopped firing and motioned his partner to do the same.

Silence.

'He's stopped.'

'Maybe...'

The policeman dropped to the floor and inched through the doorway, then paused as he heard a shout.

'That's Tom Varney,' John Conway said, as he and Bill Reece joined the group, carrying powerful flashlights.

FORTY FIVE

Matthew Hardy's wife, alerted by the noise and gunfire, arrived in the hallway accompanied by two other women, the banker's elderly mother, and the housekeeper.

Mother and wife helped the banker back into his office while the housekeeper went to the aid of the shot policeman.

'Don't worry about the wounded, we'll see to them,' Karen said.

Mike Jordan nodded his thanks.

'There are more ambulances on the way,' he said. 'They shouldn't be long.'

Then the chief inspector put on the wounded policeman's body armour, picked up his Heckler and Koch submachine gun and did a mental head count. One of the ambulance men was only slightly hurt and able to give assistance to the injured outside the front of the house, and the motorcycle policeman had now snapped out of it and was giving what help he could.

Jordan ordered two of his men to guard the house and John Conway said he'd better stay to help protect his client. He handed his large flashlight to Reece, with orders to pass it on to Tom.

That left four policemen plus the chief inspector and two security guards.

A voice outside made the group of men turn.

'He's run back to the trees,' Tom Varney said, as he stood at the bottom of the steps openly holding the Browning automatic.

'Let's go then,' Jordan snapped, and raced outside into the darkness, followed by his men. Challis had been hovering in the background, his phone call for more medical help made. Silently, he and Des sprinted down the steps after them.

Brilliant lightning made jigsaw shapes in the black sky and seconds later ear-splitting loud cracks of thunder reverberated around the banker's estate. Horses in the stables were making noises. A few spots of heavy rain spattered on the grass. The storm was directly overhead.

They reached the trees but agreed not to use the flashlights yet. No point giving the gunman something to aim at.

'Now what?' Jordan asked. 'Who knows the area?'

'At the back of these trees there's a large perimeter hedge that stretches for hundreds of yards,' Varney replied. 'But he won't be able to climb over it, its hawthorn and he'd cut himself to pieces.'

They decided to split the group into two. Jordan, two policemen and Bill Reece would go in one direction, and Varney and the two remaining policemen would search in the opposite direction.

If Beckett had got in this way - then he must have an escape route planned.

'What are you two doing here?' Jordan asked, as Challis and his photographer appeared.

'We're coming,' Challis replied.

The chief inspector looked as though he might object but instead said in a strained voice, 'Okay then, I haven't got time to argue. Just stay out the way.'

Challis also thought it a good idea to split and told Des to go with Jordan's group.

There was a deep rumble of thunder, quickly followed by another, and then the threatening rain poured down in torrents. The driving water so heavy it stung the men's faces and, within a minute, the grass underfoot was as slippery as a skating rink. Challis shaded his eyes and felt the ferocity of the rain bounce off his hand as he followed in the rear.

The small group carefully eased their passage through the copse and began to work their way along the hedge in the direction away from the house. Tom Varney purposely avoiding the spot where he'd left Tessa, hoping she'd obeyed his instructions and stayed put.

But she hadn't.

When Tom left her Tessa hadn't felt scared for the first five minutes but the sound of shots, loud thunderclaps and lightning had started to play tricks with her imagination. During the brief flashes of light she was positive flickering shadows were about to attack her, and when the downpour began decided to make her way back towards the safety of the mansion.

Tessa had crept along slowly for about fifty yards when she suddenly felt a hand clamped over her mouth and something hard shoved in her back.

'Don't make a sound or I'll kill you,' Beckett snarled. 'Make no mistake about that. If you scream or shout you're dead.'

He released his hand and prodded his trembling hostage in front of him, cautiously heading towards the conifer trees hiding his escape hole. Tessa was numb with terror and blindly stumbled through the undergrowth, her mouth tight with fear, too scared to look at the man behind her.

The storm was increasing in its intensity and the woman slipped on a patch of earth and leaves, now a muddy mess, and pitched headlong.

'Get up and keep moving,' Beckett hissed, and pulled Tessa up by one elbow, pushing her forward.

The rain was now so torrential it was making it difficult to see for Beckett's pursuers, even with the lightning, so Tom Varney switched on his powerful torch, not realising how close he was to his quarry.

Beckett immediately saw the bright beam of light over to his left and knew he had to make faster time if he was going to get to his spot first. He shoved the Uzi inside his tracksuit, picked up Tessa in both arms, her short skirt riding up over her bare buttocks, and charged through the conifers until they reached the high hedge. He kicked in several places before finding the weak spot and moved back a few yards. Then, holding Tessa in front of him as protection prepared to run straight at the concealed gap but before he could do so was caught in the glare of the torch and heard shouts. He whirled around.

'Don't shoot,' Varney screamed to his companions as he recognised the human shield Beckett was holding. The two policemen with him slid to a stop and Challis fell to one knee behind a tree.

Beckett dropped Tessa's feet to the ground, pulled out the Uzi and held the gun to the side of the frightened woman's head.

'Drop your weapons,' he shouted at the three men in front of him. 'Put down your guns, or I'll shoot the woman,' and tightened his forearm over Tessa's throat.

'Don't let him kill me,' she pleaded, her voice high-pitched with fear.

'All right, all right,' Tom Varney shouted, and faced the two policemen. 'Do as he says,' and threw his Browning automatic down on the soggy grass.

'I'm not going to say it again,' Beckett yelled above the rain and thunder.

The policemen looked at each other but knew they had no choice and threw their submachine guns to the ground.

'Now move away from them,' and as they obeyed there was a sudden burst of gunfire from the Uzi and the three men felt the bullets tear through their legs, knocking them over in writhing agony.

295

'You bastard,' Tessa screamed, and grabbed Beckett's gun hand biting deep with her strong teeth. The Uzi dropped to the grass and Beckett pushed the woman from him with a curse and bent down to retrieve it.

Without hesitation Challis sprang up, covered the ten feet distance in a few strides, and kicked Beckett hard in the side of the head. The force knocked him sideways and he rolled over but came to his feet in one fluid movement. Then his eyes opened wide in amazement as he saw the face of his attacker.

'*You*,' he spat out.

Challis crouched into a fighter's stance, threw a straight left into Beckett's masked face, and quickly repeated the punch before his opponent had time to think. He felt the other man's nose break but Beckett just shook his head and hurled himself forward at the journalist. Challis moved slightly to one side and whacked Beckett hard on the jaw knocking him once more to the ground. This time he stayed down, but as Challis closed in on him, Beckett ferociously threw out his arms and upended the reporter. They grappled on the sodden ground, their clothes and hair plastered to them by the pelting rain, but Challis managed to get in a head butt before being pushed to one side as Beckett's hand fastened on the dropped Uzi. The feeling of the gun seemed to give him extra strength and he pushed himself upwards. Challis, quickly seeing the danger, leapt up too. Beckett didn't have time to aim and swung the gun hard against Challis's temple, who fell back on the grass, and wisely kept rolling to make himself a difficult target from any bullets.

But Beckett had turned away and grabbed Tessa who was still sprawled on the grass praying to stay alive. She offered no resistance as she was lifted up into the gunman's arms and couldn't help but stare in terror as Beckett rushed straight at the concealed gap in the hedge. Although the cut hawthorn had been loosely put back only as camouflage it still slashed into Tessa's face and she screamed out loud in pain.

As Beckett disappeared Challis got to his feet and put a hand on his throbbing head where the Uzi had caught him. Then he heard one of the policemen talking to Chief Inspector Jordan over his radio phone asking for help.

'Get a fucking gun,' the other policeman shouted, as he tried to crawl to one of the weapons laying on the grass, his face grimacing with pain.

'I'm not sure how to use one,' Challis shouted back over the thunder, but picked up one of the Heckler and Koch submachine guns.

'Here, give it the fuck to me,' and the policeman checked to see the safety catch was off. 'All you've got to do is aim and pull the trigger.'

He returned the weapon to Challis.

'Better take this too,' and Tom Varney thrust the heavy torch into his other hand.

As Challis ran through the hole in the hedge he heard a voice shout, 'The others will be following any minute.'

When he reached the other side of the gap Challis paused and crouched. He was in a field and apprehensive about switching on the torch and giving away his position.

Another massive crack of thunder followed by a brilliant flash of light illuminated the open space and the journalist saw two figures less than a hundred yards in front of him. Challis ran bent double towards them and after fifty yards he stopped and switched on the flashlight. Then there was a sudden burst of gunfire and the journalist flung himself face down. More lightning and Challis cautiously looked upwards. The figures were much closer, but one was now on the ground being dragged along by the other.

Challis got to his feet and moved forward, this time more slowly and carefully. He couldn't be far away. He stuck out his left arm away from his body and flicked on the torch, ready to drop it if Beckett fired. Then another beam of light stabbed through the darkness and Challis followed it, pinpointing the masked figure standing erect. Challis lowered his torch and lifted the submachine gun to his shoulder as the Uzi opened fire again. The journalist aimed high, scared of hitting the woman laying on the ground, and pulled the trigger, the unfamiliar object jumping in his hands.

Challis heard gunfire coming from behind him and saw Beckett stagger and fall. Then the wounded man levered himself up to his feet, cupped a hand to his mouth and shouted, the words lost in a rumble of thunder. Continuous streaks of white lightning lit up the night like flares above a battleground.

Beckett held the Uzi once more in front of him spitting streams of bullets, drawing returning fire from the kneeling police marksmen. Challis kept his finger on the trigger as bullets thudded into the lone figure sending him flying backwards onto the saturated earth.

This time Beckett didn't get up.

Challis sank to his knees and turned his face upwards into the lashing rain, but twisted around when his name was called.

'Give me the gun, Challis,' and Chief Inspector Jordan stood there with one arm outstretched. 'You didn't fire this weapon, understand?'

The journalist did as he was told and handed over the Heckler and Koch as he got to his feet.

'What's the matter? Scared you might not get all the credit?'

'Don't be a stupid prick,' Jordan retorted, 'this case is complicated enough without me explaining what a civilian was doing shooting at a member of the public with police property. So, you didn't even touch this gun. You got that?'

Challis suddenly realised the chief inspector was doing him a favour and gave a grateful smile.

'Of course,' he replied, and added, 'thanks.'

The policeman returned the smile, the tension gone from his face.

'I must say you're a brave bastard,' he said. 'Anyway, don't let it bother you. You probably missed him.'

The journalist stared hard at the ground for a long moment before he lifted his eyes and looked directly at Jordan.

'But I'll never know for sure. Will I?'

And that bothered Challis.

FORTY SIX

Challis threw back the duvet, headed straight for the shower and stood under the stinging spray washing the cobwebs from his mind. It had been a hectic night and he hadn't got to bed until four. But at least he'd been able to sleep peacefully in his own flat knowing Frank Beckett was dead.

Fortunately, Tessa Seddon was alive when they'd reached her. She'd passed out with fear and her worst injuries were a few deep scratches on her face which should soon heal.

Chief Inspector Mike Jordan had shown great organizing skills once the shooting stopped and very soon had the situation under control.

Des had got some graphic pictures and Steve had arrived, annoyed that he'd missed the excitement, but with the news Shirley Quinn had agreed to talk only to Challis. Then Jordan made it plain that he'd appreciate it if the press were out of the way as soon as possible. So they'd headed back to London.

But when Challis had got inside his flat, bed was the last thing on his mind. His adrenaline was flowing and he'd immediately gone into his office and started writing.

It was still only seven o'clock and, even after only three hours sleep, Challis was still pumping energy. He finished dressing, and went back behind his desk, all the time going over the story he'd written in the early hours. There were still bits to add, but he'd broken the back of it, and the journalist was satisfied with his work. However, he did need more background on Beckett. More family stuff. Challis flicked through his notes until he found his interview with Pauline

Fountain and the names of Beckett's brother, Randolph, and his family company.

The journalist looked at his watch. It was a bit early to start tracking him down and decided to phone later in the morning.

He sat back in his chair thinking about the previous evening. That had been packed with enough excitement to last most people a lifetime. But thankfully, most things had turned out pretty good.

Matthew Hardy would be out of hospital later today and the wounded from the grenade attack were recovering well. The worst injuries had been sustained by the two policemen and Tom Varney when Beckett had callously shot them in the legs.

Chief Inspector Mike Jordan had been tactful enough not to make a big issue about the security guards being armed. In fact, Varney had probably saved the day, but Jordan was going to get all the credit. It would be simpler that way the chief inspector's superiors decided, and Challis had agreed to go along with that because it wouldn't make much difference to his story.

So the police just gave Gerry Cassidy a private warning, and told him his men mustn't carry guns in the future, *or else*. The warning hadn't bothered the security boss. He'd done the job he was supposed to do and knew word of his success would reach the right people. A grateful Matthew Hardy would see to that.

Shirley Quinn was also on the mend and Challis was going to the hospital this afternoon for a heart to heart. She'd spoken further to the police and told them about the strong painkillers and her suspicions that Beckett might have suffered from a brain tumour. The police said they'd tell the pathologist before he did the post-mortem.

Chief Inspector Mike Jordan was now happy and so were his hierarchy. The London, Southampton, Sheffield and other murders up north had been solved, and the .22 Ruger and commando knife found on Beckett's body had been identified as two of the murder weapons. The police were sticking with Bernie Harris's theory for the motive although there was one question they still couldn't answer.

Why had Beckett taken on the role as Giles Faraday's avenger?

Challis felt slightly guilty because of the favour Jordan had done him, but they would have to wait and find out at the same time as the public. Otherwise it wouldn't be an *exclusive* - and there was no way he was going to lose out on that.

The ringing of the phone interrupted his thoughts. It was Keely.

'I've just had breakfast with Steve and he told me all about last night. Sounded pretty scary to me.'

Challis laughed.

'You can say that again. In future I think I'll stick to good old fashioned sex scandals, and leave the murders to the police...much safer.'

'Are you sure you're all right?'

'I'm fine,' he assured her.

Keely said Steve had offered to take her home and she'd speak to Challis later in the day.

'Don't forget, Keely, today's Friday, and by tomorrow night I want both of us out of the country for a two week holiday at least. So start thinking about somewhere you'd like to go, and let me know.'

After he put down the phone Challis checked through his copy changing a bit here and there. As he read the words he began to understand how Bernie Harris had felt when he'd wondered if it had been his bullet which had killed Faraday all those years ago.

Challis now had the same thoughts about Beckett. Had it been his bullet?

But at least the old soldier had been in the army, at war, where death was a common occurrence, and men were trained to kill, expected to. But the journalist couldn't allow himself the luxury of those thoughts, and he'd just have to live with it. It had never crossed Challis's mind that he'd ever take another person's life - not even when he stepped in the ring for a boxing match. He knew such accidents happened - but always to someone else.

However, this wasn't an accident, and the journalist's finger had been on the trigger.

Challis put a hand to his temple, which was still tender to the touch, and his mind grasped at one consolatory thought. Beckett had been a murdering bastard and deserved to die. So did it really matter who the executioner was?

The radio was on and there was a brief mention of a shooting at Matthew Hardy's mansion in the country. But it was early yet and Challis knew more would come out over the next two days.

However, he wasn't bothered because nobody had what he had. Or was likely to get it.

In fact, the interest created today and tomorrow would only make his story all the more valuable.

The journalist knew his business well enough to go straight to the largest selling Sunday tabloid and offer his story exclusively to them. He wasn't going to mess about auctioning his story around the other papers because he knew who would pay the most anyway. At eight thirty he spoke to Alex Mulrooney, the news editor, explained what he'd got and the price he wanted.

'As long as you can stand up what you've told me,' Mulrooney said, enthusiasm in his voice, 'there's no problem with the money as far as I'm concerned. And the pics are okay?'

'Yeah, I've got everything. Family ones as well.'

'I'll go and have a word with the editor and speak to you soon. And no bull shittin', you haven't tried to sell this to anyone else?'

'No. It's yours exclusive.'

Nine fifteen Mulrooney called back and said it was a deal, including an agreement regarding worldwide syndication. Challis would probably make a normal year's money out of this one story.

'I'll see you in about an hour,' Challis said. Then he called Steve.

'Can you be at the paper in about an hour, with all the photographs?'

'No problem,' Steve replied.

'Right, see you there.'

Challis printed out his finished copy and put it in his briefcase. The Shirley Quinn stuff he'd file later in the day and anything he got from the psychologist, John Andrews. He looked at his watch again and decided he'd wait until he was at the Sunday paper's office before trying to get hold of Randolph Beckett.

Forty five minutes later Challis pushed open one of the large glass door's to the newsroom and saw Steve had arrived first and was chatting to the picture editor. The large open plan room, with the features department at the other end, was starting to get busy, reporters already working on their VDU's and busy making phone calls from their cluttered desks. Today and tomorrow would be frantic.

Alex Mulrooney stood up from the news desk as soon as he saw Challis.

'If you give me your copy I'll go and read it in my office,' he said, and held out a hand. Challis took a buff coloured folder from his case and called Steve over to get the photographs.

'There's still a bit more to come,' Challis said, 'but you'll have the lot by the end of the day.'

While Mulrooney went to his office, Steve decided to go to the paper's canteen to get a couple of coffees and Challis scrounged a London BT business directory to look up the head office of Beckett's family business. He found an unoccupied desk and phone, and pressed nine to get an outside line. But it took a couple of calls before he got anywhere because there were several companies connected to each other with different names. Then he was told Randolph Beckett wasn't available because he was in Canada but he could leave a message with his secretary.

'Do you have a press office?' Challis asked, and was informed they didn't but they did have a public relations department. And finally Challis was talking to a pleasant sounding woman called, Janice.

'I wanted to speak to Randolph Beckett but I'm told he's in Canada.'

'Then you know more than me, Mr Challis. Have you spoken to his secretary?'

'No,' Challis replied. 'I could have left a message with her but I thought it might be better if you arrange something for me.'

'Why?'

'Because there is a big story just about to break which will involve the Beckett family name. It's very personal and I'm sure your boss will appreciate it if he knows he can get a chance to state the family's side of things. Good public relations, and all that. Besides, once he's made a statement, that should be the end of it.'

'What's the story about?' Janice asked in a puzzled voice.

'Murder, quite a few of them.'

'And this is to do with Mr Beckett?' amazement now in the woman's tone.

'Take my word for it that the family is directly involved. There will be something about it in the papers later today, and tomorrow, but I have the exclusive story which will reveal everything on Sunday. And it's a big one. So if I were you I really would try and get hold of Mr Beckett for me.'

'Okay, Mr Challis, I'm sure I'll be able to contact him. But I can't promise what his reaction will be.' Janice paused. 'Is there anything else you can tell me? Something more I can pass on to him?'

Challis thought carefully before answering.

'Tell him it concerns a close member of his family. His brother, Frank Beckett.'

The journalist gave the PR woman his telephone numbers and she promised she would call him later in the day.

'Thanks,' he said.

As Challis put down the phone he felt a tap on his shoulder and turned to see a smiling Alex Mulrooney.

'That's quite some read,' he said.

'It'll put up your circulation,' Challis grinned. 'Nobody will have anything near what I've got.

'So what are you going to do now?' and the news editor listened carefully as the journalist explained.

'I'll file whatever extra I've got tonight with your copy taker, then get some rest,' Challis added, knowing that he would have to be at the newspaper early tomorrow until the middle of the afternoon to answer any last minute queries from the subs.

'It'll be our splash,' Mulrooney said, 'with another three to four pages inside.'

*

The interview with Shirley Quinn in the hospital was a great success and she wasn't at all perturbed about discussing her intimate love life. She also told Challis she had some sexy photographs he could use of her dressed in black leather outfits, and gave Steve her key and a short note addressed to

306

her air hostess friend giving the photographer permission to take away the pics.

She admitted she was heartbroken over the death of Frank Beckett, even though he had tried to kill her and murdered all those other people. She really had loved Beckett all the years she'd been with him.

The power of love was strange - but she realised she'd have to get over it. The money she was getting for her story would help somewhat.

Challis drove back to London, dropped off Steve at the studio, and then went on to Victoria. Last night's violent storm had finished about midnight but a heavy rain had continued, off and on, for another six hours, leaving the air fresh and clean during the morning. But the sun was once again a brilliant ball of fire in the sky and the mugginess had returned after lunch.

The journalist looked at the time as he parked the BMW and decided he'd be able to manage another quick shower before leaving for his appointment with the psychologist. Now that Beckett was dead he'd been tempted to cancel but knew he'd have to see it through. Especially after all the fuss he'd caused.

But he'd go by taxi. Last night was starting to catch up on him and he was beginning to feel knackered.

Challis had just entered his flat and walked into the kitchen for a beer when his mobile rang. It was Janice, the PR lady.

'Sorry to be so long getting back to you,' she said.

'That's okay.'

'Mr Beckett had left Canada and I had to track him down in New York. Anyway, I must say he sounded very intrigued when I repeated what you'd told me.'

'When can I speak to him?' Challis asked.

'He's flying back to this country and he'll be in London sometime this evening. He said he'd probably call you about eleven o'clock. He'll try your home number first. But he'll definitely phone you.'

'Thanks, you've been a great help.'

'It's a pleasure,' Janice said, and the line went dead.

FORTY SEVEN

Pathologist, Dr Fabian Cook, was looking forward to a relaxing weekend after the busy end to the week.

The doctor's sister, Wendy, and her husband were on a month's visit from the States and the two men were going fishing for the next two days. The families took it in turn for alternate holidays between the two countries, and had been doing so for years.

Wendy had been on a visit to Chicago when she'd fallen in love with an American, also a physician. A year later she married Dr Bruce Malone and was very happy with her new husband and country. In fact, it was her love which helped him overcome his nightmares.

Before their marriage her husband had been a doctor in the American Army stationed in Vietnam. He'd been working in a forward field hospital when they had been attacked by the Viet Cong and in the ensuing battle he'd been severely wounded. But the wounds on his body had healed much more quickly than his mind.

*

Dr Cook had been in the mortuary most of Friday afternoon finishing the post mortem of a man called, Frank Beckett. During the morning he'd done a preliminary examination with several police officers present and established the deceased's life had been terminated by five 9 millimetre bullets fired from a Heckler and Koch MP5 submachine gun. The bullets had penetrated Beckett's heart, lungs and liver.

And now he'd confirmed the police information that the man did have an astrocytoma tumour on the brain which would have caused death in a matter of months.

Dr Cook looked up as the doors of the mortuary swung open and his brother-in-law walked towards him. They were having a drink together later.

'I should imagine you saw enough of these type of wounds when you were in Vietnam,' the pathologist said, pointing to the naked cadaver laying on the stainless steel slab.

The American looked at the familiar bullet wounds which sent a shiver down his back.

'But what do you make of this?' Dr Cook asked, touching a scar on Frank Beckett's right shoulder.

Bruce Malone bent forward and looked carefully at the body, something stirring in the memories of his past.

'Could be a knife...or even an old bayonet wound...and it looks as though it happened a long time ago.'

The doctor's voice sounded puzzled.

'I wonder which war he was in?'

FORTY EIGHT

Challis got out of the cab in Wimpole Street, crossed the busy road, and rang the doorbell to the psychologist's consulting rooms.

'Who is it?' a woman's voice enquired from the small brass grill mounted on the wall. Challis recognised the voice and grinned.

'I've got an appointment with Mr Andrews,' he replied.

'Oh, it's *you*,' and the front door clicked open. The journalist walked into a large hallway and saw a frosty faced woman behind a reception desk getting ready to leave.

'I was hoping to be gone before you arrived,' she glared.

'What, and *miss* meeting me?'

'You were very rude to me yesterday,' she said.

'You weren't exactly a bundle of laughs either. Now, where is Mr Andrews?'

The woman indicated with her arm towards a small lift.

'The first floor, turn right and it's the door directly in front of you.'

As Challis got out of the lift John Andrews was waiting for him and a minute later they were seated in a large comfortably furnished room.

'I believe you want to discuss one of my patients with me,' Andrews said. 'Frank Beckett, is that right?'

'That's correct.'

'You made some pretty outrageous claims when we spoke yesterday. Even so, I don't know what I can do for you because ethically, I shouldn't help you.'

'Even if the patient is dead?'

The psychologist looked puzzled.

'I don't understand,' he said.

'Frank Beckett was killed last night.'

'How? What happened?' Andrews asked in a shocked voice.

'He was shot by the police after he killed and wounded several people. And the police have absolute proof that he murdered a lot of people this summer and over the last five years.'

Challis gave the psychologist a penetrating look.

'Those tapes were the cause of all the murders. He believed he was the reincarnation of Giles Faraday, didn't he?'

'Why did Beckett kill Brody?' Andrews asked.

'To stop him talking to me,' Challis replied. 'Brody was going to tell me about the tapes.'

'You're a journalist, Mr Challis, and I take it you're doing a story. I presume that's the reason you're here.'

'Yes, my story will be out this Sunday, and to be honest, it really doesn't matter if you speak to me or not because I have plenty of information already. One other thing, the police will be paying you a visit sometime, anyway.'

'Why's that?'

'Because they'll find your name and address in the same place I did. In one of Beckett's flats.'

'I see. Supposing I do tell you about Beckett, does my name have to appear?'

Challis shook his head.

'Not at all. I can write...*a specialist said*...and then go into your quotes. I won't give your name, if that's the way you want it.'

'Okay, Mr Challis, leave my name out of it and I will try to explain Frank Beckett's condition in the simplest of terms. But, his case was complicated, in fact, one of the most fascinating I've ever come across.'

'All right, it's a deal,' Challis said.

Andrews settled back in his chair and rested his arms on his leather topped desk.

'When Beckett first came to me he explained about his sessions with James Brody and brought along the tapes. Each week he would play one and then we would discuss the contents. I suppose it took about six months of weekly visits to comprehensively discuss all the tapes. You see, right from his very first visit he was convinced he had lived before as Giles Faraday.'

'Do you believe in reincarnation?' Challis asked.

The psychologist smiled.

'Let's just say I've got an open mind. But it is a fact that over two thirds of the Earth's population believe in reincarnation and is one of man's oldest beliefs. And this is not limited to Buddhists and Hindus, it also exists among some Christians. Also, several eminent doctors have written on this subject in serious scientific publications. Many people believe we have a soul which is immortal and survives an earthly death.'

'Have you got copies of the tapes?' Challis asked.

'No, Beckett wouldn't let me make copies.'

'Did you ever hypnotise him?'

'No, Beckett wouldn't agree. I *can* hypnotise people and I've helped many of my patients in this way. But I do have to have co-operation.'

'Any of your other patients ever claim to have lived a previous existence?'

'No, but I have attended sessions run by colleagues of mine who have regressed people under hypnosis. And some of these people claim that they've not just lived *once* before, but have had *several previous lives.*'

'Do they remember these lives when they're not in an hypnotic state?'

'Usually not, though some say they do have flashbacks. But nothing that lasts very long, and certainly doesn't interfere with their daily business.'

'What about Beckett's behaviour? What kind of pattern did he fit into?' Challis asked.

'I believe Frank Beckett began to live two lives, the other one being Giles Faraday. It didn't happen overnight, it was a gradual process, but it appears now that the Faraday character became more predominant in the end. However, don't let's jump too far ahead.'

John Andrews sat quiet for a moment gathering his thoughts.

'It was about three years after I first saw him that I really began to worry about Beckett and realized he'd developed a dual personality.' Andrews continued. 'How many times he sat by himself and played those tapes is anybody's guess, but as time went by I became more and more convinced he believed he was two people. He also told me he was experiencing mood swings, aggressiveness and that sort of thing. He told me he had a girlfriend, a masochist, and beating her got rid of a lot of his anger. He also said he didn't go out very much and had dropped all his friends, except the girl. These symptoms all pointed to schizophrenia...as well as having a dual personality. That, coupled with his claim of reincarnation, made Beckett's case most unusual. In fact, I'd never come across anything like it.'

'So why did he keep coming to see you, if he felt so anti-social?' Challis asked.

'Simply because he wanted someone to talk with about his other life, and I had become part of that life, probably the *only* one he could talk to.'

Challis stared hard at Andrews before his next question.

'But he conned you, didn't he?'

'What do you mean?'

'Well, he never trusted you enough to tell you about the murders.'

There was a long pause before Andrews spoke again.

'No, Mr Challis, he never told me about the murders.'

'And you never suspected anything?'

'No, nothing.'

'When was the last time you saw Beckett?'

'About three months ago. For the last two years he only made appointments every couple of months or so, but there *was* something special about his last visit.'

'What was that?'

'He told me he was dying...he said he'd been seeing a specialist and by this Christmas he would be dead.'

'He had a tumour,' Challis said.

'You know?'

'Yes, I found a letter from his doctor.'

'It was a malignant tumour on the brain,' Andrews said. 'He'd had all the tests and it was inoperable.'

'I think that's the reason Beckett suddenly became in such a hurry to finish his killing spree,' the journalist said.

'From what you've told me you're probably right, Mr Challis.'

'One last question, Mr Andrews. Did you believe in Frank Beckett's claim that he was the reincarnation of Giles Faraday?'

The psychologist shrugged his shoulders.

'I truthfully can't give you an answer to that question. Who knows? But I am firmly convinced that, in the end, Frank Beckett drove himself insane.'

*

When Challis arrived back home he found a message from John Mason on his answer machine. 'Pissed as a newt and enjoying myself.' But this time he'd left the name of the hotel and where he was staying, and that decided where Challis would go. Hawaii.

After he'd phoned Keely and asked her to book the flights and accommodation, to which she happily agreed, he called Seton to remind him to contact Chief Inspector Jordan tomorrow evening at seven o'clock and tell him about the tapes. By then the first editions would be printed - and the journalist should be on his way to Heathrow Airport.

'Don't worry, Challis, you go and have a good holiday, and don't forget, Matthew said to put it on your expenses. He insists it's a present for the both of you.'

*

Challis had just about finished packing a suitcase and large shoulder bag when his phone rang just after eleven.

'Challis here,' he answered.

'I'm Randolph Beckett,' a well spoken man's voice said. 'I understand you've been trying get hold of me.'

'Yes, Mr Beckett. I appreciate you calling me.'

'I'm told it's something to do with murders and my brother, Frank. I'm sorry, but I don't know what you're referring to,' the man paused, 'and the name Frank...surely you mean my Father. His name is Frank.'

'Your father? How old is he?'

'Over seventy.'

'No, it's definitely not him. Look, Mr Beckett, have the police been in touch with you yet?'

'The police, Mr Challis? What on earth for?'

Challis hesitated as he tried to think of an easy way to break the bad news.

'I'm sorry to tell you, Mr Beckett, but your brother, Frank, is dead.'

'Of course he's dead. My brother died when he was two years old.'

'What did you say?' and Challis couldn't keep the shock from his voice.

'Frank, was my older brother, named after my Father, but he drowned thirty eight years ago.'

'He can't have. He lived in Knightsbridge, drove a white Porsche. He was married at one time to a French Canadian woman called, Ghislaine.'

'No, Mr Challis, you've got your facts mixed up. My *Father* married a French Canadian woman by the name of Ghislaine. And they're still together. They live in Montreal. I've just spent the last week with them. So who is this Frank Beckett *you're* talking about?'

There was a stunned silence and the journalist gripped the receiver as though in a trance. The room seemed very quiet as he sat there, the question still ringing in his ears.

But Challis didn't know the answer.

'I'm sorry, but it seems I've made a mistake,' he mumbled, then ventured one more question.

'Do you remember the date your brother died?' he asked in a faltering voice.

'Yes I do...all very sad really...something the family's never forgotten.'

What the hell was the date? the journalist felt like screaming, but instead, asked in a whisper.

'And the date?'

'July the twenty eighth. Why?'

Challis didn't know the answer to that either.

FORTY NINE

'So who *was* Frank Beckett?' Keely asked, as she settled into the corner of the taxi seat. They were on their way to the airport.

Challis shrugged his shoulders.

'Who knows,' he replied. 'It's weird.'

The reporter had added the rest of his copy that afternoon. In the story he'd said that Beckett had assumed the identity of a dead man to cover his tracks and police investigations were continuing.

That would get right up Chief Inspector Jordan's nose, Challis thought, and gave a small grin. But the journalist was bothered. He didn't like leaving loose ends.

In a way, it gave the ending a mysterious twist, and the news editor had assured Challis they would find out the murderer's real name for next Sunday's edition of the paper.

But would they? The journalist wasn't as sure.

'So, did this man think he was the reincarnation of Beckett as well as Giles Faraday?' Keely asked.

Once again the journalist shrugged his shoulders.

'I definitely believe he thought he was the reincarnation of Faraday…but Beckett?' Challis paused for a moment. 'He could have just assumed Beckett's identity. A lot of conmen do that. That's easy enough and that's nothing to do with living another life. But…' and the journalist's voice tailed off.

'But what?' his companion asked.

'Well, it seems strange that this unknown man should have chosen the identity of a man who died on the same date.'

'Same date?' Keely's voice sounded puzzled.

'Beckett died on the twenty eighth of July, the same date as Faraday. And this man also claimed that was his birthday, the date he was born. It all seems too much of a coincidence.'

'I'm sure everything will work out in the end,' Keely said reassuringly, and gave Challis a kiss on the cheek. 'At least the killings have stopped. We're all safe in our beds now.'

The journalist nodded but didn't say anything and sat staring out of the taxi window feeling frustrated.

Something wasn't quite right – but he wasn't sure what.

*

The Air France plane touched down and taxied to a stop.

Forty five minutes later a tall dark haired man in his late thirties, carrying a small suitcase, strode through the crowded airport concourse heading for the taxi rank.

Reaching the automatic plate glass doors his suitcase accidentally caught a trolley being pushed towards him.

'Pardon,' the man said, bending down to pick up a small bag which had fallen on the floor. 'I am sorry,' he apologised in a distinctive French accent, as he returned the bag to the trolley.

'That's okay,' Challis smiled. 'No harm done,' and continued pushing his way deeper into the airport, Keely walking by his side.

The Frenchman stood looking at the backs of the couple for a few moments before turning and joining the queue for taxis. Fifteen minutes later he was speeding on his way into London. When the cab reached Hammersmith it stopped outside a car rental service where the Frenchman picked up the Peugeot car he'd ordered from Paris.

Before setting off he studied a map, working out his route, and then headed towards the Kings Cross area. He finally found the address he was looking for, a road leading to a row of graffiti covered lockup garages, and parked his car.

Taking a bunch of keys from his pocket he opened one of the garages and entered. A few minutes later he emerged carrying a canvas holdall bag and long wooden case painted camouflage green and brown. He opened the boot of the Peugeot and put them inside.

Carefully locking the garage a few minutes later he was driving towards north London. Passing through the suburbs he got on to the A1 road heading into Hertfordshire, finally stopping at a motel on the outskirts of Hatfield.

Yes, there *were* a few vacancies the cheerful blonde receptionist informed the Frenchman, in answer to his question, and opened the registration book for him to sign.

'Are you here on business?' she asked with a smile, handing over a key.

'Oui,' the man replied, 'unfinished business,' and turned to walk away.

'I see you're from Paris,' the young woman said, glancing down at the registration book, 'Mr...I'm sorry, but I can't read your signature.'

The man stopped in mid-stride and looked back over his shoulder.

'It's *Fabere*. My name is *Henri Fabere*.'